Praise for Gabriella Hewitt's *Dark Waters*

4 cups "This story has it all."
~ *Coffee Time Romance*

4.5 Blue Ribbon "If you like edge of your seat suspense, hunky heroes and heroines you can relate to, then DARK WATERS is the story for you. Filled with a gripping suspense tale, I found myself thoroughly enthralled with the story, unable to put it down. Ms. Hewitt doesn't disappoint her readers."
~ *Romance Junkies Review*

Dark Waters

Gabriella Hewitt

A Samhain Publishing, Ltd. publication.

Samhain Publishing, Ltd.
577 Mulberry Street, Suite 1520
Macon, GA 31201
www.samhainpublishing.com

Dark Waters
Copyright © 2008 by Gabriella Hewitt
Print ISBN: 978-1-59998-817-7
Digital ISBN: 1-59998-606-X

Editing by Laurie Rauch
Cover by Vanessa Hawthorne

First Samhain Publishing, Ltd. electronic publication: September 2007
First Samhain Publishing, Ltd. print publication: July 2008

Dedication

To my husband Konrad, for your love and support.

* * *

To my wonderful husband B with much love, always.

Prologue

"*M'ijo*, are you listening to me?"

Swallowing a groan, Rico took a last lingering look at the blonde bikini-wearing bombshell. She had mile-long legs and a body that would make any man forget his name. She offered oblivion far better than the whiskey bottle he'd been crawling into these past several nights.

With a sigh, Rico shoved the blonde and all her possibilities to the back of his mind and braced himself for his unexpected visitor.

Or make that *visitors*.

The black-clad woman on the left looked vaguely familiar. The way she wrung a red handkerchief between her fingers boded ill for his peace of mind.

The woman on the right he knew only too well. Hands on her wide hips, her foot tapping against the weather-beaten pier, she stood below his battered boat like an oversized piñata ready to burst at the seams.

Forcing a grin, he turned his attention to her. "*Sí, Mami.*"

"Then come down here and give your *mami* a hug."

Rico easily descended the ladder and jumped to the dock where he bent down to gather his mother into a strong embrace.

She hugged him fiercely. Then, putting space between them, she reached up and clasped his face between her hands. "You've gotten thin, *m'ijo.*"

Motherly concern rang through, reminding him of why, when he'd run away, he'd chosen to run home.

"I'm fine, *Mami.*"

"You expect me to believe that? Since when, *m'ijo*, do you walk around with your shirt hanging open and hair all over your face, looking like a *borracho*? And take off those sunglasses so I can see my boy's beautiful brown eyes."

Rico slipped off his Ray-Bans and slid them into his shirt pocket. "It took time to get here from Miami. I didn't bother shaving." He'd reduced his life down to the essentials—his boat and a bottomless glass. Shaving wasn't on the list.

The trip down the Atlantic had been smooth. The secondhand, small sailing boat he had bought from a colleague had cut through the water like a dream. Granted, the head didn't always flush, the sail on his mast was a bit frayed and salt clung to his clothes and skin, but overall he felt invigorated that he had made it to Vieques, the small island off Puerto Rico, in one piece. Wind-blown waves slapped against his boat and ruffled his shaggy black hair. Conscious of his appearance, he scrubbed at the stubble on his chin. It was no wonder his mother called him a *borracho*—a drunkard.

Folding her arms over her ample bosom, his mother gave him the look that usually had him and his six siblings running for cover.

"Rico Tomás Miguel Lopez, you would tell me if you were in trouble, wouldn't you?"

For an instant, he saw fear replace concern in her eyes.

"I'm not in trouble. I simply took some time off."

"Then why haven't you come home?"

Rico's jaw tightened. "I am home."

"Ah, *sí*? Today's Sunday, Gloria came to lunch with her husband and your nieces. Roberto is home from university. He hasn't seen you in how long? And what about *Papi*? You think he doesn't want to see his son? You think we didn't know you've been hiding out on this floating tin can for a week?"

Rico pressed his lips together. He should've known his presence would be reported by the town's lightning-quick gossip network. But he wasn't about to get into explanations in front of a stranger. Why hadn't his mother introduced him?

"And did you forget your manners? Say hello to Maria. You remember Maria Santos? She married your *Tío* Alonso's nephew's cousin on his mother's side. We're practically related."

He didn't bother trying to untangle that bit of speech. Taking the relationship as a given, he stepped forward to greet the woman, who already looked wilted by the afternoon sun, with a kiss to both cheeks. Other than a brief hello, she spoke not a word. Unease rippled through him. Why had his mother brought her?

"What do you think of the town?" his mother said, gesturing with her hand to the storefronts doing a brisk trade at the edge of the marina. Rico took a moment to really look. On some level he'd been aware that several new bars, restaurants and a few new hotels had sprung up on the old sleepy strip. Noting the changes, he almost didn't recognize the stomping grounds of his youth. Had he been away so long? Before, the only people who'd bothered to visit the small island off the shore of Puerto Rico were relatives or military personnel. Judging from the blonde he'd been admiring and other strangers he'd glimpsed over the past few days, tourism had declared Isabel Segunda the latest best-kept secret.

"We've doubled capacity at the bakery and even put in a café. We're as good as Starducks."

Her face beamed with such pride, he didn't have the heart to tell her she'd mangled the name of the famous coffeehouse chain. Then again, with his mother, her selective use of English was highly suspect. The woman was as smart as a whip and every Lopez knew it, which made him wonder what her purpose today was. Somehow he doubted it was to visit the prodigal son.

But he really didn't want to deal with anyone right now. "Look, *Mami*, I'm not good company. How about I visit the house tomorrow?" Or the day after, though he doubted he'd be allowed to get away with that. If he didn't show up tomorrow, the entire Lopez clan would probably board his boat and drag him home.

Familia. A heavy weight descended upon him just thinking about it. He shrugged it off and looked out into the bay. The forecast called for sunshine and warm temps, but the dark cloud slung low on the horizon told him the weather was about to change.

He longed to get back on his boat. Rico squinted against the sun glinting off the sea-green ocean and sighted a manatee rolling slowly in the water as boats passed by.

"*Oye?*" Mama jabbed him in the chest with her finger.

"Ow!" He rubbed the sore spot and stepped back to put more space between them. "I'm listening." He turned his attention back to the women.

The wind picked up, carrying the smell of sea, hibiscus and saffron from the restaurant across the street.

The bright red handkerchief Maria carried in her hand blew limply in the breeze. She looked up at him with sad eyes. He looked away. He knew that look. He swallowed hard. In his line of work, he had come across women like her much too often. If he was right, and he hoped he wasn't, his mother had brought Maria to the wrong person.

He fixed his stare on his mother. "Mama, what's the real reason for your visit?"

Mama Lopez planted her feet. She was not a woman easily intimidated or one to mince words, as he knew only too well. Mentally, he braced himself for her response.

"Maria's daughter is missing. She didn't come home last night. The police think she's run away."

Damn. He'd been right. In this case, he hated being right.

"I'm sorry, *Señora*. I can't help you."

Maria rushed forward. "*Por favor!*" she cried and pleaded at the same time, her words a rush of Spanish. She raised her fist up to his face, and he saw that the handkerchief she'd been clutching was really a bandana. "Chita wore this around her hair. She loved it." She clung desperately to him. "She would never run away. *El chupacabra* took her! Other girls have disappeared. One of them was found along the roadside, her body drained of blood. Please, you must help."

Rico avoided the woman's eyes. Ashamed, he stepped back toward his boat. "I'm sorry," he could only repeat. His chest tight, he gazed out over the ocean and wished he could leap back on his boat and lose himself in the wide blue expanse. He couldn't do this. Not even for *Mami*.

Behind him, he heard his mother furiously whispering. Maybe she would leave and take Maria with her. *Dios mio*, he hoped so. His *madre* didn't know what she was asking. Neither of them did.

A moment later, he felt a warm hand grasp his arm and turn him. From the corner of his eye, he saw Maria walking back down the pier. If his mother had gone with her, he might have thought they'd given up. But when had his mother ever given up? Every Lopez knew that while *Papi's* talent for bread and pastries could not be matched, it was *Mami's* vision and ambition that made the bakery profitable and popular.

"You want to tell me why you came back, *m'ijo*?"

Blood. Death. Failure. The images flashed through his mind. "No."

Her hand dropped to her side. He knew she debated whether to press him or not.

"Don't, *Mami*. I really don't want to talk about it."

Air puffed out on a sigh. "*Muy bien*. I won't ask for now. But I will say this to you. You are wounded—"

He opened his mouth to protest when his *madre* silenced him by placing her hand on his heart.

"You are wounded in here," she insisted. "Your soul cries out in pain. A mother knows these things. The bond between mother and child is never severed. You are my firstborn, my pride. Not a day has gone by that I don't think about you. Worry about you."

Rico's fists clenched at his sides. He didn't want to hear this. Not now. But he couldn't find it in him to walk away.

"Papa and I hoped that you would choose to take over the bakery, but that was not to be." She shrugged her shoulders. "But I always knew that you would come if the *familia* needed you. Maria is *familia*. Her husband died from a heart attack. Her son, Pablo, got permission from his army *capitán* to come back for the funeral. That was the last she saw him. He died somewhere in Iraq, doing his duty. You know about duty."

His mother paused for breath and all he could think was that she wasn't fighting fair. Yeah, he knew about duty.

"Chita is all Maria has left. There is no one to watch out for either of them. Papa has agreed that if you won't look for Chita, then he will."

Rico's head snapped up. "He can't—"

"He will. He must."

11

"You don't know what you're asking."

"*Sí*, I do. But an honorable man does what must be done, no matter the cost."

Rico winced, feeling the shaft hit home. "You sound like *Papi*."

His mother's features softened and she smiled. "Of course I do. He is the most honorable man I know. That's why I married him."

Defeat settled on Rico's shoulder, weighing him down. "All right, *Mami*, I'll look for Chita." God knew he didn't want to. His gut hurt just thinking about where it might lead. "But no promises."

Promises were something he would never give out again.

Chapter 1

The overhead fan twirled listlessly in the day's heat. Rico sat on the bar stool nursing his beer. The best way to get information was to blend in with the locals. With the sun at its peak, those who didn't go home for the *siesta* sought the comfort of the local bar.

Rico sat quietly, soaking up the atmosphere, making his presence known. He'd been gratified to see one local man nod to him upon entering the bar. His second stop for the day. If there was any place to get the local gossip, this was it.

So far, though, he'd learned little. No sign of Chita. Only whispers and fragmented talk of the legendary *el chupacabra*— the goatsucker—island lore of an elusive creature that sucked all the blood out of its victims.

The only monsters Rico believed in were the human kind.

One quick phone call back to his Immigrations and Customs Enforcement office in New Jersey had confirmed his suspicions. Jared Colton, a hotshot ICE special agent hadn't questioned Rico's request when it had come—something he was grateful for. The email he had received on his Blackberry last night spoke volumes. Chita wasn't the only girl to disappear. And, as Maria had said, one girl had indeed been found with the blood drained from her body. With that news, speculation about the blood-sucking beast spread like wildfire and, at the same time, it scared most people off from investigating further.

A legend made good cover for something dirty. Legends were for history books and fairytales, but in the real world there was very little room for heroes. He had played that role and the ending hadn't been very happy. Rico fingered the wallet in his pocket. Disturbed by his thinking, he went back to nursing his beer.

The reports Jared had compiled didn't give Rico much to go on, but it was enough information for him to leave Isabel Segunda and travel south to the other side of Vieques.

The door opened behind him. All talk stopped. A glance in the mirror above the bar told him why.

Lord have mercy.

Every eye on the place remained glued to the beauty who'd walked in. Either she was completely oblivious to the looks she was getting or good at hiding it.

He suspected the latter by the very faint tremble he noted in her hand as she tucked a springy curl behind her ear.

"Excuse me," she said to the bartender. "Can you tell me where I can find a mechanic? I'm having car trouble."

She had a low husky voice and spoke in a Spanish rhythm that told him she wasn't local. Her choice of clothes also spoke volumes—the cut and style screamed mainland tourist. But from the neck up, she was pure Latina. Olive skin. Wide lips meant for kissing. Eyes that could knock a man to his knees.

"*Sí, Señorita.* Carlos is the mechanic you want."

"Great. Where can I find him?"

"Over there," the bartender waved her towards a table in the corner where four men sat talking and drinking.

"Oh, thank you." She walked over to the table, her hips in those tight hip-hugging jeans swaying to a beat that had Rico swallowing a bigger gulp of beer than he intended. He didn't have to hear the conversation to guess what was happening. The lady wanted her car fixed now, but Carlos wasn't about to be separated from his meal and gossip. He watched the beauty gesture with her hands. No dice. Carlos went back to his meal.

The woman came back and slid onto a barstool. "Coca-Cola, please."

Rico watched her from the corner of his eye. One of the young guys with bulging biceps swaggered up to her side and snaked an arm around her shoulder. "Hey, beautiful, how about letting me show you a good time."

"Yeah?" she replied. She hooked a finger into his shirt and pulled him closer until she could whisper in the guy's ear. Fascinated, Rico forgot about his beer. The guy's face went white. He apologized and backed away.

The woman faced the bar again. She thanked the bartender for the Coke and paid him. He saw her lips moving and leaned over to better catch what she was saying.

"...swear the next man who lays his dirty paws on me is going to be wearing his testicles for a tie."

Rico coughed to cover the fit of laughter that erupted in his throat. She'd spoken in English with a notable New York accent, probably thinking no one would understand. Fire, passion, and strength crackled in the air around her. A man would have his hands full with this one.

And, he suspected, no man would ever tame her completely. Like the wild chestnut curls that spilled down her shoulders and back, she would resist any form of control.

His blood heated at the challenge, surprising him. He scowled at his drink, tamping down the emotion. He didn't need that kind of distraction. Besides, for all her sex appeal, he had the feeling she wouldn't be the kind of woman you could walk away from after a night of burning up the sheets.

No, this one had *the look*.

The kind that reeled you in softly until, before you knew it, you were hooked, landed and gutted. He had four sisters. His poor brothers-in-law hadn't stood a chance.

The woman finished the last of her Coke and slipped off the stool. Good, she was leaving. "Is there a taxi service?" she asked the bartender.

"*Sí*, of course. Where do you wish to go?"

"Casa Verde."

The bartender's eyes widened and he crossed himself. "You must go *Señorita*. I have no wish for trouble. Please go."

"What?" She stared at him in disbelief, but the bartender continued making shooing gestures with his hands and insisting he wanted no trouble.

Anger flashed across her face, but she left the bar.

"*Què pasó?*" Rico casually asked, more than curious to

know what was up.

The bartender leaned over and dropped his voice. "Strange things happen at Casa Verde. Flashing lights, screams, and some say they've even seen *el chupacabra*. No sane man will go there."

Rico tossed the money he owed towards the bartender, telling him to keep the change.

His best lead to tracking down Chita Santos had just walked out the door. Though the Latina beauty didn't know it yet, the two of them were about to become better acquainted. And, unlike other men, he couldn't be scared off.

౪

"Yo!" Frankie stuck out her thumb. The taxi rolled right past her.

The midday sun pelted down on her head as she scanned the block for another cab. *Nada.* Nothing.

Punta Negra wasn't exactly a hot spot. The southeastern town was a sleepy village on the threshold of the Wildlife Preserves. Once it had been a stopping area for military personnel to pick up groceries and other items, but since the US military pulled out a few years ago, the town had fallen into a lull.

Frustrated, she swiped at several wayward strands and tried to tame the unruly mass. Another cab sailed by. She put out her arm to wave it down.

"You're never going to get a taxi like that." One of the patrons from the bar stepped out onto the street. He put his fingers in his mouth and gave a sharp whistle. The cab braked and backed up. The man on the sidewalk shot her a sly grin.

"Where to, *Señorita*?"

"Casa Verde." She reached for the door handle.

She heard the snick of locks being engaged. "Sorry, *Señorita*. That place is haunted."

Before she could protest the cabbie drove off.

Frankie vented her frustration with a few choice words.

A deep rumble of laughter caught her attention. She spun around, "What's so funny?" Actually she didn't want to know. "Forget about it." Last thing she wanted to hear was another stupid story. Talk of witches, evil spirits, and *el chupacabra* was all she'd heard since stepping foot on the island. If the locals were trying to scare her off the island they were doing a lousy job. It would take a lot more than children's tales to frighten this hardened New Yorker.

Frankie assessed her situation. She could go back into the bar and bribe someone to take her or she could trek the five miles on foot. Neither prospect seemed appealing.

Least appealing was the rusting flatbed truck laden with plywood and lumber that sat useless on the side of the road. The lumberyard she had ordered the supplies from had refused to deliver to the plantation. The manager had said it was because the roads were too soft for his trucks, but Frankie suspected it had less to do with the marshy mangroves around the plantation she had inherited and more to do with superstitious nonsense.

She walked back to her truck and tried to start it again. The ignition turned, sputtered and died.

"Your battery needs to be replaced."

"What?" Frankie leaned out the open window. Trucks this old didn't have air-conditioning.

"I said..." Six foot tall, give or take an inch, the stranger from the bar walked up to her window. He flashed her a friendly smile, white teeth contrasting with his deep tan skin. Shaggy black hair curled past his ear, thick and silky, the type of hair made for running fingers through, danced over his eyebrows. "Sounds like the battery. Why don't you pop your hood and let me take a look?"

Something about the way he said it made Frankie's stomach contract.

"Are you a mechanic?" she asked warily. Still she pulled the lever for the hood.

"No, but I'm good with my hands."

Yeah, she bet.

Tall, dark, and handsome stuck his head in and began to tinker. Frankie got out and went to take a look. "Do you know what you're doing?"

She heard him laugh, a deep rumble, masculine and sexy, just like the man. "Not really." He pulled out a glass bulb and gave it a shake. "Looks like this spark plug is shot. A jump start won't cut it."

He placed the bulb in her hand and slammed the hood shut. "Truck's old. Doubt you're going to find a replacement on the island. Probably have to order it. Takes a few days more than average for anything to be received in the mail from the mainland."

"Great, just great." Frustrated, she gave a strangled scream. "How am I supposed to get this stuff home?" Frankie pointed at the lumber sticking out the back of the truck. "Don't suppose you have a truck?"

He shook his head.

"Didn't think so." She was right back to square one.

"Give me a minute." The helpful stranger grinned and went into the bar. Frankie stood outside contemplating a new strategy when her mystery man reappeared.

"Got us a truck."

"Us?" Alarms went off in her head. "I don't recall me inviting you..."

He cut her off, "Figured you might need the help loading and unloading this stuff."

True, she did. "Let's just make one thing clear buddy. I don't have a lot of cash on me and I'm not the type of girl who repays favors, know what I mean?"

"*No problema.*" He shot her another smile. Frankie had to wonder about the guy.

"Look, um, I didn't catch your name."

"Rico Lopez." He stuck out his hand.

"Frankie Montalvo." She gave his hand a shake. "I just want to make it clear that I appreciate your help and all."

"*Bueno.* Then it's settled." He started to pull wood off the back of the truck.

Frankie couldn't believe this guy. "I'm not sure you understand."

"Look, *Señorita. Mi mami* always told me to help women, especially beautiful ones." He gave her a wink.

This guy was too much.

A small truck pulled up before she could give Rico a piece of her mind. The driver hopped out and started to load up the back of his truck. Frankie shrugged her shoulders and went to help. Who was she to complain? This was the closest anyone had come to helping her out. So used to doing stuff on her own, she felt slightly uncomfortable and it must have shown.

"Frankie, don't worry. Here on Vieques everyone helps everyone."

She wanted to believe him, but her experience this past week since coming here had proven otherwise. Still, afraid to bite the hand that fed her, she kept her mouth closed.

After everything was loaded up, she slid into the front cab, sandwiched between Rico and the driver.

"*Dónde va?*"

"Casa Verde."

The driver blanched. He stared over her head at Rico. Rico nodded his head. The driver put the truck in gear and mumbled under his breath in Spanish. Even though the dialect was too thick for Frankie to understand, she had a feeling the man didn't agree.

She looked at Rico, who stared straight ahead, his body and face relaxed.

Frankie wondered what she had just agreed to.

A trickle of sweat slowly rolled its way down to the valley between her breasts. Frankie grimaced. Even with both windows of the truck cab open, there was no escaping the heat and humidity.

Or the company.

The truck hit a particularly brutal pothole, throwing her half on top of Rico. "Sorry," she mumbled, as she tried to peel herself off.

He glanced down into her face, a disturbing gleam in his dark, melt-in-your-mouth chocolate eyes. She'd always had a weakness for chocolate. "*No problema.*"

For an eternal second, she couldn't move, caught up in his gaze. Oh, man. Big *problema*. Frankie sucked in a breath, trying to make herself smaller—like it made a difference—and wondering why she'd never noticed the truck's definite list to the right. No matter what she did, her legs still rubbed against the guy's jeans. He might look lean and wiry, but Rico's rock-hard biceps and muscular thighs told her he wasn't a guy to mess with.

Frankie dragged in a breath and turned her attention to the scenery. Dense vegetation lined the road. A bird flew up and was soon joined by others. Brilliant colors dotted the landscape.

Beautiful. Frightening.

Nothing like the skyscrapers, traffic noise, and crowds she'd lived with daily. This would be her home now. Could she adjust?

She had to.

The truck swerved, throwing her once again into Rico. "Don't you know how to drive?" Irritated, she pushed herself back into place.

"Sorry, *Señorita.*"

A chuckle rumbled from Rico's chest. Frankie gave him her meanest glare, but it didn't seem to faze him.

Crossing her arms in front of her, she stared out the front of the window and willed them to arrive at the plantation.

Her plantation.

She still couldn't believe it. Who would've thought that she, Frankie Montalvo, would inherit such a place? She hadn't even known she'd had a grandmother. She'd lost her mom when she was little and then her dad when she was thirteen. Placed in New York's foster care system, she'd assumed it was her against the world. And it had been.

But not any more. Now, she was a homeowner. Her grandmother's legacy gave her the chance to make her dream a reality. The thought of settling unsettled her, while at the same time, it gave her hope. Hope for what she still didn't know, but with each passing day and each nail she hammered into the structure, she felt something. Something concrete. And nothing was going to stop her. Certainly not a bunch of superstitious nonsense.

Finally, the driver pulled into the plantation's long driveway. When the manor came into view, she heard Rico suck in a breath and felt him stiffen.

"This is it?"

She saw incredulity in his eyes.

"Yeah. Why?"

Casa Verde. Green House.

Unlike what the name suggested, there was very little in the way of greenery. Nothing but a long dirt road led up to the palatial house. The white stucco outside had faded to a dirty gray that would take more than a power wash to remove the mix of saltwater buildup and air-baked dust. The brick porch sagged, the foundation had cracks, the red ceramic Spanish-style roof begged for repairs, and the inside looked even worse, if that were possible. But it was hers and she hugged that knowledge to her heart.

"Please tell me the realtor gave it to you for free."

"For your information, I inherited it." She didn't care that others saw it as an eyesore. She owned it and that was all that mattered. "I'm going to turn this place into a home if it kills me." She turned to the driver. "Please pull up behind the house. Thanks."

The driver began muttering in Spanish, his grip on the wheel so tight, she wondered if his knuckles could get any whiter. The truck rolled slowly along the overgrown dirt driveway.

As soon the truck stopped, Frankie resisted the urge to push Rico out the door or climb over him, wanting out of the truck's close confines.

"Where do you want this stuff?" Rico gestured to the load, waiting for her to descend from the cab.

"Right over there will do." She'd need the supplies close enough to the house to use. She didn't want to have to drag the wood planks farther than necessary.

"So, who do you have doing the work?" Rico asked as he moved to the back of the truck to start unloading the lumber.

"I'm going to do it myself for now."

"You're kidding."

Frankie bristled at the disbelief in his eyes. "Look, what I can't do, I'll hire someone. Anyway, it's none of your business." Assuming she could get anyone out here. The driver had pried himself away from the wheel, but she hadn't missed him making the sign of the cross, or the way his eyes darted left and right as if he thought he might be attacked at any second.

Rico didn't seem spooked. He worked smoothly. Efficiently. His lean muscles rippled with each movement. Mesmerized, Frankie watched. He bent over to lay down his load on the ground and Frankie couldn't help noticing how his jeans molded to his butt. A really nice butt.

"So, how much you paying?"

"Wh-What?" She dragged her eyes up to his face. His eyebrow quirked. Her face flamed.

"How much you paying to fix the house?"

"Why? You thinking of applying for the job?"

He shrugged. "Maybe."

Have Rico make-Frankie-drool Lopez here everyday? No way. She didn't need the distraction. Besides, he was probably all brawn and no brain. She'd wasted enough of her dating years on guys like that.

"I don't think so. Look," she said, waving towards the house, "I'm going to get us some drinks. I'll be back."

She could feel his eyes drill into her back as she hurried towards the house. She'd have to be really desperate to hire Rico Lopez.

Really, really desperate.

"*Tostao.*"

Rico turned to see José, their driver, twirling his finger around his ear. "You think she's crazy? Why?"

José didn't pause a beat as he grabbed another stack of wood and piled it on the ground. "Has to be," he grunted, "to live here. If I'd have known when you offered me fifty bucks for transportation that you were coming here..."

Though José left the rest unsaid, Rico could fill in the blanks. Screams, strange noises, a goat carcass and a girl's body, both found without a trace of blood inside, and a spooky house—put all the pieces together and throw in some missing girls and it made for a bad horror movie.

Six girls in total, including Chita. All were late teens, early twenties. All had disappeared while partying at various clubs. Friends assumed they'd gone home with someone else. The police were inclined to believe the girls had simply run away. And when one girl had been discovered dead, her body drained of blood, the islanders thought they knew the truth—*el chupacabra* had returned.

Rico's stomach cramped as he thought of what the pattern meant to him.

He dumped the last load on the ground and looked up at the plantation manor. What the hell was this woman thinking? José had it right. She had to be *tostao*. Only a crazy person would consider taking on this fixer-upper by herself. His eyes roamed over the large structure. Was she really staying here by herself? Hadn't she heard the rumors? More likely that in-your-face New York attitude of hers assumed she could handle anything.

Even *el chupacabra.*

Rico shook his head. A movement on the second story caught his eye. Frankie stood at a window. Her eyes met his briefly before turning back into the room. What was taking her so long? And what was she doing upstairs when she'd said she was going to get drinks? He could use a glass of something cold, though it was near impossible to escape the heat and humidity. Glancing over his shoulder, he saw José dust off his hands and then nervously check his watch against the darkening sky.

"We go now, yes?"

"In a minute, I want to check on—" but he never finished.

A piercing shriek rent the air.

Frankie dawdled over the preparations. She really should go back outside. She at least owed the men some drinks, if not cash. Frowning, she calculated how much the job had been worth. She had just enough cash on her.

She arranged the ice tea onto the chipped tray she'd discovered in one of the cabinets. Slicing up a lemon she'd picked up in town a few days ago, she added it to each glass.

Her stomach rumbled, reminding her that she hadn't eaten in a while. The men were probably hungry, too. She'd bought chocolate chip cookies on her grocery run. She'd give them a few of those.

A loud creak sounded from above. Frankie sucked in a breath. She could hear her heart pounding as she strained to listening. Surely it was the house settling. Old houses did that.

She glanced towards the back door. The men were outside. Just to be sure, she crossed the uneven kitchen planks and peered out a window. They stood by the truck. They'd almost finished.

The creaking sound came again. Frankie bit her bottom lip. She'd have to go upstairs sooner or later. Better to go now while she had help nearby.

Firming her shoulders, she marched across the kitchen to the swinging door. Taking a deep breath, she pushed the door. As it swung open, she let out a breath, aware that the dining room was empty. Stepping into the room, she noted the signs of neglect in the threadbare carpet, listing chandelier and cobwebs.

Her eyes riveted on the door leading out of the room, she purposefully made her way to it. Her hand trembled as she reached for the handle.

Get a grip, Frankie.

She yanked open the door. Nothing. Okay. Good. Her eyes viewed the main staircase. The sound had come from upstairs. She'd have to go.

You could have asked one of the guys to do it.

"And risk them going back to town and telling everyone that the place is haunted or some other silly story," she muttered under her breath. "Not a chance." She'd discovered practically upon her arrival that her grandmother's plantation had a rather colorful history. If her plans for the place were to succeed, she couldn't afford giving fuel to further stories.

Her feet hit the last tread and she stepped onto the landing. She headed in the direction of the kitchen. Her bedroom lay that way.

She reached her bedroom door. It stood closed. Had she left it that way? She couldn't remember. She'd been in such a hurry to get to town and pick up the materials she needed.

"C'mon, Frankie. Just turn the knob."

Flexing her fingers, she wrapped them around the knob and slowly turned. The door creaked open. Sweat ran from her temples down her neck. Briefly, she squeezed her eyes tight, then opened them.

She pushed the door in all the way and stood on the threshold. Nothing. The air whooshed out of her. The room appeared undisturbed. Exactly as she'd left it this morning.

She stepped inside and moved to the window. Flicking back the curtain, she saw the men had finished. Rico glanced up and his eyes met hers. Those eyes should be outlawed. She withdrew and returned her gaze to the room. She really should get downstairs and give them their tea.

Her eyes swept the room one last time for signs of anything out of place. Something niggled at her.

The bed hangings.

She'd fallen in love with this room when she'd seen the old-fashioned canopy bed. The hangings were frayed, but they'd represented every princess dream she'd ever had as a child.

The loose bed hangings shielded the bed from view. She'd left them tied back this morning.

The ties probably just came undone, she thought, as she hesitantly stepped towards the bed.

All four of them?

There were no such things as ghosts or monsters. They were stories made up by people with overactive imaginations and too much time on their hands. With each step, she repeated the explanation. Unfortunately, it wasn't bringing a lot of comfort.

Her shirt stuck to her front and back. Her mouth felt dry. And if her pulse shot up any higher, she'd probably blast off.

Her hand shook as she reached for the hanging and drew it back. Slowly, she released the breath she'd been holding. Nothing but her nightgown in the middle of the bed.

And then her nightgown moved.

Chapter 2

Rico's feet pounded on the stairs. At the top he paused, crouched low and examined the surroundings. All the doors on either side of the landing remained closed—except for one.

With his back to the wall, he sidestepped down the hall, his eyes constantly moving, searching for signs of a threat. He itched to have his Glock in his hand, but drawing a gun like that would only generate more questions than a supposed beach bum like Rico wanted to answer.

When he reached the door, he plastered himself to the side and glanced inside. Crablike, Frankie scrambled back from the bed. Her eyes wide, mouth open, she sobbed in a breath.

Where was the threat?

His eyes searched the room, then moved back to the bed. Curtains blocked his view, but judging from the way Frankie's eyes stayed glued in that direction, whatever had her frightened had to be there.

He slipped into the room. She saw him and whimpered. Her eyes glazed with terror.

Rico whipped his head around and in disbelief watched a fat mother of a snake slide off the bed. It paused, its tongue darting out. Then it reared up.

Crap.

He didn't have time to think. Reaching into his pocket, he flicked open the knife he carried and let it sail through the air.

The blade sliced into the beast's neck. Frankie jumped to her feet and slammed into him, her arms strangling his neck.

"Oh, God. Oh, God. Oh, God," she repeated over and over again, her body trembling with little shocks.

Rico rubbed her back with a circular motion, telling her that she would be fine. His eyes, though, continued to search every corner. How had the snake gotten in here? Were there any others?

The damn thing was huge. If she'd been bitten...the muscle in his jaw tightened. He didn't need to finish the thought. Out here alone, the woman was a walking target. Anything could happen and no one would have a clue for days, months or even longer.

"You need to come back to town."

"What?"

"You can't stay here alone." He looked down into her face, relieved to see the frozen look gone.

"Of course I'm staying. It was just a snake. I can handle that."

"Like you handled it this time?"

Her eyes flashed fire and he wondered when she'd realize she still stood in the circle of his embrace. Her body felt good flush up against his. Her womanly scent combined with a light perfume was doing stuff to his head. His eyes zeroed in on her mouth.

Damn if he didn't want to kiss her.

And then she shoved him.

"What was that for?" He glared at her.

She had the grace to blush. "Uh, thank you for, uh, helping me, but you and your friend need to go."

"You're kicking me out?"

"Yes. No. I mean, you're here to unload the lumber. That's it. Job's finished. Time to go."

Rico couldn't believe her. She'd been so scared she'd nearly climbed into his skin. Now she was acting like they'd shared a cup of tea and visiting time was over. He shook his head in disbelief.

"You going to clean that up by yourself?"

She looked at the carcass and shuddered. "Do you suppose

you could get rid of that for me?"

Rico stalked across the room, then looked down at the dead snake. Brown-black in color, close to seven feet long, an adult. And not indigenous to the island. "Nasty sucker." he commented.

"That thing wanted to eat me." Frankie stood in the doorway with her arms wrapped around her middle.

"I doubt it. Not enough meat on your bones." He gathered the snake in the top sheet. Since he didn't think she'd want the bedding back, he pulled out his knife and wiped the blade on the sheet before tying it up. A sound behind him made him look at her. She stared at the knife and then him. Her tongue licked her lips, making him think of that kiss he'd foregone.

"You're pretty good with that," she said, nodding towards the black-handled switchblade he held.

"A skill I picked up." He put the knife back in his pocket. "You got a bag or something I can put this in?"

"Yeah, sure." She hurried from the room, but not before he glimpsed the borderline fear in her eyes.

Only this time, she was afraid of him.

Frankie had known guys and girls who were good with knives. There were those who used them for protection and those who used them to slice. She shuddered at the last thought. Having been shuttled from place to place in foster care, she spent a lot of layover time in state-run institutions and she saw her fair share of knives. Right now, she didn't want to think about it. Rico had to go and he had to go now.

Quickly, she grabbed a big black contractor bag from the room across the hall, which she had been cleaning out. "Here you go."

He took the bag and shoved the bloody sheet in the garbage bag.

"José is probably wondering if *el chupacabra* ate us." He laughed.

"Oh, please, tell me you don't believe in that crap." Frankie rolled her eyes.

His expression hardened. "No." He threw the bag over his

shoulder and walked past her.

She followed behind. "Finally, someone with some common sense."

"Vieques is a small island. Most of the people are natives, *borinqueños* who have never left the island. Puerto Ricans like to tell stories. Maybe you should listen to some of them."

Frankie folded her arms. "Oh, really. I thought you said you didn't believe in monsters."

"I believe there are monsters out there." He patted the bag on his back. "Just not the imaginary kind."

A horn blew from outside. "José is waiting." She started down the stairs, her insides in turmoil. She was glad he was leaving. But once Rico and the horn-blowing driver left, she'd be all alone. Just her and any other creatures calling this place home. Ugh.

Her sneakers hit the bottom step when a loud crack sounded from behind her.

Frankie whirled around and stared in horror at the sight of Rico several steps above her. One of his feet had gone through the stair tread.

She fisted her hands into her hair and let out a scream of frustration. "What else in this God-forsaken deathtrap could possibly go wrong?"

Rico tugged on his pant leg. The fabric tore loose and his sneaker-clad foot pulled out from under the splintered wood.

Frankie put a lid on her emotions. She could have a breakdown later. "Are you all right?" she asked.

"Yeah. I'm fine." He dusted the shards of rotted wood from his pant leg. The material was ripped from the knee down. He fingered the jeans. "Guess these are becoming work shorts." He took the rest of the stairs gingerly, testing his weight on each one as he came down.

"Sorry. This place is a disaster." She shook her head.

Rico tentatively took the last steps down, the bag containing the snake still in his hand. He looked out onto the porch. Frankie knew it was in no better condition.

"I should have warned you. I've been meaning to put some new boards down, but the lumberyard that promised to deliver supplies reneged, which is why I had to go into town to get it, and still I could only pick up half the load. The manager told me this place is cursed and he doesn't want to come near it. Can you believe this nonsense?" Her left eye twitched.

Rico placed a hand on her shoulder and softly caressed it. "Relax. No harm done. We can drive out there tomorrow and pick up what we need."

There was that "we" again. She liked the way his hand felt warm and rough against her skin. So calm and reassuring. She wanted to lean into his touch, but pulled away.

His hand dropped down to his side. "It's going to take more than twice the wood you got outside to fix this place."

"I know, but the lumberyard won't deliver here and I'm short on cash. What I ordered will have to do." She looked at the gaping hole and moved it to the top of her list of jobs to tackle. Why had her grandmother let the place deteriorate like this? Why had her grandmother waited until she was dead to contact Frankie? Too many unanswered questions. Shaking her head, she turned back to Rico. "I'm sorry. You could have broken your leg." She looked into eyes as tranquil as the Caribbean Sea, aware that he wasn't the least bit frazzled.

"But I didn't." He smiled wickedly and leaned on the banister, their mouths inches apart.

"You need to be more careful," she said breathlessly as his hand slid up the banister to cover hers.

"I'll keep that in mind, but I'm usually reckless by nature." He stroked his thumb over the back of her hand.

She gripped the solid polished wood. "I have iced tea in the kitchen," she said, her mouth suddenly parched and dry. Quickly extracting her hand from the heat of his touch, she tried to put more space between them. "Excuse me."

Rico took a step back, allowing her room to move. She squeezed past him. Her breasts accidentally brushed against his T-shirt. Her nipples hardened in response. She crossed her arms over her chest and hurried through the parlor doors into the kitchen.

Get a grip. The man was way too hot and she wasn't about to get burned. She grabbed one of the glasses and downed the icy liquid, aware of Rico's eyes on her as he passed through the kitchen and out the back door.

Once composed, she picked up the tray with refreshments and headed outside. Rico circled to the back of the truck and threw the garbage bag onto the truck bed. José sat in the driver's seat, impatient to leave.

"Thought you might like a drink." José politely took the glass and gulped it down almost in one swallow.

Rico smiled and took a glass from the tray. "*Gracias.*"

She watched his Adam's apple bob as he thirstily drank the iced tea. He swiped his lips with the back of his hand. "The land looks like it needs a drink too."

Frankie knew what he meant. Long ago, the grounds had been fertile and used as a sugar cane plantation. But that had been nearly half a century ago, according to the lawyer who had handled the execution of the will. Neglect and lack of funds had left a good portion of the land hard-caked dirt. Aside from weeds and the occasional prickly poinciana bush with its brilliant reddish blossoms, there was little vegetation. A few ceibo trees grew on the property. Their large green fronds offered some shade from the sun and, on occasion, she found herself sitting beneath them, listening to the breeze through the leaves. Overall, since arriving, she had put her effort into restoring the house and had little time to explore the sixty-plus acres, much less take care of the grounds.

He gave the house a once over and handed the glass back to her. "Why don't you come back into town with us? You'll be safer there."

"Safer?" Frankie's spine stiffened. "I'm not about to be driven off my property by stupid stories or anything else." She'd toughed it out nearly all her life. This place was a piece of cake compared to the cold streets of the Big Apple. "Your ride's leaving."

Rico's head whipped around. Sure enough, José had put the truck in gear and was starting to back up. Rico cursed. Frankie grinned.

"Better jump in. It's a long walk back."

Clearly frustrated, he grabbed for the door handle. It swung open and he leaped inside. Hanging out the window, he called out to her. "I'll be back later."

"No, you won't," she screamed back. "You're not needed or wanted."

He simply waved.

Hands fisted on her hips, she watched the truck tear down the drive. She didn't know who was the bigger snake. The dead one in the back or the live one sitting up front.

Frankie stomped back to the house. She had work to do and only a few more hours left of daylight to get it done.

She stepped through the back door and closed it behind her. Silence greeted her. Taking a deep breath, she tried to calm her emotions.

She would not let the day get her down. She had to stay focused. Already she had lost enough daylight. Putting the tray aside she grabbed a hammer. Maybe a few good whacks to some nails would drive out the frustration she felt. And drive out a certain islander with bedroom eyes, strong, capable hands, and entirely too much attitude.

She groaned out loud, her grip tightened on the hammer. Who did he think he was anyway? Superman?

For a moment, he came across that way, swooping down and helping her. He didn't even know her. Frankie shook her head. Experience taught her to never rely on anyone. Nothing in life came free. He'd probably be back demanding money or...she didn't finish the thought. If he thought she was some naïve *turista*, he'd better think again.

Her social worker had called her spunky. Her foster families had called her a fighter, a troublemaker, and uncontrollable. The system had deemed her unadoptable. Frankie Montalvo was more than that—she was a survivor.

She tested the weight of the hammer in her hand. No one or nothing was going to stop her from making Casa Verde her home. Not some goat-sucking legend, or a man-eating snake, and especially not some macho Latino with a superhero complex.

છ

Rico drove slowly up the rutted driveway, the truck's

headlights slicing through the darkness. The place seemed even more isolated than it had earlier. The land immediately surrounding the house lay clear, but the encroaching forest left plenty of places for a predator to hide.

Frankie Montalvo could've disappeared at any time and no one would've been the wiser.

For all her gutsy, in-your-face attitude, the woman was out of her element. Now if only he could convince her to walk away without blowing his cover.

The manor lay in darkness. He supposed she'd gone to bed since it was nearly midnight. He hadn't intended to be this late, but he'd had to bully the mechanic into fixing her truck and then persuade the manager of the lumberyard to keep the place open long enough to load Frankie's order.

The mechanic must've used duct tape to put the damn vehicle together, because every time Rico went above thirty, the contraption rattled and shook as if it were shedding pieces of itself along the road. He'd practically crawled the whole way.

Somehow he didn't think Frankie was going to be happy to see him.

He grinned in the darkness, recalling her standing in the driveway yelling at him as he'd left her place earlier in the afternoon. The woman had the lungs of a fishwife.

She'd fit right in with his family.

Whoa. Rico rubbed a hand over his face. He didn't want to know where that thought came from. Lack of sleep, probably.

Around the back of the house, he stopped the truck and set the emergency brake. In the beam of the lights, off to the corner and veering around the side of the house, he caught signs of tire tracks. Rico climbed out of the vehicle but kept the headlights on, the illumination penetrating the darkness. *Coquí* frogs sang their songs high up in the canopy of trees. Sweat rolled down the sides of his face from the sticky humidity. He put all his weight into closing the truck's door, surprised the damn thing didn't fall off. The creaky hinges sounded like a shotgun blast in the night. No lights came on. She mustn't have heard him.

Rolling his head, he tried to ease the tension in his shoulders. Rico walked in the deep ruts. No dust. His sneakers sunk into the mud. José had parked in the back of the house and these tire markings were too big to be from the small flatbed truck. He crouched down and measured the depth of the impression with his hand. Fresh. Deep. Definitely a heavier vehicle. A van or an SUV. He followed the tracks. They led straight back into the mangroves. It was too dark. The headlight beams could no longer penetrate the thick foliage. He'd have to come back with a flashlight. Turning around, he jogged back to the truck and opened the toolbox in the back.

Wrench. Nuts and bolts. Electric drill. No flashlight. He cursed. Rico stared at the wall of overgrown vegetation. "Tomorrow morning," he promised. "If you're out there, Chita, I'll find you."

At the back door, Rico knocked loudly and waited. No lights or sound indicated she'd heard him. He banged again with a fist. No one could sleep through the noise.

He jiggled the door handle. Locked.

Rico backed away and looked up at the windows. All of them were dark. Was Frankie all right? He'd only put his foot through a board. What if she'd fallen through the floor? She could be lying inside broken and bleeding. He should have simply tossed her over his shoulder this afternoon and forced her to go into town.

God save him from stubborn females.

He pulled a lock pick out of his pocket and went back to the kitchen door. In a matter of minutes he was inside. His eyes swept the kitchen, noting the clean counters and dishes lying in the draining board. The scent of onions and garlic lingered in the air. Well, she'd obviously eaten.

He retraced his steps from the afternoon until he was at the bottom of the staircase. He could see where Frankie covered over the hole he'd made with a patch of plywood. As much as he wanted to run up the stairs, he didn't dare. Carefully, he tested each tread before taking a step.

While moonlight filtered into the rooms downstairs, up here, with all the doors to the hallway closed, he could barely see his hand in front of his face. Quietly, Rico made his way down the hall until he came to Frankie's door.

He rapped lightly. Still no answer.

Moving to the side of the door, he reached over, turned the handle and gave it a small push inward. He glanced in and then slowly stepped over the threshold, grateful for the moonlight that enabled him to see.

Fresh sheets covered the bed. The room looked neat and tidy.

No Frankie.

What the hell had happened to her? God help him if she'd been snatched...

He didn't pause to wonder why his fear she'd had an accident had morphed into something worse. He didn't have to.

This house had him on edge, while his mother's request had him balled up so tight he could bounce.

A sound caught his ears. Exiting the room, he moved silently down the corridor. The noise grew louder, like a herd of sick cows. When he reached the room where the sound came the loudest, he threw open the door and went in low and fast, ready to deal with the threat.

Frankie rose before him, moonlight casting its soft glow on the water droplets sliding down her torso and into the claw foot tub she stood in. Her mouth opened and closed and, in that second, Rico catalogued every gorgeous inch of her, from her perfect, dusky-tipped breasts to her shapely thighs.

"What do you want?" Her voice came out reed thin, her eyes wide.

He'd terrified her. Rico held his hands out, palms open. "I brought your truck back, Frankie. When you didn't answer the door, I got worried and let myself in. I'm not here to hurt you." He spoke low and soft, willing her to listen to his words. He almost missed the change in her eyes from fear to majorly ticked off, but he wasn't left in doubt long.

Frankie exploded into action. She grabbed a bar of soap and hurled it at him, hitting him smack in the chest.

Instinctively, he caught the soap before it fell to the tiled floor. "Want me to get your back?" Relief coursed through him. Not only was she okay, she was in kick-butt NY mode. He could live with that.

"Get out!" she screamed. "Out! Out! Out!"

The gentleman in him grabbed up a towel and held it out to her. The other side of him wanted to wipe every drop of water off her sexy body, but he highly doubted she would let him.

Frankie seized the towel and wrapped it around her. "Get out!"

"I'm going. But, why are you taking a bath in the dark?"

"Because the damn fuse blew and I wasn't about to go traipsing around the house wet and naked. Satisfied?"

Hell, no! But, feeling a definite tightening in his groin at the image, he decided not to answer. Safer that way. At least with this woman.

"Now are you leaving or do I have to get mean?"

"You got a weapon on you? All I saw—"

"Shut up, Lopez. I swear you're dead meat." Her hands tightened into fists at her sides.

"Need a hand getting out of the tub?" he asked hopefully.

"That's it. You have five seconds to get out of this room or you and that toilet brush are going to become personally acquainted."

"Okay, you win," he said, holding his hands up in the air in mock surrender. "Anything but the toilet brush." He winked at her and left the room, shutting the door with an audible snap. Leaning against it, he closed his eyes. He could hear her stepping out of the tub. Could imagine her rubbing that lithe body down and wished he were the towel. The image of Frankie rising up from the water like some goddess out of a Greek myth would stay burned onto the back of his eyelids for a long time. And if he told her, she'd probably try to have them surgically removed.

He grinned so hard the sides of his mouth hurt.

The bathroom echoed with her creative curses in both Spanish and English. The woman sure had a mouth on her.

Feeling incredibly lighter, Rico spoke through the closed door. "Frankie?"

"What?"

"Would it make you feel better if I got naked too?"

"You're not forgiven. I'll pay you back for the repairs on the truck and we will forget that tonight's episode ever happened."

Frankie slapped the coffee mug down in front of her uninvited guest and took the seat farthest away from him as she could. She didn't know if she believed Rico's glib explanation that he'd simply been trying to help her out. In her experience, people only helped you out when they wanted something in return. By the glint of humor in his chocolate brown eyes, she had a feeling she knew what he wanted. She crossed her legs under the table.

At least he'd had the decency to find the fuse box and get the lights back on. She really hadn't relished the idea of making her way through the house in the darkness. Now she didn't have to, but that didn't mean she was happy about Rico dropping in unannounced.

Frankie studied him over the rim of her cup. He sat kicked back in the kitchen chair, one hand wrapped around the chipped mug she'd scrounged up. His eyes moved constantly, the mirth evident, though something deeper lay under his gaze.

"A job this big is too much for you to do on your own. What about your family? They must be worried about you, down here, all alone." He spoke casually, but she sensed he was probing. Similar to tactics her social worker had used whenever she got kicked out of another home.

"My problem. Not yours," she retorted evasively. With both forearms on the scratched kitchen table, Frankie leaned forward. "Look, I don't know what you want. If it's cash, I told you, I'm low. Maybe tomorrow I can get some from the bank to repay you for fixing the truck and the supplies." She pushed away from the table. "Want some more coffee?"

"No. I'm good." Rico stretched his arms, sinewy roped muscle rippling beneath the thin, sweaty T-shirt fabric. She turned to pour herself another cup before she got caught gawking.

"So, when are you returning to New York?"

Frankie stopped mid-pour. Other than her name, she hadn't told him about herself. "What makes you think I'm from New York?"

He shrugged. "I must've heard it in town."

Frankie chewed her lip. She supposed he could have. She did recall mentioning it to one or two townspeople she'd met.

"What part?" he asked.

"Brooklyn."

"What about your parents?" He watched her carefully even as he rubbed at a scar on the table. Her eyes fixed on his hand. Long, strong, calloused hands, good for construction work or strangling women.

Frankie blinked and tried to remember what he'd asked.

God, she must be more tired than she'd thought. She shoved the vision away.

"What is this? Twenty questions?"

He laughed, a deep rumbling sound, and he relaxed more into the chair. How anyone could look that stress-free, she had no idea. Must be Caribbean life. Frankie hoped in a year from now, when the renovations were over—if they ever would be— she could kick back and relax as easily as Rico.

"Just some friendly talk to pass the time."

Frankie took her mug back to the table. "Time is something I don't have much of." She looked at the sunshine-yellow clock on the whitewashed plaster wall of the kitchen. "It's late. You should be going."

"Wish I could, but the roads up here are treacherous. Besides, I need a lift back into town and I don't think Old Yeller out there can make anymore trips."

"Guess you'll have to walk."

"Aw, you'd kick me out after all the nice things I did for you?" His hand over his heart, he gave her a fake pained look.

Frankie didn't want to smile but she couldn't help it. "Anyone ever tell you that you're charming?"

"*Mi mami.*" He flashed her a smile.

Frankie rolled her eyes. "Fine. You can stay the night in one of the guest rooms. Might as well get used to strangers sleeping under the roof if I ever want to make Casa Verde a successful bed-and-breakfast."

Rico gave a low whistle. "Ambitious."

"You're not kidding." She held the warm mug between her hands and looked down into the dark swirling water, hoping to see a vision of her future, but it remained black. "When I inherited this place, I had no idea what I was in for, but it's all I have." She swallowed the uncertainty that lodged in her throat. "I'm determined to make something good here." Her voice came out hard, even to her ears.

When she looked up from her beverage, she saw Rico studying her. "What?"

"Nothing." He grinned. "Just thinking what a gutsy girl you are."

"Gutsy. Never been called that before," she mumbled under her breath before taking a sip of her coffee.

"What are your dreams for this place?" he asked.

A simple enough question, no harm in telling him. Yeah, right. People had a way of tearing your dreams down before you even had a chance to build them. Was Rico the type? He observed her with friendly interest. But so had a number of do-gooders who always wanted what they thought was in her best interest. All her years riding the system, based on feigned concern for her future, ultimately to be spit out on the street. Dreams? She had no dreams. Frankie Montalvo was a hard-core realist. Working her way from a simple cleaning maid to the front desk manager at one of New York City's premier boutique hotels. She may not have the fancy degrees or the wads of cash to make Casa Verde a smashing success, but she did have determination.

And the reality was that if she couldn't make Casa Verde work for her, she'd be out on the street again, or worse, crawling back on hands and knees to her old boss to beg for her desk manager job back. If there was one thing Frankie Montalvo did not do, it was beg. But she also knew the deep chill of being broke, homeless and desperate.

Not this time. Never again.

She eyed Rico warily. Uncertain if she really wanted to hear his opinion. Frankie took a chance. "I was hoping to renovate and open up in six months for the tourist season."

"You and what army? This place doesn't need a repair here and there. It needs to be torn down and rebuilt. Do you have any idea how much time, effort and money—"

"Yeah, I know." Frankie jumped to her feet. God, she had been a fool to believe he would understand. "It won't be easy. I'm working on the money. I figure to get a loan. As for time, well, I've got plenty of it." She wanted to walk away. Just turn around and forget Rico and his stupid questions.

No! This was her house. Her rules. "You know what? This is none of your business. You need to go."

Rico stood up and faced her across the table. "Anything could happen to you out here. Who the hell would even know? If I'd really been some kind of rapist back in that bathroom, do you really think you would've stood a chance? You could scream all you wanted but it would be just one more story to add to the others about this place and not a damn person would have the guts to come out here and check on you."

Okay, he had a point. She'd been terrified when he stormed into her bathroom. Had even thought *el chupacabra* had come to get her. But she wouldn't be scared out of her own home by some guy she'd just met. "I've taken care of myself for a long time. I don't need a babysitter."

"Well, you're going to get one."

"Don't even think about it."

She skewered him with her eyes. He didn't blink. Anger arced between them, each trying to assert authority. As tired as she felt, Frankie could almost reach out and touch the energy zinging back and forth. Sparks charged the air.

A cat, she suddenly thought. Rico reminded her of a large jungle cat. Sleek, powerful, ever watchful and ready to pounce.

It was too much. This man. This situation. This damn attraction. She didn't want any of it.

"Who are you? I mean for an unemployed laborer you seem too interested in me and mine. What is it to you?"

She'd struck a nerve. His eyes became remote and the muscles around his mouth tightened.

"What you see is what you get. I told you before, *mi mami* raised me to be a gentleman. She'd never let me live it down if I left you all alone out here."

"Now, wait one minute. No disrespect to your *mami*, but

this is my house, my life. And you're not wanted. You can stay here for the night and then get the hell out." Not wanting to give him the last word, she stalked out of the kitchen. Climbing the stairs, she told herself that if he didn't leave tomorrow she'd call the cops. She didn't know why Rico was so desperate to attach himself to her. She didn't care.

Her feet dragged as she reached her bedroom. She was so tired. Having worked all afternoon with only a short break for supper, her muscles begged for sleep. She'd even dozed off in the tub, which is why she never heard Rico come in.

Inside her room she closed the door and locked it for good measure. She tossed her robe onto a chair and pulled back the sheets, examining them carefully. She'd put fresh sheets on earlier, but wasn't about to discount some creepy crawly thing finding its way inside. A knock sounded at the door.

"What?" she called out.

"I'm going to bunk down in the room across the hall. If you need anything, call me."

"Not likely," she muttered under her breath. "You're out of here in the morning, Rico Lopez," she said, this time in a voice loud enough to be heard.

The damn man laughed. Fuming, Frankie slipped under the sheets. The deep timber of his laugh rolled under with her. She punched her pillow. Argh, why did her get under her skin? Shutting down her mind, she turned off the lamp and lay her head down. And then clicked it back on. How had he gotten inside? She had been exhausted when she had been locking up. Frankie tried to think if she had missed a section of the house. She kicked off the sheets. Rico would tell her how he got in. On second thought, it might be better to just go downstairs and test all the locks.

Sleepily, she rubbed at her eyes and made her way to the door. She opened it slowly so as not to make a sound and have him come running. Knowing him and his superman-have-to-protect-weak-and-desperate-women issues, he'd come running if the door squeaked. With equal care, she turned around to shut the door when a hand clamped down over her mouth from behind. Frankie opened her eyes wide, willing them to see in the dark. She struggled forward but was pulled back into a warm, broad chest. Her heart thundered loudly in her chest. Survival instinct kicked in. She felt something cold press up against her bare arm.

He had his knife in his hand.

Oh God, he was going to slice her. *Stupid! Stupid! Stupid!* She should have insisted he go.

She was going to die.

Right here.

Right now.

Chapter 3

"There's someone in the house," Rico whispered.

Frankie's body vibrated against his. She breathed hard through her nose, his hand still clamped over her mouth. Suddenly, she jabbed her elbow into his ribs. "Umph!" he grunted, but didn't budge. His ribs would be sore for days. He ignored the sharp pain. Instead, he pulled her in closer, not giving her an advantage to hit him again.

"Frankie, there's someone in the house," he repeated, this time slower, into her ear. She must have registered his warning because she dropped her arms and the tension stilled in her body.

"Don't make any noise. I don't know how many there are. I want you to stay behind me." She'd be a sitting duck in her room without a weapon. He had no choice but to have her tag along. "Do exactly what I say and if I say run, you get the hell away. *Comprende?*"

She nodded her head. Slowly he removed his hand.

"You could have just told me that in the first place," she seethed.

He put his fingers to his lips. So much for being quiet. The woman had to fight him at every turn. He didn't waste time arguing back. With his ears tuned to any sounds below, he retreated, pushing her back into the bedroom. He stayed near the door, keeping it slightly ajar to view anyone that might come up the hallway. "You expecting visitors?"

She shook her head.

Whoever was in the house hadn't bothered to hide their presence. He'd been lying on a lumpy mattress, unable to get the image of Frankie clad in nothing but water droplets out of his head, when he'd heard someone bumping into a piece of furniture and cursing. He'd been across the hall in seconds, not even taking time for his shirt or shoes. Though he figured Frankie would scream bloody murder if anyone so much as laid a finger on her, he needed to make sure she was safe.

One dead woman on his conscience was all he could take.

A hand touched his bare back, scalding him with unexpected heat. Rico nearly leaped out of his skin. "Damn it, woman, don't do that," he growled.

"What? What'd you see?" Frankie asked, leaning over his shoulder to try to get a better look.

Rico blew out a breath. "Is there another way down to the first floor other than the main stairs?"

"The back stairs, but I don't know what kind of shape they're in."

"We'll chance it."

Rico slipped into the hall. He glanced over his shoulder to see Frankie following him. Corkscrew curls shot out in every direction and her eyes were spitting mad. It was all he could do to force his foot forward rather than turning back and dragging her to him for a taste of those luscious lips.

God, how he wanted a taste.

Later. For now, if he wanted her to live long enough, he had to find out who'd broken in.

He retracted the knife and stuck it in his waistband for easy retrieval. Cautiously, he made his way forward. When one board creaked loudly, he paused, but another loud crash from below made him doubt the intruders were paying any attention to the floor above.

Frankie glided up and laid her hand on his bicep. "What's your plan?" she whispered.

"When we get downstairs, I want you to go out to the truck and wait there. I left the keys under the foot mat. If I don't come get you within fifteen minutes, you get the hell away. Drive into town and report to the police. Got it?" He saw all the arguments spinning in her head. He covered her mouth with his hand before she could voice a single one.

"Nod if you understand." He waited, ignoring the way her eyes shot darts at him, until she finally nodded.

"Good." He took his hand away. "Let's move."

Sweat poured down his back by the time they made it down the narrow staircase. It'd been slow going as each board had to be tested before they dared step on it.

Relief hit him once his feet touched cool tile. The kitchen lay in darkness, but enough moonlight cleared a path through the obstacles. Reaching out, he grasped Frankie's shoulders through the thin cotton of her nightgown. Her scent intoxicated him, clouding his thoughts. "Do as I said," he ordered. "Get to the truck. If I'm not there in fifteen minutes, get the hell out of here."

"But—"

"No buts." He squeezed her shoulders and then, calling himself every kind of fool, he did what he'd been wanting to do ever since he'd seen her in the bar mirror, looking ready to take on the world despite the vulnerability lurking in the back of her eyes. He closed the distance between them. With his feet braced apart, she fit snug against him. Sliding his fingers up to spear them into those glorious curls, he lowered his lips to hers.

He wouldn't have been surprised if she'd belted him one for the liberty he was taking. He deserved it.

But she did nothing. No, not nothing. She leaned into him. Her lips parted slightly and warm breath touched his.

She tasted of honey and spice. Of heaven.

It ended too quickly, but now wasn't the time. Not when bad guys were prowling around.

And not when he was being less than honest with her.

"Go. Now," he ordered in a harsh whisper.

She looked up at him, questions swimming in her large doe eyes. "Why'd you do that?" Her fingers came up and touched her mouth.

"Never mind. Go." He turned her and gave her a little shove to the back door. She went, but he knew she wouldn't let what had just happened go. She had questions and she would expect answers.

Frankie Montalvo was nothing if not persistent.

He'd definitely learned that in the short time they'd known one another. But he didn't have time to dissect the kiss and didn't want to. The creak of a door told him the enemy was close. With his hands up and fisted and his knife easy to retrieve at his waist, Rico rested on the balls of his feet and waited.

The blast of cool night air provided the shock to reality Frankie needed. She couldn't believe she'd kissed him. Intruders had entered her home and all she could think about was how great Rico's butt looked in those jeans. What was wrong with her?

She did not trust him. Did not know him.

Frankie strode over to the truck listing all the reasons why kissing Rico was bad. When she reached the vehicle, she wrapped her arms around herself and leaned against the door. Stars winked at her from above.

Her breath came out on a sigh. Who was she kidding?

Kissing Rico might've been wrong, but nothing had ever felt that right.

She'd felt safe, protected. Like she'd found a home.

Frankie shook her head in denial, her curls slapping at her face. Dangerous thoughts. Stupid ones.

Rico could be a drifter for all she knew. A man without a home and a woman in every port. He could be trouble with a capital T.

She scrubbed her face with her hands, willing for some sanity to return, because deep down, she wasn't sure she could push Rico away if he tried to kiss her again.

She'd always had a soft spot for a bad boy.

A crash from inside the house had her head whipping around. Rico was in there. Fighting her battle. And he expected her to obey him. It was the smart thing to do.

Yeah, but for who?

Sometimes smart had to take a backseat. This was her home. Rico's macho attitude might tick her off, but she didn't want the guy hurt because of her.

She pushed away from the truck and turned her attention to the flatbed. Just as Rico had said, her order of lumber lay piled in back. She undid the ties holding the load down and reached up to grab a two-foot piece of a two-by-four.

Shouts carried over the night air. Frankie hefted the piece of wood in her hand and ran back to the house. At the back door, she slipped inside and, on tiptoes, made for a vantage point that would give her a view of what was happening.

A cry of pain sounded and Frankie winced. Please don't let Rico be hurt, she repeated over and over.

Shadows moved. Rico's bare back came into view. The sound of flesh pounding on flesh sickened her. It looked like two against one.

Make that two against two she amended and stepped in swinging. She brought the wood down on one intruder. She'd meant to whomp him in the head, but he moved at the last minute and the board clipped him on the shoulder. He went down with a howl anyway.

Rico took advantage of the distraction and made short work of the remaining intruder. Frankie ran to the wall and flipped on the light. Chairs lay on their side and one of the flowerpots she'd set out on a sill had fallen and shattered, but the overall damage seemed minimal.

Her gaze took in the two strangers on the floor. No blood. At least nothing more than a split lip and a bloody nose. Her eyes flew to Rico. He was wiping a trickle of blood from the corner of his mouth. His knife lay closed at his waistband.

Something inside her loosened. A man who lived by the knife would've had no hesitation in using it against two unknown assailants. Why hadn't Rico? She stared at him as if seeing him for the first time. His tan chest radiated strength. His jaw line indicated a stubbornness that matched her own. His eyes that had only a few hours ago glowed a molten caramel now snapped with anger.

"Why the hell didn't you listen to me?" his voice thundered through the kitchen.

"I couldn't leave you here by yourself. You could've gotten hurt." She stomped her foot in emphasis. "I keep telling you, but you don't seem to get it. This is my home and it's my job to protect it." Then, realizing she probably sounded ungrateful, Frankie backpedaled. "Of course, I appreciate what you did—" Rico snorted, which she ignored—"and you're hurt." She pointed at his bare arm.

He turned and looked at the back of his hand. A thin layer of blood smeared over his knuckles. "It's not mine," he said gruffly.

Frankie turned her attention back to the two men groaning on the floor. One looked to be in his fifties, while the other was several years younger than her. They didn't fit her image of burglars. Then again, in foster care, she'd seen all sorts of desperate acts. Anger rose in her chest. She finally had something of her own and some idiots were trying to take it away.

Well, if they thought they were going to get away with it, they could think again. She took a step forward and raised the wood plank. Rico grabbed her before she could teach the two fools a lesson.

"Francesca!" the older man yelled. The stench of alcohol rent the air. He staggered up and made a run at her. With unprecedented speed, Rico intercepted him and knocked the man down. The older man floundered under Rico's weight. "Francesca!"

Frankie paused, the two-by-four angled above her head, ready to strike out.

Francesca. It had been a long time since she had last heard that name. A vision of a happy moment popped in her mind—her with her arms out swinging as her mother and father held on to each of her hands. Her mother's dimpled cheek as she laughed at the child's antics, her father's fierce embrace as he scooped her up over his head and deposited her onto his shoulders.

"Francesca!" The drunken slur of her name brought her back to reality.

Rico put the man in a headlock, his grip daring the man to get away.

Frankie lowered the board. "Rico, stop! You're hurting him."

Rico gritted his teeth. "He's a burglar." The man cried out her name again.

She dropped the board. "Please," Frankie grabbed Rico's upper arm, his muscles tight and hard. He held the man fast. "You're going to kill him!" Desperately, she tried to wrestle the man free.

Rico's head snapped in her direction, "What are you doing?"

A loud crash brought their attention to the second man. Younger and filled with bravado, he swung Frankie's discarded wood plank like a baseball bat. "Step away from my father and nobody gets hurt."

"You know this guy?" Rico interrupted, jerking his thumb at his captive even as he let loose and shoved the guy away.

Frankie shook her head. "I've never seen him before in my life."

"That's not true," the man denied, staggering to stay upright. Finally, he gave up, dragged out a kitchen chair and sat. Blood trickled from one nostril. "When last I saw you, you were a *niña*. Don't you remember me?"

Frankie stared at the man. Her memory fought hard for a recollection from her youth. Scattered images of faces slid through her mind, too many, too fast. She shook her head to clear the onslaught.

"I'm sorry, but I don't remember..."

She searched the thin, aged face for signs of recognition and found it in the dimpled, lopsided smile he gave her, so reminiscent of her mother's smile.

"Francesca, it has been many years since I last saw my sister, Ana, and your father, Tito."

He knew her parents' names. Frankie sucked in her breath.

Rico eyed the newcomer warily. He put his hand on her shoulder. She leaned into it for support. "Be careful," he whispered to her.

The older man smiled, his teeth yellowed from cigarettes and booze, a combination that wafted off him in waves. "I'm your uncle Hector and this is my son, Armando, your cousin. You won't remember him as he was born long after your mother took you off the island."

Frankie shook her head, still trying to absorb all the new information being thrown at her.

"No worries. We'll have plenty of time to get to know each other. We've come for a visit." The man belched and Frankie nearly reeled back from the fumes. She settled for waving her hand in front of her face.

"He's your uncle?" Disgust and disbelief dripped from Rico's mouth.

"Maybe. Yeah, I guess." She didn't like how she sounded—defensive, uncertain. First, a grandmother she hadn't known about who'd left her this place. Now, an uncle and a cousin. How many other relatives were there?

Rico gave a noncommittal grunt as he moved back to stand sentry over the man who claimed to be her uncle.

With bloodshot eyes matched by marks of dissipation, the man looked more like the homeless guys on the streets of New York, which might explain why he and Armando were sneaking into the house in the middle of the night. Still, they were strangers.

"Look, it's really late," she said pointedly. "Maybe if you had called or something. I'm really not prepared for guests."

"I told you, *Papi*, but you never listen."

Frankie turned her head to the cousin who still held the board loosely. The clothes he wore were clean but threadbare. The young man refused to meet her eyes, embarrassment clear on his face. He didn't seem to know whether he needed the weapon or not, his eyes darting back and forth between his father and Rico.

"You can put that down now." She smiled and tried her best for levity. "We thought you were burglars. Superman over there gets cranky when he has to fight without his tights."

"Yeah, well, Wonder Woman better watch it or she's going to learn what Superman does when his orders aren't followed."

For a moment, Frankie forgot about her unexpected guests. Her gaze dueled with Rico's. No way was she going to let him think he could boss her around. But his eyes hardened with a ferocity that made her rethink the wisdom of baiting a tiger.

"Francesca, your boyfriend has a mean right hook." Her uncle struggled to his feet. He patted his pockets and finally dug out a handkerchief that he used to plug his nose.

"You know, Uncle Hector," said Frankie, trying out the name on her tongue, "he's not my boyfriend—"

Rico flashed Hector a smile. Not like the ones he reserved for her. This smile reminded her of a jaguar. "What Frankie here meant is that I'm her contractor, Rico Lopez."

"Now wait a minute—"

"Francesca, I don't understand any of this." Her uncle put his hand to his temple. He swooned on his feet. "I really need to go to my room."

"Uncle Hector, you can't stay—" The stricken look she caught on Armando's face, combined with Hector's obvious issues with gravity took all the air out of her argument.

"We understand," Armando said. "Come on, *Papi*. Let's go."

"Wait!" Frankie put her hand up to stop them. "Look, do you have someplace else you can go?" she asked almost desperately.

Armando's eyes dropped to the floor. Frankie groaned inwardly at the unspoken response. She already had Rico staying the night. Would it hurt to let these two stay as well? She'd kick them all out in the morning.

"Are you out of your mind, woman?" Rico hissed beside her.

Frankie shot Rico a look that should have singed his chest hairs. Instead, she focused on the glimpse of relief that flashed in Armando's eyes, the sight dredging up memories she'd prefer to forget. "I'll take you to your room, Uncle." Except she didn't have any idea which room was his. Hopefully, not the one she'd chosen. She didn't know if she could give it up, even for a newfound relative. But he could have the room across from hers with her blessing. Rico could sleep in the basement for all she cared. Let his charm keep him warm tonight.

"Armando, go get the suitcases." Her uncle wavered, nearly losing his balance, and then wove his way to the stairs.

Frankie choked down a laugh. Looked like Casa Verde's guest list was growing and she hadn't even opened the doors yet. Go figure.

51

"So, you're Frankie's cousin." Rico observed the youth, who'd finally let go of the board. The boy blanched further as Rico flexed his hand. His knuckles hurt like crazy.

"You put up some fight, kid."

The boy puffed up his chest. He stood a little taller but his shoulders remained hunched. Skinny. Barely out of puberty. Rico figured the boy to be sixteen or so, if that. Nervous, given the way his fingers kept twitching.

"I should go get the bags." He looked to the door, ready to bolt.

Rico placed his hand on the boy's shoulder. The kid jumped under his touch. Rico held on.

"I didn't hear a car." And that bothered him. The two men had gotten too close to the house without Rico hearing it.

"We don't own a car. We bummed a ride." The boy looked down at the tops of his scuffed sneakers. "Nobody'll come up the drive, so we had to walk it."

Rico nodded his head, but he couldn't help recalling the tire tracks he'd seen earlier. Someone didn't have a problem with coming up to the house. "Forget the luggage." He moved Armando further into the kitchen. "You hungry?"

Armando's stomach growled. "We missed dinner."

Rico had a feeling the kid missed meals frequently.

Rico reached up and grabbed a glass from a cabinet and filled it with water. "Want some?"

The kid nodded his head and took the glass. Rico poured himself a glass and chugged down the water, his eyes never off Armando's. The kid didn't seem to be lying, but he sure was nervous. His fingers wouldn't stay still.

"You planning to stay long?"

"It's up to my father. I mean, my cousin Francesca." Armando shuffled from foot to foot, then rubbed his hands on his pants. He had the beginnings of a nice shiner. Rico almost felt sorry for him.

He walked over to the refrigerator, aware of the step back the boy took. He opened it and checked the contents. "Looks like your cousin is out of steak. Too bad." He opened the freezer next. "You're still in luck, kid. Hand me that towel."

Armando thrust the towel in Rico's hand and retreated. "*Gracias*," Rico said. He dumped some ice cubes onto the cloth, and wrapped it. "Put this on that eye of yours. I guarantee it's going to look beautiful tomorrow."

Armando's fingers twitched some more before he reached out for the bundle. "*Gracias*," he mumbled, applying the cold compress to his left eye. While Armando nursed his eye, Rico made a quick sandwich for him.

He placed the plate in front of the kid.

Armando looked up for a second and then quickly devoured the food.

"Can I go now?"

"Yeah, sure." Rico watched the kid scurry out of the room.

His eyes strayed to the pale yellow clock on the wall and he swore. It was almost two in the morning. Odd visiting hours.

He heard Frankie say goodnight, playing Miss Hospitality to the uninvited houseguests.

He shook his head. The woman needed a keeper.

Rico turned and braced his arms against the counter. He was getting in way too deep. All for a skinny *chica* with wild hair and a mouth that wouldn't quit.

But what a mouth.

Rico grinned. He'd learned one thing tonight of value. Kissing Frankie was the surest way to get her to shut up.

Just as quickly his grin faded. What was he thinking? She wasn't a woman to play with. She might wear her attitude like a shield, but he wasn't fooled. Get past that prickliness and a man would find himself knee-deep in passion and on his way to the altar.

Frankie wanted a home.

She wanted it so badly she was willing to turn this albatross into a bed-and-breakfast.

Rico glanced from the chipped green counter tile, to the dingy cream walls, down to the faded who-knew-what-color-it-once-had-been linoleum. How was she going to do the job herself? The woman was too stubborn for her own good.

"Way too deep, Lopez." Rico shook his head, trying to clear it. He shoved his hand into his back pocket and pulled out his wallet, staring at the worn leather. He didn't need to open it to know what lay inside.

He'd inserted the photo of Carla and Lourdes the day of the funeral. Carla and Lourdes had had each other. Now Lourdes had no one. And all because of him.

The guilt and pain ripped through him.

He had so much to answer for. Too much.

He'd find Chita. He'd even keep an eye on Frankie while he searched for the girl. But once he had the answers he needed, he was out of here.

Like the woman and child he carried in his wallet, Frankie and this place would be nothing more than a memory.

&

Sunlight bathed her face. Her head pounded. No, make that the door. Frankie shoved curls off her face and struggled to sit up. "Who is it?"

"Wake up, sleepyhead. Rise and shine."

"Drop dead, Lopez."

Frankie pummeled her pillow and slid back down. Forty more winks and she'd be good to go.

"I'd love to oblige, *querida*, but it would break too many women's hearts. Now, get that cute little tail of yours in gear. There's work to be done."

Frankie rolled over and glared at the door. *Querida?* She wasn't his darling. How had a simple ride home turned into...into... "This!" she spat into the air. Once she had a shower and a cup of coffee, she'd let Rico know who was boss.

She swung her feet over the side of the bed, only to pause. She wasn't seriously considering hiring Rico, was she? Twenty-four hours ago, she'd sworn she'd have to be desperate.

Frankie fell back on the bed. God help her. She really was desperate.

If the price was right, she couldn't afford to be picky. The job was too big for one person. And somehow, she didn't see Uncle Hector and cousin Armando swinging a hammer to turn her inheritance into a B&B. Of course, what did she really know about them anyway? All of them were strangers.

But then, a good portion of her life had been spent among strangers. Never sticking around long enough to get to know anyone.

A smile came to her face. Not this time. This time she was here to stay.

Frankie got up and headed to the bathroom. She'd have to feed her uncle and cousin before sending them on their way, but if they really had no place else to go, could she just kick them out?

Inside the bathroom, she went to the sink before she remembered the faucets had rusted shut and only a sledgehammer would fix it. Frankie turned on the faucet that hung over the claw foot tub. A loud clanging sounded, accompanied by a moan that no longer freaked her out like it had the first time she'd showered. The pipes needed to be replaced. Along with the stairs, the kitchen, the porch, the roof. *Don't think about it.*

Frankie splashed water on her face, her mind returning to last night's events. She'd thought her grandmother to be the only relative she'd had. Now, she found herself with an uncle and cousin. Where had these people been when she'd been dumped in the foster system? Hadn't they cared?

Not that it mattered anymore.

She'd survived. She wasn't anyone's pushover and she'd learned to fight for every inch that was hers. She'd turned out just fine.

But, she couldn't help question, as she dried her face, why her grandmother had left everything to her. Why not them? Surely they needed it as much as she did.

When her uncle woke up, she'd ask him. Until then, she wouldn't let it bother her.

Back in her room, she threw on a purple tank top over a pair of black pedal pushers and stuffed her feet into her favorite sneakers. Chunky gems glittered from an old wooden jewelry box. Frankie fingered her grandmother's estate jewelry, almost all of it costume, except for a strand of pearls and a diamond engagement and wedding ring set, which she'd tucked inside her suitcase now sitting in the back of the closet, and one piece, which she'd fallen in love with and decided to leave out.

Her eyes fell on the long braided gold chain with a starburst of gold inlaid with amethysts. It beckoned her to put it on, but she resisted. All her life she'd wanted beautiful things, but her budget had always only allowed for the basics. Struggling to make something of herself, she'd had an instinctive fear of falling back into poverty and had socked away every penny she could, foregoing even the simplest pleasures. Inheriting the estate, a small sum of money and everything inside had been a dream come true. Only now she had to wonder what else besides semi-precious stones had she inherited. Noise of clanking pots and pans brought her attention back to reality.

Quickly, she grabbed up the gel and gave it a shake. Just her luck, it was empty. Knowing she'd regret it later, she left her hair alone to dry in the heat. In a couple of hours it'd be mistaken for a bush, but she'd deal with it then.

She tread lightly down the backstairs and into the kitchen. Rico sat at the table scribbling something. The smell of coffee brewing drew Frankie to the counter.

"I see you made yourself at home." She snagged a cup from an overhead cupboard and poured herself a cup. She dumped in a spoonful of sugar. Stirring the brew, she took a sip, savoring the flavor.

"Puerto Rican coffee. *Te gusta*?" Rico asked.

"Mmm." She voiced her pleasure, the cup warm and fragrant in her hands. "I like."

"You having any breakfast to go with that?" Rico leaned back in his chair, looking entirely too comfortable and at ease.

"I don't do breakfast."

"That's why you're too skinny. Nothing for a man to grab onto."

"That's twice you called me skinny. And I'll have you know that no man who's gotten close enough to grab any part of me has ever complained."

"You would've cut him off at the knees if he had. Now, sit."

His eyes gleamed with amusement and a hint of desire. Frankie felt the knot of need in her stomach coil tight. She was in way over her head with this guy. For a first, she decided not to argue with him. Sitting sounded like a safe thing to do.

Very, very safe.

Rico stood up, tucking the small notebook into his pocket, and then started pulling things out of her refrigerator and stacking them on the counter.

"You know how to cook?" That was a definite surprise. A lot of the Latino men she knew had caveman principles when it came to the kitchen.

"Mi mami made sure I knew how." Rico winked at her.

"I'd like meet your *mami*, someday." She didn't know where that came from. She held up her coffee mug in front of her face, hoping he wouldn't see her blush. "I mean, she sounds like quite a lady."

"She is that. Raised seven of us." He started cracking eggs into a bowl.

"Seven of you?" Frankie tried to imagine seven Ricos running around the island. There went that coil of need tightening again. The room certainly seemed warmer. Frankie took another sip of her coffee and shoved the image of seven buff-looking Ricos from her mind.

"Tell me about your family." Better than talking about hers.

Rico beat the eggs and stayed silent for a long time, his back to her the whole time. "They're simple people. Coming from a big city like New York, you'd find little about them to interest you."

Frankie put down her cup on the table. "That's pretty low even for you." She pushed her chair back and stood up. "You know what they say about people who assume." She turned to leave, ready to start ripping up the front porch. "It makes an ass out of "u" and me."

"Wait, Frankie. Sit back down."

"I don't think so." She held herself rigid, not sure why the words of a guy she barely knew hurt so bad.

He dropped the fork he'd been using into the egg mixture. He thrust his hands into his hair. "You're right. I'm sorry. I shouldn't have said that."

"So why did you?"

He came over, stopping only when he was a foot away. "I don't want to talk about my family. Can we leave it at that?"

Frankie shrugged. "Yeah, sure." He looked surprised. She didn't know why. She understood all too well the need for privacy and space. She'd had little of either growing up. She protected hers and respected that of others.

"I'm forgiven?" He took a step forward.

Frankie held up a hand. "Ask me later. For that low blow you're going to have to work your butt off to pay for me to forget."

Rico didn't argue. A rumble rose from his chest, bursting forth in a full-bodied laugh. "You're all right, Frankie Montalvo." He returned to the counter and continued with the preparations.

Frankie watched him. The man sure knew how to move. And yes, he definitely had a nice butt, which she wasn't going to notice because the only relationship they were going to have was employer to employee.

"Have you seen my uncle or cousin this morning?"

"You're joking right?" Rico grabbed a fry pan and put it on the stove. "Your uncle will be lucky to make it up by noon. As for the kid, haven't seen him either. Would've figured him to be sitting at the table first thing this morning." He shrugged his shoulders. "Saw him come out of the bathroom earlier. I know he's up."

Frankie frowned.

"Here you go, Omelet à la Rico." He flipped the omelet out of the pan into the air and onto a plate.

Frankie laughed, "Don't think this gets you off the hook."

"Wouldn't dream of it." He brought the two plates over and sat down next to her. The fabric of his denim scraped against her calf, sending an electric jolt through her system.

She tried scooting over, but with the wall on her other side, there was no place to go. Frankie angled her knees away, only to find his shoulder rubbing hers as he reached for the salt. Those long fingers wrapped around the container and she could see the strength in the muscles of his arm as they flexed. She recalled clearly how it felt being held in those arms last night when he'd kissed her.

"Want some?"

"No, thanks," she croaked out. Why couldn't he have taken a seat across from her? Better yet, in a totally different room? Why did she have to be so aware of him? What was wrong with her?

Frankie dug into the omelet set before her, desperate to regain some control. "This is really good." Catching Rico's smug expression, she merely rolled her eyes, but it didn't stop her from finishing every bite.

Though her awareness of him never truly diminished, she managed to channel their conversation into safer topics. Mostly, they talked about how to tackle the work ahead, concluding that their smartest move would be to go through each room in the house, listing what needed to be done and then doing the same for the outside.

"Hope you don't mind but I want to take a look around outside," Rico said, "make some notes."

"Sure." Frankie bit her lip. She didn't want to discuss the next topic but it was necessary. "Rico, let's talk about money."

Before she could go on a loud squeal of brakes came from outside.

"You expecting anyone?" Rico moved his chair back.

Frankie shook her head. "As of yesterday, I couldn't get anyone out here. Now it's Grand Central."

Loud yelling ripped through the house.

Rico moved fast. He tore out of the kitchen, Frankie nipping at his heels. They ran out the front door and skidded to a stop. Standing on the dried-out lawn was a woman with long black hair in a flowing gauzy dress, one hand crossed over her body while the other clutched her necklace. A stream of Spanish burst from her lips, rising into a wail. Her hand came up shaking and she pointed behind them.

Frankie turned, almost afraid of what she would see.

"Oh my..." her breath caught in her chest.

Blindly she reached back and grasped Rico's shirt, tugging on it to get his attention.

"Please tell me it isn't—"

"Blood," he finished for her.

Chapter 4

Claw marks gouged deep into the wood. Bloody handprints haphazardly smudged over the dirty white door. Flies buzzed around, landing on the sticky surface. Dark red splotches emphasized the deep gashes, and anger rolled through Frankie at this petty act of destruction.

The heat of the morning sun baked the handprints into the wood. "Why would someone do this?" Her throat clogged.

Rico pulled her loosely into his arms and held her. The tension in his arms belied the words of assurance he tried to give her.

Frankie savored the feeling, unsure whether to cry or be angry. She chose anger. "Whoever did this is messing with the wrong girl." She stepped out of Rico's embrace.

The strange woman stared wide-eyed at her. Frankie wanted to talk with her, but the sound of uneven steps pounding down the stairs drew her attention back to the house. Hector staggered out the door, his shirt half tucked into his pants, gray stubble all over his jaw.

"What does a man have to do to get some sleep?" He grabbed his head. Before Frankie could say anything, he saw the woman. "You!" he shouted.

Words erupted like a volcano. The woman spoke in rapid-fire Spanish. Hector spoke simultaneously in English. The louder Hector got the more animated the woman became.

Rico stormed over to the two of them. "*Basta*! Enough!"

Frankie fisted her hands on her hips. It seemed that today would be another eventful day. She seriously had to wonder what exactly she had inherited when she'd signed the deed for Casa Verde.

She'd let Rico handle it for now. More than likely the woman was Hector's ex-wife or something. The two seemed familiar with each other. What other reason would they be screaming at each other? But if the woman was behind the mess on the front door, Frankie would let her have it.

"*Mira!* Look what she did." Hector gestured towards the house. "She's crazy!"

The woman crossed herself again, this time more elaborately. "We need to invoke the saints to cleanse the veil of evil that shrouds this home." She chanted some unfamiliar words.

"You see. She's nuts." Hector threw up his arms in disgust and pulled out a flask from his back pocket and took a swig. He looked toward the house, his face screwed up in distaste. The woman continued to offer some kind of incantation.

"Both of you shut up." Rico glowered at them. "You, Hector, care to introduce our guest?"

"Believe me, you're better off not knowing—"

"Damn it, Hector, do we need to go nine rounds every time I ask a question?" Rico's fierce scowl and the mention of his fists did the trick. Hector folded.

"Meet my sister, Margarita. Don't say I didn't warn you," he continued to mumble before taking another swig.

Tía Margarita? "I have an aunt as well?" Bewildered by yet another relative, Frankie still managed to walk forward, holding out her hands to greet her so-called aunt.

"*Hola,* Francesca." The woman's face stretched into a warm smile as her hands came up to cradle Frankie's face. "You have grown so much since I last saw you. And you have a strong husband to protect you. That is good. You will need that for there is great evil here." She shuddered and, dropping her hands, she once again fingered her necklace.

Frankie stepped back. "Uh, he is not my husband. He's a...a..."

"Her boyfriend," Hector slurred.

"He's not my boyfriend." She raised her hands in exasperation.

Margarita's hand suddenly shot out, gripping Frankie's arm. Her nails dug into Frankie's skin. Before she could protest, her newly found aunt spoke. "You are in great danger. He is coming for you. He will—" Her eyes rolled back in her head and she slumped to the ground.

Rico took his knife out and scraped shavings of the blood into a plastic bag he'd grabbed from the kitchen. With Frankie busy seeing to her aunt and Hector happily drowning in his whiskey, this was the perfect time.

Ideally, he'd prefer taking photos of the door and even cutting out a section of the wood for a thorough analysis. But aside from the fact that Frankie would probably cut off his *cojones* if he hacked up her door, he couldn't afford to act like anything other than a guy looking for a job. Plus, he really liked his testicles.

He stood up and stretched his legs. Automatically, he surveyed the surroundings, scanning for more signs. Blood droplets trailed off the porch and were lost in the dirt. Whoever had done this was long gone. The question, though, was why?

The snake. The door. Were they pranks or was someone sending Frankie a message?

He had to get her back to town where she'd be safe. Except the woman was too stubborn for her own good. She'd never go for it. Not unless he tied her up and delivered her there himself.

Rico moved into the shadows of the long porch and pulled out his Blackberry, grateful to have one bar. Service could be spotty out here. While he waited for his call to be picked up, his eyes scanned the area.

"Special Agent Colton."

"Jared. Rico here. I need a favor."

"Shoot."

Quickly, Rico filled his ICE colleague on what had been happening. "I'll have the blood sample sent overnight to you. See what the lab can come up with. Also, I need maps and any aerial shots if you can get them of Casa Verde and the town. Send them to my email."

"I'll see what I can do. One more thing. I did more research on the missing girls. Rosa Diaz, the dead girl, was diabetic."

"If the girl had gone into insulin shock, the bastards who kidnapped her could've used the legend of *el chupacabra* to cover up her death. What does the autopsy report say?"

"That's where it gets interesting. The autopsy report has been sealed. I'll need more time to get you a look at it."

ICE's best technophile, Jared could hack through systems like a hot knife through butter. Rico swallowed hard. "No, *amigo*. This operation isn't legit. Let's not send up red flags. If I need the info, I'll call in some favors down here. Just get me the stuff I requested. And thanks. I owe you."

They spent a few more minutes discussing delivery and then Rico disconnected. He didn't doubt Jared would come through for him.

Only one more person to call. He took a deep breath dreading the conversation. Rico punched in another number and waited. Pulling a bandana from his back pocket, he wiped the sweat off his brow. The phone picked up on the other end and he held his breath.

"*Dígame.*"

Rico groaned as he heard his sister's voice. "Diana, it's Rico. I need to talk to Roberto." Diana and her husband lived in San Juan. Since it was summer vacation, she must have come over with the kids to be with the family.

"Is that all you have to say? Where are you? Why haven't you come to say hello?"

Rico squinted into the distance. He could imagine his sister pacing in front of the phone in those silly high heels she always wore in order to stretch her five-foot-two-inch height. But along with being the shortest in the family, Diana was also the most tenacious. She'd never let him near Roberto if he didn't throw her a bone.

"Look, Di, I'm working on a case."

"Does this have to do with Chita?"

"Yeah, it does. So, could you get Roberto for me? I don't have a lot of time."

"All right. But, you know, Rico, at some point you're going

to have to come home. You can't keep hiding out forever."

Rico mentally braced himself for more of a lecture, but God must have been with him because next he heard his youngest brother's voice.

"Bro, what's up?"

At least one member of his family didn't feel the need to rip into him. Now, if Roberto would simply do as he was told. "Listen up and listen good, 'cause I don't have time to repeat this. I want you to meet me this afternoon and whatever you do, don't tell *Mami*."

Frankie reminded herself to keep her cool. Hector had taken Margarita into the sitting room. The woman sat on the dust-covered green velvet sofa, a beaded necklace between her palms, while she silently mouthed a prayer. Uncle Hector lounged across from his sister, his hand on his head and a sour expression on his face. The tension in the air nearly drove Frankie from the room. Years of working in a hotel had taught her patience. If she could handle an irate, snobby old rich woman and her over-fluffed poodle, she definitely could handle these two.

Before she could open her mouth, her relatives launched into attack mode. Hector accused his sister of spying on him, throwing blood on the door, and a host of other stuff Frankie couldn't make heads nor tails of. Margarita screeched back that he was a drunkard who suffered from hallucinations and an inability to succeed.

Frankie winced. She wiped her palms on her pants and took a deep breath. This called for tact.

"Hector, Margarita, I think you—"

Neither of them listened. The yelling continued. Okay, so diplomacy bites the dust. This called for some old-fashioned tactics, Brooklyn style. Frankie walked into the middle of the room and stood between them. Hands on her hips, she glared them down. "Shut up!"

It worked. They both stopped. Her uncle grumbled and plopped back into his chair, a plume of dust erupted into the air. He coughed and grumbled some more.

"You know, Uncle. I just realized you haven't had breakfast.

How about I fix you eggs with some bacon or sausages. Or how about a tortilla filled with cheese and refried beans and lots of salsa..." Hector's face turned green. At least he stopped grumbling.

He lurched to his feet, cast a glance filled with reproach and headed for the door. "I think I'll go lay down. Please try not to make a lot of noise."

"How am I supposed to fix the house without making noise?" she asked in exasperation to his retreating back.

"Ignore him." Her aunt rearranged the folds of her gauzy dress and settled more comfortably on the sofa. "Sit down and tell me about yourself."

Frankie stared at the woman and hoped the horror she felt didn't show on her face. She didn't know her aunt. The woman might be kind and everything else under the sun. She could also be the nut who'd left that calling card on her door. Mostly, though, she was a stranger.

Frankie had no intention of getting up close and personal with someone she'd just met—even if the woman was her aunt.

"Aunt Margarita, how did you know I was here?"

"I had this strong premonition I should come home. When I returned, I learned of your visit." Margarita fingered another extravagant row of beads that hung around her neck.

Frankie decided not to go anywhere near the premonition talk. That was a losing proposition for sure. "I'm not visiting. I intend to stay. To put down roots." Even to her own ears she sounded defensive.

"I'm glad you've returned, Francesca. But wouldn't you prefer to come home with me? I have plenty of room. This house..." Margarita's small hand fluttered in the air.

Francesca was reminded of a sparrow. Small, delicate, yet ready to fly away at any moment. For all the grace her aunt displayed, Frankie sensed the woman's discomfort and desire to flee this house.

"You don't like it here, do you?"

Her aunt's hand touched the beads again. "No, Francesca, I don't. This place is cold. Inhospitable. Full of dark emotions." Margarita's mind seemed to travel back and Frankie wondered where she'd gone. Margarita shook her head as if to clear it.

"You don't believe me. I can see it. But take heed. There is greater evil coming."

Frankie suddenly felt chilled and stopped herself from rubbing her arms. She wouldn't give her aunt the satisfaction of knowing she'd been affected. Her aunt was talking nonsense. That's all. Sure the place was probably full of bad memories. But they weren't hers.

She'd left all hers behind in NY. She was starting fresh. And she'd make over this manor house and fill it with good memories. New ones.

"Look, I appreciate you stopping by and for the invitation. But I'm fine and I'm staying. This is my home now."

"Yes, it is, isn't it?" Margarita stood up. She raised her eyes to Francesca's. "You are very like your mother and yet..." She lapsed into silence and Frankie found herself wanting to know more and at the same time not wanting to hear another word. Then Margarita spoke again. "My sister was lucky to escape, you know. And my mother hated her for that. But it looks like she's found the perfect revenge."

She shouldn't ask. She shouldn't listen to a word this woman said. Maybe Hector was right. Maybe Margarita was crazy. But the words came out anyway. "What are you talking about?"

Margarita smiled sadly. "There is no point in my telling you. You will need to learn for yourself. So very like your mother," she whispered. She started walking to the door and Frankie fell into step beside her. "If you need anything, Francesca, I'm in town. Ask anyone and they can give you directions." In front of her sedan, she grasped Frankie's hand, gave it a brief squeeze and left.

As Frankie watched her aunt drive away, Rico came to stand next to her. "What'd your aunt have to say?"

"Nothing. Absolutely nothing." At least nothing that mattered. Frankie wouldn't let it.

Rico's face turned serious. "I'll see about getting the door cleaned."

"Don't worry I got it." Frankie started up the drive. She dragged her feet in the dirt.

"Hey, you're not in this alone."

Wasn't she? Frankie didn't remember inheriting a house complete with family and a hot-bodied contractor. Though, looking at the blood-smeared door, she was glad Rico was here. She'd intended on tossing everyone out this morning, but maybe having a few able-bodied men around would prevent the joker who was doing this from pulling another stunt.

"Going to need a new coat of paint." Rico pulled a bucket of soapy water out onto the porch. He handed her a sponge.

"Thanks." With a sigh she took the sponge and started to attack the door. Rico knelt down beside her and silently they washed away the offending marks.

Sun poured down onto the porch and sweat rolled between her breasts, but the soft breeze of the Caribbean Sea floating through the air took the sting out of the humidity. Their arms moved simultaneously working at the gouged wood. Rico flashed a smile at Frankie. Though she hated to admit it, even to herself, it felt good to have company. The past years on her own, she had done everything by herself. Having Rico by her side, helping her, felt foreign and yet so familiar.

"All done." Task complete, Rico picked up the bucket and threw the fouled water over the railing into a sun-baked bush on the side of the porch.

Frankie got up and dusted off her knees. "Thanks, again."

"*De nada.*" Rico leaned back and stretched his arms. "You know, I think that's the second time you thanked me today." He leaned forward and placed his arms on both sides of her hips, trapping her between the porch railing and his body. He flashed her a wicked smile. "A man might get used to it."

Frankie dodged under his arm. "Yeah, well don't." She couldn't keep the smile from creeping on to her face. The dream of keeping Rico around was way too tempting. But it was just that, a dream. People didn't stick around in Frankie's life and she'd accepted it long ago. No hope in thinking a drifter like Rico would stay on long after the project was finished. He'd take his money and run.

"We got a lot of work to do." Frankie pointed to the sagging floorboards beneath their feet. It was a miracle the porch had held them both.

"*Sí.*" He looked off into the distance over the driveway.

Frankie followed his eyes. Overgrown and choked with weeds, the mangroves looked dark and foreboding against the bright sunlight. "Beautiful, yet dangerous."

"Exactly."

Frankie turned her head and realized Rico was no longer looking at the mangroves but at her. She turned her eyes down.

"There's a lot to do and very little time."

Rico nodded his head and pushed off the railing. He was about to pick up the bucket when he stopped.

Armando pushed aside thick fronds and emerged from the neglected path. He carried a backpack slung over one shoulder and his pants were wet and muddy. The kid must have gone for a casual hike in the mangroves, but there was nothing casual about his movements. His face, sporting a nice shiner, swiveled from side to side. Frankie went to wave to him but Rico caught her arm and pinned it to her side.

Together they watched Armando disappear around the side of the house.

"Bet he's hungry. He's going to be disappointed that he missed out on your omelets."

Rico pointed to the mangroves. Leaves snapped and moved. "Looks like Armando isn't the only one out for a stroll."

Rico dropped the bucket and bounded down the steps. He headed straight for the mangroves.

"Hey, wait up." Frankie took off after him. If that was the prankster who'd damaged her door she wanted a piece of him, too.

Rico didn't have a Superman complex. He was Superman. Rico crashed through the foliage, swiping at leaves and branches. Frankie struggled to keep up. Her feet caught a few times on tree roots. She stumbled and tripped, falling farther and farther behind. Soon she no longer saw him. She stopped to catch her breath. "Damn it, Rico!" Her voice got lost in the thick vegetation. Her feet squished in the soft, spongy ground. "Ewww." Dead leaves, bugs, moss-covered rotting fruit lay scattered around. Unidentifiable goop covered her sneakers to the laces.

She turned to go back and found herself completely lost. "What happened to the path?" Frankie tried to retrace her steps but there were too many footprints scattered all around. She had no idea which were hers.

Frankie wished that she had taken more time to explore her land and make a clear path to and from the house. She put it on the top of her to-do list. "All right, no need to panic. I'm sure this is easier than navigating the city subway system."

The groves at night were pitch black and scary. During the day they were no less friendly looking. Very little light filtered down through the thick canopy of leaves. Frankie figured it was around nine in the morning and the sun rose in the east. The mangroves ran out to the beaches and they faced east but using the sun for direction proved to be useless. The sunlight that did make it through bounced all around. Instead, she looked down at the ground. Tangled roots protruded from the marshy floor, extending their fingers into a running channel of water. "I bet that leads to the sea." She turned her toes in the opposite direction and picked her way carefully back through the dense bacteria-laden sea grass beds.

"Rico!" she shouted. Her eyes trained on the floor, looking for the easiest route. Fallen leaves squished underfoot, her sneakers sucked at the mud, and her ankle twisted as she tried to stay on the edge of the swampy land. She stepped high, maneuvering over the roots, using her hands and nails to hold onto the slimy bark of the trees. "Lucky I didn't break my neck," she muttered to herself, at the same time cursing Rico for running ahead of her. Macho man could have waited. It was her property. Her problem.

She called out again louder this time as she stepped across another stream of water. Crickets and cicadas chirped loudly and then stopped. Alarm bells went off inside Frankie. Her eyes darted around. Shadows danced all around. Thick cloying heat pressed down on her. The overripe smell of decaying oranges and stagnant water choked her.

Somewhere, off to her left, a branch snapped. She whirled around. "Rico?" she whispered.

Two pairs of huge red eyes stared at her from the leaves. She let out a yelp. The animal croaked and scurried up the tree.

"Red-eyed tree frog," she giggled nervously.

The tree above her rustled. Instinctively, she looked up. Frankie hadn't encountered much wildlife in the city, unless she counted the school trip to the Bronx Zoo. Oranges tumbled down to the ground and one fell on her head. She brought her hand up and massaged her scalp. A ray of light filtered down through the leaves framing a dark silhouette. Either the tree frog had grown enormously large or someone was in the tree.

"Whoever you are, come down out of the tree now," she said with false bravado. Where the heck was Superman when she needed him?

Frankie kept her neck craned. The figure in the tree didn't stir.

She wondered if frogs came that large. "I'm warning you," Frankie shouted up. "Don't make me come up there and get you."

Nothing happened. She tried to see up into the branches, but the foliage was too thick. There was no movement in the tree. She inched closer to the tree trunk to get a better view.

Black eyes glowed down at her.

El chupacabra! the voice inside her mind screamed. All the stupid village tales of a little hairy beast with hooked claws and dripping fangs covered in blood flooded her mind.

She reeled back from the tree, stumbling over exposed roots. Her legs slipped from under her and she went down backwards, landing flat on her back and bumping her head. Groggily, Frankie tried to stare into the tree. Paralyzed with fear, she watched as a large hulking figure climbed down through the leaves, the sound of claws tearing into the wood. Her hands sloshed in the mud searching for a rock, a stick, anything to defend herself.

"Rico!" she screamed at the top of her lungs.

Frankie pushed backwards with her feet to get out of the way. The dark creature landed on the ground and hissed at her. She grabbed a rotten orange and pelted it at the monster. *El chupa* crouched down and sprang off its back legs and landed on top of her. She screamed and pounded the monster with her fists. *El chupa* pushed her down into the muck. She could feel the creature's hot breath on her neck. Slicing teeth cut into her neck. *El chupa* was going to suck her blood!

Chapter 5

He'd lost him. Rico cursed and dragged his hand through his damp hair. His pants were soaked with muddy water and his T-shirt soaked with sweat. Gnats buzzed around biting into exposed flesh. One sucker took a nasty bite. He cursed double time.

The mangroves hummed with life. Sixty-foot-tall trees pressed in around him. His legs throbbed from running through the muck and his arms stung from the numerous scratches. For a while, Rico had kept up with his quarry. Then, he'd vanished.

How any man could run so fast through the mangroves without breaking his neck, Rico had no idea. Copious amounts of dead leaves, bark, twigs, root material, guano from birds roosting in the trees, dead animals and loose sea grass trapped in the maze of roots made for impossible navigation. The best way through the mangroves was by kayak. Something Rico wished he had. The black mangrove trees were impenetrable, his visibility low. Anyone or anything could be hiding in the tangle of roots and seawater.

Birds squawked and flew past him in a flurry of colors. Something or someone had disturbed them. He turned around and headed back into the water. Hip-deep, he dove into the channel and swam through the murky water.

"Rico!"

He pulled himself up onto the bank of the lagoon. "I'm coming!" His heart raced.

Frankie! What was she doing out here? She must have followed him into the mangroves when he gave chase. Stubborn woman. The mangroves were no place for *turistas*. Growing up on Vieques, he knew better than to play around in them.

Her screams were getting louder.

"Frankie!" he shouted. A barrier of black grove trees stood between him and Frankie. Through the roots, he could see her lying on the ground. Rico grabbed hold of the nearest tree and pulled himself over. He tumbled down into the sea grass on the other side and struggled to gain purchase on the marshy seafloor. Rico splashed through the mud and knelt down beside her. "Frankie." He breathed a sigh of relief to see her unharmed.

She finally looked up at him, fear dancing in her amber eyes. His gut clenched. He gathered her into his arms. Mud mixed with sticks and leaves oozed down her back. Gently, he wiped the debris off.

"Something attacked me," Frankie croaked into his sweaty shirt.

His blood filled with ice. "Who?"

"*El chupa.*" She shook her head on his shoulder. "I know it sounds crazy, but it's true. It wanted to suck my blood." She shuddered against him. He felt her fear clear to his bones.

She tipped her head back to look up at him. Her eyes—wide and distressed—dominated her face. A streak of mud marred her pure, olive complexion, while her dark tresses lay in a tangled, matted mess around her shoulders.

She'd never appeared more beautiful and his heart tripped when he thought of what had almost been done to her. "You're safe, *querida*," he said to her as he gently rubbed away the dirt on her face.

"I am now." She ducked her head and tucked herself against him. His grip automatically tightened and he cursed himself for not having protected her better. Once again, he'd been too late. His only saving grace was that Frankie had survived. But memories of another woman who hadn't crowded in. In his mind's eye he saw all the blood, could even recall the stunned look in her lifeless eyes. He'd failed and it had cost Carla her life.

This time it could have been Frankie.

He closed his eyes briefly, trying to push the rage he felt down. While the anger gave him purpose, left uncontrolled it could lead to deadly mistakes in judgment and he could not let that happen.

He didn't know what had attacked Frankie, but he'd bet his badge that it hadn't been a creature of the forest.

Someone played a deadly game. Using the legend of *el chupacabra*, some bastard preyed on young women, knowing that village superstition would prevent people from digging for the truth. Chita could've turned into another statistic if his mother hadn't guilted him into searching for the girl.

And if he hadn't given in to his mother, what would've happened to Frankie? God help him, he would not let her turn into a statistic, too.

"I swear to you, Frankie. I'm not going to let this monster get away." Rico would see the bastard in hell before he'd let Frankie be harmed.

And this was one vow he intended to keep.

Frankie clung to Rico's shirt, her nose buried in the crook of his neck. He smelled of earth, sweat and saltwater. Rico held her tight in his arms. She felt safe, something she hadn't believed possible since her parents' death.

For so long, it had been her against the world. No one picked her up, brushed her off and set her on her feet when she fell. No one offered a shoulder to lean when she needed it. Inside the foster system and out, she'd learned to rely on herself, had even persuaded herself that it was a sign of strength.

But at this moment, she didn't feel very strong. She needed Rico in a way she'd never needed anyone before. It should've spooked her, but she couldn't work up the emotion.

She didn't want to be anywhere but where she was—in his arms.

"Frankie," Rico said softly in her ear. "Talk to me. Describe what happened."

Frankie shook her head even as words clogged her throat. She licked her lips, noting how parched they felt. "He came down from the tree. He was big and black and—" Words failed

73

her. The images blurred in her head. "I don't know. I mean he had these claws and huge teeth, like a werewolf or something. He jumped me and I thought... I thought..." She squeezed her eyes shut, wanting the fear to go away. She didn't think she'd ever been that scared before in her life.

She really hadn't noticed any details. All she'd been focused on was saving herself from being ripped to shreds by those claws or its teeth.

Why hadn't she paid more attention to the stories the villagers had told? *Because you thought it a lot of superstitious nonsense, that's why.* In fact, she'd tried to change the subject whenever someone brought up *el chupacabra*. Big bad girl from NY. She knew better than a bunch of bumpkins from the Puerto Rican wilds. She'd witnessed scarier things in her lifetime—or so she'd thought.

She'd never been more wrong.

Rico stirred against her and she had the ridiculous urge to wrap herself around him and never let go.

"We should get moving. Whoever attacked you might come back to finish the job."

His words brought fresh terror to her heart. Goosebumps broke out along her skin. She fought the fear, concentrating on the fact that she had Rico beside her now. She wasn't alone.

Rico released his arms and Frankie immediately felt the void. She wanted to crawl back into the safety of his embrace. She restrained herself.

Rico stood up, his eyes surveying the groves. Deep-set lines of worry furrowed his otherwise smooth brow.

"A little help here." Frankie held out her arm and he pulled her up from the muck. Mud stuck to her pant bottoms in clumps. "I call dibs on the shower first." She picked a few leaves out of her hair.

Rico laughed. "*No problema.* Need someone to scrub your back?"

The thought of Rico's hands lathering soap on her wet, naked body made her skin tingle. She swiped some mud from her neck.

Rico stopped smiling. He stepped close to her and ran his hand down over her throat. Frankie held her breath. His fingers skimmed over her neck and then along her collarbone. His touch brought every one of her nerve endings to life. She wanted to beg him for more, but having never asked for anything in her life that she hadn't worked hard for herself, she stayed silent, pleading with her eyes instead.

He moved his head closer and his fingers danced around her neck...

"Ouch!" Frankie pulled back. Her hand flew to protect her throat. "What do you think you're doing?" They obviously hadn't been on the same page, which was just fine. Stupid jungle made her think crazy thoughts.

"You have two small puncture marks." He showed Frankie his fingertips. Small amounts of blood marked the tips.

Visions of *el chupa* swam through her mind. "Okay, playtime is over." She grabbed Rico's hand. "Let's get outta here." Without asking, she turned and proceeded to pull him through the trees. She came up short. "What is it with you?"

Rico stood rooted to the spot. "You're going the wrong way."

"No." She jutted out her chin. "The house is this way."

"Are you certain?"

Frankie wasn't certain of anything anymore. Up until two weeks ago she had been certain she had no family. She had been certain there was no such thing as *el chupacabra,* that is until one decided to munch on her. And, oh yes, she had been certain that she could never want or need another person in her life until a minute ago. So, no, she wasn't certain of anything anymore. Damned if she'd tell Rico about it.

Instead, she kept quiet and defied him to prove her wrong.

"That's what I thought." He tugged on her arm. "We'll follow the water. All the channels lead out to the Caribbean Sea. Bound to come out at a lagoon or a beach."

"What makes you such an expert?"

He turned them around and headed off in the opposite direction. "I grew up in Vieques. Sooner or later every young boy goes exploring."

They picked their way carefully around trees and vegetation until they had no choice left but to wade down into the water. She swallowed hard. The brackish water had God knew what hiding and waiting beneath the surface to come and devour her up. She hesitated on the embankment.

"You coming or not?" Rico slipped into the water effortlessly. Chest-high in the water, he sloshed through flotsam, using his arms to paddle through the water.

Frankie shook her head. "No way." She turned to head back into the snarl of trees.

"If you're afraid of alligators or snakes, don't be. Vieques has no poisonous animals. Only small Caymans, and trust me, they are more afraid of you." He beckoned her to come down.

"I'm not scared of anything." Frankie crossed her arms over her chest and stuck out her chin. "Just that I can't swim."

Rico nodded his head. "*No problema.*"

He reached up his arms and placed them on both sides of her hips. He gently guided her into the water. A moment of fear struck her as half her body disappeared beneath the murky water.

"Put your feet down." Rico instructed never taking his hands off her hips.

The soft mushy bottom slid under the soles of her shoes, sucking her legs down into the muddy floor. Frankie jumped up and wrapped her legs around his hips like a child seeking safety. She rested her head against his chest. "I can't do it."

Rico spoke soft in to her ear. "Yes, you can. I promise I won't let you go. Trust me, Frankie."

Slowly and cautiously she followed his instructions. With a few more attempts, she felt comfortable enough to stand on her own. At first they took it easy, each step slow and sluggish.

"We have to pick it up. Otherwise we won't get out of here before nightfall." Rico tested the ground in front of them. Frankie followed close behind, holding onto the back of his T-shirt. Once or twice she attempted to swim, but it proved to be more of a task—her wet clothes hindered her and kept snagging on extended branches in the water. If she could go back into the past, she would have taken swim lesson at the YMCA.

Little fishes darted in and out around the trees roots that dipped into the water. More times than she could remember, her foot caught on the roots underwater. Bugs danced across the water while cranes foraged for food below the surface.

Above, in the treetops, birds sang out and flew from tree to tree. The groves were alive with color and sound. Eerie as they were, they held a strange haunting beauty. Frankie understood why they called Puerto Rico the land of enchantment, everything around her seemed surreal, even the attack by *el chupa.*

Finally, Rico pointed to a large opening in the mangroves. Bright sunlight illuminated it. As they drew closer, the view came into focus. Frankie had to shield her eyes from the shining rays bouncing off the white sandbars. "An estuary."

The sound of gulls and waves washing up on the shore beckoned them on. Frankie moved with a purpose. Within minutes, Rico pulled her up onto a shallow sandbar. Tiny silver fish darted around her ankles.

"You did it!"

She embraced Rico and smacked a kiss right on his salty lips. He smiled and kissed her back twice as hard. Too excited to be out of the tangled webbed maze of trees and the muddy water, she didn't complain. Instead, she leaned into his embrace, toppling them both over back into the water. They came up for air sputtering. Rico pulled her up before she could drown in a foot of water.

Frankie laughed till her belly hurt. When she regained her composure, she took in the spectacular sight. A crescent-shaped alcove of pure white sand cut off from the rest of the island by the mangroves. Not a soul in sight. No condos, no boats, nothing to mar the pristine beauty of the secluded beach—a perfect romantic hideaway for a couple seeking discretion. She looked at Rico and frowned.

"Now what?"

He squinted against the sun. "We walk along the beach." He put out his hand. For a second she hesitated. Then she placed her hand in his.

The sun glinted off the white sand. Seagulls called to each other on the beach. Her muddy sneakers in her hand, she savored the sand between her toes. Too bad that she couldn't rest and soak in some sun. Rico set a grueling pace.

"Could you slow down?" The words scratched against her parched throat. Despite the gallons of water all around, none of it was drinkable. Her lips were chapped and her cheeks burned from salt and sun.

She envied Rico for being able to take off his shirt. She would have done the same, but the utilitarian bra she wore didn't exactly look like a bikini top.

Rico rubbed at his arm, a few scratch marks marred his tanned skin. Unconsciously, she ran her finger along her neck.

He gave her hand a squeeze. "Come." Rico led her along the water's edge. Gentle rolling waves lapped up onto the beach.

"We should wash off some of this mud." He stepped into the water up to his knees and sloshed off the muck from his pants, arms and legs.

Frankie followed his lead walking into the warm waters up to her knees. The water was so clear, she could see her toes wriggle. She bent down and rinsed off the goop that clung to her calves and arms.

The warm crystalline blue water shimmered and danced around her, tempting her to come and take a dip. She shied back, afraid to test her newfound ability to brave the water.

"It's incredible, isn't it?"

She turned her head to see Rico gesture toward the sea. Sunlight reflected down into the water, making it visible all the way to the reef on the bottom. Birds bobbed on the crests of waves. In the far distance, a boat sailed near the horizon. Peace beckoned.

"No matter where I am, this place always calls me back."

"You've lived off the island?"

"What?" He flashed her a smile. "A *borinqueño* who left Puerto Rico?" He feigned shock.

Frankie laughed and splashed him with some water. "You're too much."

He splashed her back. She couldn't let him get away with it.

They launched into all out war. Frankie found herself losing the battle. She moved back to shallow water. Rico dove beneath the lapis-colored waves and swam away from her.

"Hey! No fair. I can't swim."

He swam between her feet and grabbed onto her ankles. She shouted as he stood up, carrying her on top his shoulders.

"Put me down!" she screamed, holding onto his head for dear life.

"If you insist." Rico crouched down in the water. She felt his muscles bunch in his arms under her thighs before he launched her off his shoulders.

Frankie went flying. Splash!

Kicking and sputtering she came up for air. Her hair hung down over eyes. "You are so dead, Lopez!"

He laughed at her. The sun shining down on his glistening chest and his boyish enthusiasm drained away at her indignation. She laughed along with him. They both splashed through the water, she pursued and he dodged.

She knew they were wasting time but she couldn't remember the last time she had had so much fun. Her life in foster care had been far from carefree. Things like going to the beach or wading in a pool were a luxury that rarely happened. Once she'd been emancipated from the system, all her time had been consumed with work, school and paying the bills. With each splash, each dive through the waves, she felt her worries wash away.

Nothing mattered but enjoying this one moment in time.

"You win," she said, out of breath. She hiked her thumb back toward the shore. "I'm going in." Frankie dragged her weary but satisfied body through the waves and collapsed on shore.

She sat with her knees folded up to her chest and watched as Rico effortlessly swam through the water like a dolphin and bodysurfed onto shore.

"Show off."

His tan, muscular torso glistened with droplets, marking a trail downward to meet the thin line of black hair that disappeared at his waistband.

Her already dry mouth became even drier. She licked her lips, thirsting for something far wetter than water.

Not wanting to let him see how he affected her, Frankie closed her eyes and raised her face to the sun to dry.

She felt his shadow fall over her. She opened her eyes and watched him kneel down in the sand in front of her.

"I want to see your wound."

"It's nothing." She drew her knees up further into her chest. "I don't even feel it." Her fingers skimmed over the puncture marks.

Rico brushed aside her hand. "Still, I want to see for myself."

He tilted her head and leaned in close to examine the marks.

Rico cursed and got to his feet. His shoulders tight and his back straight, he stared off into the sea.

Frankie dug her feet into the sand. "Probably was some wild animal or something. I got too close and it bit me." Her mind fuzzed, the image of fangs and glowing eyes popped. She shook them away just like the sand on her feet. "*El chupacabra.* Ha!" She dismissed the silly notion. "I've been listening to too many stories. I guess they finally got to me."

Rico turned around. His eyes narrowed. He pegged her with his stare. The words on her tongue dried up in her mouth. "You think this is a game?" He swept his hand wide. "All you see is paradise." He moved in close, stalking her. She didn't dare move a muscle.

Rico crouched down behind her. He placed his mouth next to her ear. "Even in paradise there are predators."

His words chilled her. She shivered despite the tropical sun beating down on her. Instinct told her to run, but her stubborn will wouldn't let Rico scare her from the only home she could call her own.

"Don't think I scare easy, Rico."

"*Querida*, I'm not trying to scare you." He backed off, putting distance between him and her. With all the lazy effort of a jungle cat he found his spot next to her and stretched out in the sun. "Just don't want to see you end up *el chupa's* prey."

"I've heard about the dead farm animals, but has *el chupa* ever attacked humans before?"

"In Vieques, never." With his hand shielding his eyes, he looked at Frankie "Until recently."

She swallowed hard. "Am I the only one?" Her voice came out small as if she truly didn't want to know the answer to the question.

"No." Rico's expression grew hard. "Six other girls on the island have gone missing. One of them dead. Drained dry."

She shuddered.

Rico grunted. He turned away and looked out at the sea as if all the answers to the world lay there.

Her stomach growled, reminding her she hadn't eaten in a while and she was feeling thirsty. The trek through the mangroves had exhausted her reserves. "I guess we should try to find our way back."

Frankie got up and dusted the sand off the back of her pants. A bird called out. She looked up to see three approaching figures in the distance.

"*Mira.*" She motioned for Rico to get up and look.

Rico was by her side in a flash. He peered down the length of the beach.

He moved in front of her, blocking her view. "Looks like we might be getting off this beach soon." Rico bent down and gathered up his shirt. He took her hand. "Come on, let's go meet the locals."

Relief burst through Frankie at the sight of the three people moving down the shoreline.

"Come on," she urged Rico, pulling him along. She couldn't wait to get out of this heat. Despite the impromptu swim, her body itched. She'd gotten rid of the worst of the muck, but sand still clung in places better left unmentioned. And she desperately wanted water—first to drink and then to dunk in.

She waved to the trio as they got closer. An older man, judging from the white hair, sat in a specially designed wheelchair with large plastic wheels. Behind him, a towering hulk of a man pushed. Alongside, a well-dressed, muscular younger man accompanied them. He offered Frankie and Rico a short salute in return, then turned to speak to his companions.

"They must have a car since I don't see a boat. I mean, you don't think they pushed that chair all the way from wherever they started, do you?"

Rico kept his eyes on the people ahead, glancing at her only briefly. "Doubtful. I imagine they've got a vehicle tucked away somewhere."

"Well, it's either them or hoofing it all the way home." The thought of running into *el chupacabra* once more slid through her mind. She shuddered. She'd rather take her chances with these strangers. At least Rico would be with her this time.

"Wait, Frankie." Rico yanked on her arm, halting her in her steps. "We don't know these people, so let's play this low key, okay?"

Using her hand to shade her eyes, Frankie studied him. The man who'd teased her as they'd jumped in and out of the waves no longer existed. His face had gone serious again, leaving her with no clue as to what was going on in his head. "I don't understand. What is it you think I'm going to do?"

He rubbed his jaw, which in her experience with men usually indicated frustration over something only they understood. "Don't announce what happened back there. The less people who know—"

"Well, duh. You think I want the whole town to know? Give me some credit here." She swiveled away and plastered a big smile on her face. "Smile, Lopez. We want them to give us a ride. One look at your ugly mug and they might just leave us here."

"Lead the way, *querida*. You are the boss after all."

Somehow she didn't think he meant it.

"*Buenos días*," she called out. "*Perdón, Señores.*" They came to a stop a few feet in front of the group. "I'm Francesca Montalvo and this is my...friend Rico Lopez." From the smirk on Rico's face she knew he'd noticed her hesitation. But who went out walking on the beach with their contractor? Resisting the urge to roll her eyes, she held out her hand to the young man. Manners dictated she address the older gentleman, but given the vacant look in his eyes, she doubted he was aware of much. "We're new to the area. And we got lost. Could you tell us how to get back to the main road?"

"A pleasure, *Señorita*." The handsome stranger took her hand and, rather than shake it, brought it to his lips in a courtly gesture. Frankie blushed and politely took her hand back.

"I'm Salvador Torres and this is my father. We own property

a few miles inland." With his smooth voice and *GQ* looks—down to the expensive leather sandals—Frankie bet he was every island girl's dream.

"And your friend is?" Rico spoke up beside her.

"Julio? He's my father's attendant. He sees to all my father's needs," Salvador said dismissively.

Frankie tried to imagine the large silent man with the pockmarked face and crooked nose tenderly taking care of his charge but it stretched her imagination. She smiled at him. He flicked his eyes over her. Though the man did it fairly quickly Frankie had a feeling she had just been assessed. He did the same for Rico. The chill the man gave off couldn't have been clearer—don't mess with me.

"Did we perhaps interrupt something?" Salvador asked, his eyebrows arching, a gleam in his eye.

"Come again?" Frankie broke off as his meaning sank in. Given their rumpled condition, she figured Salvador had added one plus one and come up with three. "Oh, no. We're not...that is..." Next to her Rico snorted. Her foot nearly connected with his calf, before she got control. "I'm afraid we became lost in the mangroves. I'm the new owner of Casa Verde. I wanted to check out my property. Unfortunately, even with Tarzan here, we couldn't find our way back home."

"So, you are the lovely granddaughter of Señora de la Varga. My condolences on the passing of your grandmother. She was a well-respected member of the community. She will be missed," he said with sincerity. He laid a smooth hand on his father's frail shoulder. "My father knew the family well."

Frankie looked at the older gentleman. He remained lost in his own world. Drool pooled at the side of his slack mouth. Aside from his debilitated health, she could see his attendant had dressed him with care. In his younger years, the man probably had been someone of great importance. Frankie looked at the son and could see the similarity. Salvador carried himself well and an air of sophistication surrounded him, yet here he was on the beach taking his invalid father for a stroll.

"It must be nice to get out," she said to the older gentleman.

"Please excuse my father. He had a stroke last year and he

has not been the same since."

"Oh, I'm sorry."

"No need to be. I am sure he is delighted to be in the company of such a beautiful woman."

Frankie blushed. She had to give it to Salvador. He was definitely smooth. She threw a look at Rico. Unfortunately, she didn't think Rico found Salvador as entertaining.

"I hate to interrupt this nice little conversation you two are having but we really should be going. Can you point us in the right direction to get off this beach?"

Frankie really wanted to kick him.

"Please, let us take you home. It's a long walk otherwise and you might become lost again." Ignoring Rico, Salvador took Frankie's arm and placed it in the crook of his elbow. Conscious of her looks, she brushed the sand off her clothes so as not to mar his shirt.

Salvador simply laughed, showing a line of straight white teeth.

"Do not worry. The clothes will wash. Now, shall we?"

"Sure. Thanks." She snatched a quick look back at Rico. His lips were thin and tight. He sent her a cold look. She didn't have time to deal with his moods. They were going home and that's all that counted.

The five of them made their way slowly across the sparkling white sand and into the shadows of the trees lining the edge of the beach. They hadn't gone more than a few feet when they came upon a top-of-the-line black minivan.

"Sweet ride," Frankie commented.

"The vehicle has been specially modified to accommodate my father's wheelchair. If you will wait a moment, please."

Frankie stood silently and watched as a side door slid open. The vehicle opened up and a ramp lowered to the ground. Julio rolled the wheelchair onto the ramp, and he snapped the chair in. With a press of a button, Señor Torres and the chair were lifted up and positioned into place. The door of the van slid silently closed.

Rico gave a low whistle. "That would've come in handy lifting some of that wood yesterday." Salvador didn't appear impressed.

Julio opened the other side door and Frankie slid into the back seat. Salvador sat next to her. Rico rode upfront with Julio, who also acted as chauffeur.

Rico twisted in his front seat to look back. He maintained a pleasant expression, but Frankie sensed darker emotions underneath. "So, Salvador, what is it you do?"

Salvador leaned back, stretching his arm across the back of her seat. Though he wasn't touching her, Frankie found herself sitting up straight to put distance with the seat back.

"I've taken over my father's business. He created an export and import trading company."

"And what is it you trade in?"

Salvador shrugged. "Coffee, sugar, wood products—a variety, you might say. I've worked hard to expand the business, so I'm always looking for new items to add to our inventory."

"Business is good?"

"I have no complaints. How about you, Señor Lopez? What do you do?"

Rico flashed his trademark grin though Frankie was probably the only one who could see it didn't quite reach his eyes. "As of right now, I'm a builder. Just ask my boss, here."

"Ah, the hired help."

Frankie shifted in her seat, feeling disturbed. She sensed a hint of mockery in Salvador's tone. Not that it was unexpected. She'd been on the receiving end of a few of those comments herself when she'd been a maid. Apparently, Salvador thought she merited a second look simply because she now owned property and had a pedigree attached.

Was that what Rico saw in her too? A leg up in the world? The thought left her unsettled.

"*Querida*, you are much too lovely to have such a look on your face."

"I'm fine," Frankie said quickly. Funny, how when Rico used the same term of endearment it irritated her but in a good way. With Salvador, it made her uncomfortable. His charm lost some of its shine.

"Where does this road take us?"

"Up ahead it will fork. The left branch leads to the main road and back to town. The other takes us directly to your property. My father and I live further inland. We actually share borders."

"Guess that makes us neighbors."

"Yes, I would say so."

Salvador reached over and picked up her hand. He stroked his fingers over hers as he spoke. "I like to bring my father to the ocean for the fresh air and view. He's always much refreshed after such visits."

"Oh, I'm sorry we interrupted your outing."

"Not at all." Salvador waved her apology away with his other hand, while still hanging on to her. "I'm delighted to make the acquaintance of our lovely neighbor. Maybe one of these days, we can all go together."

She smiled. "That would be nice. A definite change from being considered cursed."

Salvador raised an elegant eyebrow. "Ah, I see the locals have been sharing the colorful folklore of Vieques."

"You could say so." She laughed. "That's putting it mildly."

"I'm afraid your grandmother became a recluse in her later years. Let the house fall into disrepair. My father and I offered to help, but Señora de la Varga was a proud woman. Had a bit of a reputation for being hard and stubborn, to say the least." He stopped and carefully picked out his next words. "Though, it is unfortunate she passed away, I am glad to see that Casa Verde has fallen into such fortunate hands." Again he stroked her hand. A shiver ran up her spine.

Frankie wanted to ask more about her grandmother, but they reached the fork and, within minutes, came out of the trees and were riding along the edge of the estate. Julio brought the car up to the front door and parked.

"Here, let me." Salvador reached across Frankie, his arm sliding across her lap. He released her seat belt. She thanked him and exited the vehicle as fast as she could.

Rico walked in front of the car and came to stand by her side.

"I can't thank you enough for your assistance. We might still be wandering around out there."

"The pleasure was all mine, Francesca." He took her hand again, and with his eyes never leaving hers, raised it to his lips.

Beside her, Frankie felt Rico stiffen. Salvador covered her hand with his other palm and continued to hold it. He paused for a moment, his eyes on the house behind her. She felt ashamed and withdrew her hand from his. The contrast of his brand new, shiny expensive car parked in her dirt driveway next to a crumbling home brought everything into perspective. Her name might be on the deed, but she wasn't some fancy plantation owner and she would never be.

"Thanks again for rescuing us."

From behind her she heard Rico snort.

"Anytime." He pulled out a thin silver holder from his shirt pocket and flipped it open. He handed her a business card. "Tomorrow night I will be holding a party to celebrate a few new business ventures with some acquaintances. I would love it if you would accompany me." Julio came out of the van and opened the door for Salvador. "I look forward to our next meeting."

Julio gave them one last look before he climbed back into the vehicle. Frankie watched the dust cloud behind the new car as it drove off.

"He's out of your league, *querida.*" The words came out harsh and angry.

"What's that supposed to mean?" She pivoted, getting right into Rico's space. "Listen up, Lopez. I hired you to renovate my house, not to butt into my business."

"I'm making it my business," he said, staring down at her, his eyes flashing sparks. "You're a trouble magnet. You have no idea what that guy wants."

"Probably to get into my pants," she fired back. "But then so do you, so where's the difference?"

"The difference is I won't waste time making love to your hand when I can do better." He hauled her into his arms and brought his mouth down hard on hers.

Chapter 6

He shouldn't have grabbed her. She shouldn't have let him.

She'd had every intention of shoving him away, but somehow her hands found themselves holding onto his shoulders and, instead of pushing, they seemed to be pulling him closer.

"You can be a real jerk, Lopez," she whispered against his mouth.

"*Sí, querida*, I know," he said as he planted small kisses along her jaw line. "You can do much better than me."

"With someone like Salvador?"

Rico's head snapped up. He captured her face in both his hands, making movement impossible. His eyes glared into hers. "Anybody but him."

"You're going to have to do better than that, Lopez. I mean Salvador's got—"

"You talk too much, *querida*." Rico's mouth came down once again, drowning her words and, she had to admit, any sensible thought. How could one man turn her brain to mush so quickly?

She leaned into the kiss, loving the way his scent permeated her senses—a combination of male and sea. Her arms reached up to wrap around his neck.

She wanted to protest when his mouth left hers to pay attention to her ear. She closed her eyes and sank into the sensation. Heat and desire whirled around them. This was dangerous, a small voice warned in the back of her head, as his lips followed a path down the curve of her neck to where her tank top dipped into a small "V".

"You still haven't answered my question, Rico."

"I thought we were done talking," he murmured, spending an inordinate amount of time at the base of her neck, though she wasn't complaining. In fact, she let her head fall back to give him better access.

"Salvador has looks, money, and compassion. Why shouldn't I be attracted to him?" Once again, she was baiting the tiger, but she couldn't resist seeing how he'd react.

Rico's fingers curled around her shoulder, holding her tight. This time he didn't lift his head, though he paused in what he was doing. "You are not attracted to him, because you are attracted to me."

"Why you arrogant—"

"*Sí, querida*, I'm arrogant." This time Rico straightened. A smile played on his lips, though his eyes indicated his seriousness. "*Mi mami* raised me well. But it was from my *papi* that I learned that when a woman kisses you like you've kissed me, it means one thing."

She shouldn't ask, but she had to know. "It means what?"

He leaned in, getting right into her face. "It means you're mine."

"What?" she erupted, but before she could say more, his mouth swooped down on hers. She would kick him in the shin. Soon. Okay, maybe later. Her insides were liquefying and all her circuits screamed overload.

His tongue thrust into her mouth and she nearly melted on the spot. But she'd never been passive in her life. She gave back in equal measure and took pleasure from the way he groaned, "Woman, you're killing me."

She never heard the front door open. Never even knew her uncle stood on the porch until he spoke and it was as if all the light went out in her world. "Francesca, such displays will earn you the reputation for being fast and easy."

Rico watched the blood drain from Frankie's face. And,

though she held herself with rigid pride, he saw the hurt in her eyes. He cursed himself for putting her in the situation to begin with. He was the one who should've known better. He stepped forward, instinct propelling him to protect her, but Frankie's hand stayed him.

"Hector, this is my house. I don't have to answer to you or anyone. Now if you will both excuse me, I have things I would like to do." She walked up the steps regally, her head held high, her tail swishing, and swept inside. Not once did she turn back to look at Rico. He'd been dismissed.

He should've been angry, but he understood. Frankie's walls were up and in force. Briefly, she'd let them down and let him in.

It was wiser to let it go. He hadn't come to Casa Verde to get involved with a hot-tempered cat. He'd come to find Chita. He had to remember his duty.

Still there was one duty he had to take care of right now.

He moved up the stairs and got into the old man's space. "Don't ever talk to her that way."

"I have a right," he sputtered, fear flickering in his bloodshot eyes. "She's my niece."

Rico pressed in on the man. "That's still to be seen. You abuse her trust and you'll have to answer to me."

To Hector's credit, the man didn't back down. "I'm simply looking out for her welfare. The people in town will not condone such behavior. You should know better. Puerto Rico is full of old-fashioned values. This is not New York."

Damn. Hector was right. If Frankie chose to make her home here, she would be the subject of all kinds of gossip if she weren't careful. Growing up, he'd chaperoned his sisters, always vigilant that their virtue was kept intact. He had no right to cause Frankie further embarrassment by saddling her with a reputation. She had enough trouble with the superstitions. If he showed too much interest in Frankie, gossips would soon have them married and starting a family. For a minute, the image of his child in Frankie's arms made his throat squeeze tight until he forced reality back into his mind. He wasn't father material and he doubted he'd ever be.

He placed his hand on his back pocket and thought of the

picture he carried in his wallet. He could see the bright little smile, so innocent and peaceful, sweet, innocent, Lourdes. He dropped his hand.

"Just remember, I'm watching you," Rico said.

The old man turned and nearly stumbled over the doorsill before righting himself.

"Where are you going?" Rico called out after him.

"I came out to see if Francesca would give me a ride into town."

"Don't bother Frankie. Give me thirty minutes. I'll take you." That would give him time to shower and make it to his meeting with Roberto.

And while he was away from Frankie, he'd better come up with a plan to get her out from under his skin.

Unfortunately, he didn't think a cold shower would do it.

The old truck sputtered to life.

Rico cranked the gears and hoped for the best. He turned around to back out of the drive and the truck lurched forward. Rico slammed on the brake.

"*Bobo!*" Hector clutched at his heart. "Simple-minded fool! What are you doing? Do you know how to drive?"

Rico gritted his teeth. He corrected the gears and reversed out onto the road. Frankie bounded out the back door and intercepted them before he could make it down the drive.

"I'm coming with you," she said breathlessly and got in alongside Hector.

Bad enough he had to endure Hector even for a short while, he didn't want Frankie questioning his every move, too. "Are you sure? Because we can handle the shopping."

"No. It's okay. I want to stop by the lumberyard and pick up a few more supplies." She looked back at the house. "I think we'll need them."

Rico cursed silently in his head. He didn't have time for this.

His brother promised to meet him in the bar. He wanted to get the evidence analyzed as soon as possible. Rico didn't have time for delays. He'd figure out a way to ditch Frankie and get the plastic baggie tucked into the toolbox delivered to Roberto.

The truck bounced along until they pulled onto the town's main street and looked for parking. Hector eyed the shops on either side.

"Pull over here and drop me off."

Rico double-parked in front of a vegetable grocer.

"Don't forget to pick up everything on the list." Frankie shouted out the window at Hector's back.

Hector waved the piece of paper Frankie had handed him right before he'd gotten out of the truck. She had also handed him money for the food. Rico mentally rolled his eyes in disbelief. He couldn't figure the woman out. "You're from New York, for Pete's sake. You really think you can trust the guy with your cash?

"It's only a few bucks." She bristled beside him.

"I thought money was tight, or was I mistaken?"

"If you're worried about getting paid for the job, don't be." She folded her arms across her chest and stared straight ahead.

"I'm not—oh, hell—what's the point?" Rico threw the truck into gear and began to pull back onto the road. In the rearview mirror he caught sight of Hector weaving through the people milling around the vegetable stands in the market only to disappear into the back. Rico would make damn sure to check the change to see if all of it was used to buy food. Frankie might want to trust Hector but Rico sure as hell didn't.

They headed off for the lumberyard. He drove two blocks more and pulled in.

Rico stepped out of the cab while Frankie fished around in her purse for her account slip.

"*No, Señor.*" The manager of the yard came out of his tiny office. "Sorry, but we are closed."

Frankie came to stand next to him. She vibrated with anger. "The sign says open."

"My mistake." He crossed his short arms over his belly. The manager might have been two heads shorter than Rico but his burly arms and thick neck spoke of a man used to lifting heavy weights. "We are closed for the day," he said in earnest.

Rico pulled out his wallet and took out the last two fifty dollar bills he had to his name. "For your trouble, *Señor*."

The man scowled and refused to take the money. "Maybe you do not understand me." He nodded his head. Another man, large and wide like an ancient ceibo tree lumbered over.

The hairs on Rico's neck rose. He squared up to his opponent. He could take the other guy but he would be no good to Frankie or Chita should he be snapped in half like a twig.

Frankie waved her credit slip. "*Mira*, I didn't come here for trouble. I just want to pick up the rest of my order and buy some more supplies."

The manager stepped closer. "We don't need your cursed money. Go back to Casa Verde, *bruja*."

"Witch! Witch!" Frankie's eyes spit fire. "What is wrong with you people?" She fisted up her hands and looked ready to pop one to the manager. "You want a witch. I'll show you a witch."

Rico grabbed hold of her. "Come on. We'll take our business elsewhere."

"*Bueno, Señor.* A wise choice." The manager looked disdainfully at Frankie. "You would do well to listen to your husband."

Frankie opened her mouth and then clamped it shut. She shook off Rico and stomped backed to the truck.

Rico narrowed his eyes and stepped forward heedless of the bruiser intent on intimidating him. "*Señor*, I will leave now, but don't think this is over."

Beep! Honk! Rico laid on the horn to drive the goats off the road and to drown out Frankie's cursing. Amazing. She cursed more than his buddies back at ICE.

"Arrogant little son of a..."

Honk! "*Ven aca!*" Rico leaned out the window and called to the goat herder. A young boy no older than Armando stepped up to the window.

"Can you move these animals any faster?"

"*No, Señor.*" The boy shook his head. "Something has spooked the goats." His eyes grew big in his head, "*El chupa*," he whispered.

"Oh, not again," Frankie grumbled. But the way she wrapped her arms around herself told him she wasn't as unaffected as she pretended.

Rico turned back to the boy. *"El chupacabra, eh? Dónde?"*

The boy told a tale of a dead goat found sucked lifeless this morning and left for dead in front of his house. "My mama has forbidden my sisters from going outside."

"Why?" Frankie sat up in her seat.

The boy looked at her as if she were stupid. "It is a sign that he will come for the children next."

Frankie shivered visibly. Rico lightly touched her shoulder in a gesture of comfort, but she turned away to look out the window. Her body language loudly proclaimed she wanted to be left alone.

Rico cursed the whole situation under his breath and squeezed the steering wheel in frustration.

A shout from the road garnered his attention. The boy's father had arrived and together the two of them herded the goats onto the other side of the road. Rico lurched the truck forward. The boy's words bounced around in his head. He made a mental note to check if any of the other girls had received such calling cards from *el chupa.*

Right now, he had to figure out a way to ditch Frankie. He was late for his meeting with his brother. And knowing Roberto, his little brother's patience was wearing thin.

Rico pulled into the parking lot of the marina at the end of the street. For the first time since they'd left the goats, Frankie's eyes swiveled in his direction.

"What are we doing here?" Suspicion dripped from each word.

"My boat is over there."

Her eyes widened in disbelief. "You live on a boat. I figured you for a drifter but..." She bit back a laugh.

Rico unhooked his seatbelt and opened the rusty door. "Yes, well, not everyone is born with a silver spoon in their mouth."

"Spare me." The laughter died on her lips. "You don't know anything about me."

Rico jumped down to the ground and headed to the small gangway leading out to a few dinghies tied up.

"How long you going to be?" Frankie slid over to the driver's side and poked her head out the door. "Want me to stick around?"

Rico glanced quickly down at his watch. He was already fifteen minutes late. "No. Go ahead and run whatever other errands you have. I need to pick up a few things. I'll meet you later."

"Why? You got an appointment or something?"

"Just get going, woman, would you?"

Frankie's eyes narrowed in anger. He shouldn't have lost his cool, but he didn't have time.

"Sure," she said. "I don't have anything decent for tomorrow night's date with Salvador. I think I'll hit the shops. Catch you later."

She slammed the door, threw the truck in gear and gunned the engine, the tires squealing as she took off down the main street.

Rico would deal with her anger later. Right now, he had more pressing matters to deal with.

Rico walked into the same bar where he had first laid eyes on Frankie Montalvo. Twenty-four hours later, he was right back where he started and not a damn inch closer to finding Chita.

Roberto sat at one of the small tables in the back fidgeting with a beer bottle. A smaller version of him but not by much. The kid had sure grown up since Rico was last in Vieques. Guilt rode him. He had missed more than a few birthdays. He should have stopped in at one of the stores along the way, but he was at a loss as to what to get a twenty-one year old. Rico took the chair directly across from him.

"Hey, *nataio.*"

His brother reached across and slapped his hand in an old familial hand code that took him back in the day. He'd been so ready to shake the sand off his feet when he left Vieques for the mainland that he hadn't realized how much of his roots he'd left behind. Seeing his brother laid back and relaxed, his life carefree, made for a complete contrast to Rico's other life in New Jersey.

"You want another?" Rico nodded towards his brother's nearly finished drink.

"Yeah, thanks. This one's gotten warm."

Rico waved to the bartender. "*Dos cervezas.*"

The bartender sauntered over and popped the tops off two cold beers and smacked them in the middle of the table before he went off to attend to other patrons. Though well after the noon siesta, the bar was still packed with locals looking to ride out the heat of the afternoon sun.

Roberto leaned in close. He kept his voice low. "*Que pasó?*"

"I need you to take this." Rico pulled the baggie out of his back pocket and handed it to Roberto.

Roberto scrutinized the contents. "What's this got to do with Chita?"

Rico shrugged his shoulders. "That's why I need you." He reached back and pulled out his wallet. "Express mail it to ICE. Attention Special Agent Colton." He pulled out a business card. A beat-up picture of a woman holding a child fell onto the table.

Rico swallowed hard. The sweet smile of Lourdes stared up at him. Roberto reached for the picture. Rico snatched it up and shoved it in his wallet.

"Who are they?"

"No one." Rico picked up his beer and took a long swig. The bitter alcohol stung his tongue, just like the bitter memories of the woman and child in the picture.

"The family is worried about you." His brother fidgeted with his beer.

Rico shook his head. "Don't be. Tell everyone to keep their prayers for Chita."

Roberto drank off the last of his beer. He no longer carried the look of a boy. He had grown and filled out since Rico had last been home. His face serious, Roberto pulled his shoulders back. "The family is counting on you."

Duty. The weight bore down on him. "Don't worry, *mi hermano.* I will bring Chita back."

"Let me help you. I can be your back up."

"No!" The denial sounded harsh and loud. Rico lowered his voice. "You're helping me by doing what I asked. I've been trained for this. You and the family have to trust me."

Roberto's expression became mulish. "You still think of me as a child."

Rico examined his little brother's face. Yes, his brother had turned into a man. But there was innocence in his eyes that told its own story. Rico thought of his years with ICE, of the sexual exploitation, drug dealing and violence that had made up his world for so long. His mind flashed to Carla, to the blood seeping out of her and onto the floor. A senseless death. One he should have prevented. Only he hadn't and his failure meant Lourdes would have to grow up without a mother.

And now there was Chita, another young woman who chipped away at his conscience.

Carefully, Rico set his beer down on the table. Leaning forward, he placed both hands on the table and caught his brother's eye. "I think you should stop feeling sorry for yourself and remember what's at stake here. Playing detective could get you, me and Chita killed." If she weren't dead already. He was too experienced not to recognize that possibility. "Just do what I ask and nothing more."

"Sure, no problem *hermano.*" Roberto pushed away from the table, throwing a few bills down as he stood. "Wouldn't want to step on the Lone Ranger's toes."

Rico banged his fist down on the table as he watched his brother exit the bar. Somehow, he'd blown it, but he didn't know how to make it right. And the last thing he needed or wanted was Roberto getting mixed up in this investigation. He never wanted Roberto to see the ugliness he wallowed in almost daily and he'd die before he let his little brother step into danger. So, yeah, maybe he had blown it, but if it meant keeping Roberto alive and well, he'd live with the consequences.

Rico drained the last of his beer. He pulled out his wallet and added a few more bills to the ones already on the table. A headache nagged at his temples. In the space of an hour, he'd managed to tick off both Frankie and his brother.

Stepping outside, Rico sucked in the heat and humidity

that never seemed to go away in the summer. He'd intended to ask Roberto for a ride back to the main street. He'd have to hoof it if he wanted to catch Frankie before she headed home. Given how they departed, it wouldn't surprise him if she left him stranded in town.

Fifteen minutes later, Rico hit the town center. He walked along the sidewalk, peering into shop windows for signs of Frankie. Up ahead, he caught sight of the Casa Verde truck and breathed a sigh of relief. She was around somewhere.

At that moment he observed Hector moving rapidly down the opposite sidewalk, glancing nervously around him. Rico stepped back into the shadows and continued to watch. Rico didn't have a high opinion of Frankie's uncle and didn't know why she'd let the guy stay on, but it was her decision. That didn't mean he couldn't keep an eye on the situation.

Hector paused in front of a shop door and swiped his brow with a handkerchief he pulled from his shirt pocket. He threw one more glance over his shoulder and then stepped inside. What was the guy up to? Rico crossed the street and peeked through the dusty shop window to see Hector dangle an item in his hand. Blood roaring in his ears, Rico yanked open the door.

Chapter 7

The afternoon sun beat ruthlessly down on her shoulders. Frankie window-shopped along the strip of family-owned business fronts. One small boutique store caught her attention. In the window hung a long, gauzy, white eyelet dress with hand woven patterns of silver and gold that swirled around the hemline. Light and delicate, the simple dress would go easily with a pair of sandals.

The tinkle of a bell greeted Frankie as she pushed open the door. Incense of orchid and vanilla filled the air. Dimly lit by candles that lay on the floor and on shelves, the room glowed as light glinted off the walls. Beaded drapes hung from the windows and doorways. A diminutive glass skull sat on top of the counter next to the register. Books on the occult, herbal remedies, and spiritualism took up a large section of the wall. She picked up a copy and paged through one of the prominently displayed books.

Sketches of *el chupacabra*—some of the creature as an alien, others as a vampire—filled each page together with tales of the legendary creature's exploits. Carcasses of goats, horses, and other farm animals all graphically shown in photographs made Frankie's nose wrinkle up in distaste. But one photograph stood out among the rest, a snarling rodent-like beast with glowing red eyes sent a shiver up her spine. Only the description below noted the creature to be a foot long. A big difference from the animal that had attacked her. The creature in the mangroves had been six times larger.

"Francesca! What a surprise."

Frankie snapped the book closed and quickly put it back in the display.

Margarita came out from behind a curtain of beads dressed in white linen pants and a white button-down top, her massive amounts of hair pulled up and tied artistically in a red chiffon scarf.

"I am so glad you decided to visit me." Margarita hugged Frankie and placed a kiss on both side of her cheeks.

"Actually, Margarita..."

"*Tía, por favor.*"

"*Tía.*" The word for aunt sounded strange to her ears but it gave her a little thrill to say it out loud. "I came in to look at the dress in the window."

"*Sí*, it is beautiful."

Margarita took her hand and led her to the window. She opened the display case and took down the dress. She held it up against Frankie.

Up close the dress was even more stunning.

Frankie glimpsed the tag. "Oh, I'm sorry the price is a little out of my range."

"Nonsense." Margarita pushed Frankie to the back of the store. "You are family. I'll give you a big discount. Now, go and try it on."

The material felt soft under her fingertips. "Really, I don't want to..."

Margarita shooed her with her hands into the back room. "Come out when you put it on."

Inside the backroom, a small fountain of water trickled down into a large black iron pot on top of ember-hot coals. Steam fogged up over the sides down onto the floor. She stepped around it. The faces of patron saints on glass candles stared back at her from the floor and along shelves on the walls.

"I don't know if I can undress in front of Jesus."

Her aunt called out. "The saints are benevolent."

Frankie didn't doubt it for a moment. There was something about stripping down in front of the iconic candles, sort of like getting naked in a church.

Frankie fingered the dress, tempted further by the soft material and exquisite embroidery. Mentally, she added up her cash on hand and compared that to the list of repairs Casa

Verde needed. She nearly groaned under the weight the cost of the dress would add to the debit side of the ledger.

Still, she had nothing to wear for tomorrow night. No other shop in town offered anything nearly as beautiful. It was this or drive clear across Vieques to Isabel Segunda.

She brushed a loose strand of hair behind her ear and frowned at her visage, noting the wrinkles on her forehead, well aware of what was causing them. She might be able to afford the dress if her aunt lowered the price. Problem was, it didn't feel right. She didn't know Margarita. She didn't like the idea of being beholden to a stranger. Who knew what ties would come with the sale?

Realizing she'd stood there long enough, Frankie undressed and gently eased the dress down over her shoulders and hips.

"All done?" Margarita called through the beads. She came into the back room. "*Bonita.*" She clapped her hands. "You look beautiful."

She did feel beautiful. The soft material felt airy and light on her body. Margarita circled her finger in the air. Frankie spun around on one foot. The mid-calf-length dress swirled up and moved effortlessly with her.

Margarita beamed. "A dancer's soul you have."

The smile was contagious. "I feel like dancing in it." Mist touched her toes and slid over her feet.

"Looks like I am not the only one who believes you should have the dress. The *orishas* deem it a happy union." She pointed to the fountain bubbling over with white fog.

Frankie screwed up her face. "What is this for?"

"For divination. Mostly, I use the power of the well to protect me from harm. The amount of mist tells me if there is ill will toward me."

Frankie shook her head. Hector might be right. Her aunt was cracked. "Hector says you're a witch."

Margarita's face tightened with anger, but as quickly as it came, it disappeared. "Do not listen to him. He is unenlightened in the ways of Santeria."

Growing up in Brooklyn she had heard about the religion— cult of animal sacrificing, devil worshipping fanatics. "Santeria?

Is that like voodoo?"

"Oh, no. It is a peaceful, old world religion. Rich and symbolic, full of power, knowledge and beauty." Margarita's eyes lit up, her face glowed with pride. "The most powerful magic in existence today. It comes from Cuba and dates backs to Africa. Many people practice. Once you feel the power, you know you have been touched."

The look in Margarita's eyes told Frankie her aunt was definitely touched.

Margarita picked up a blue and white candle and held it out to Frankie. "Yemaya, Our Lady of Regla, is the patron saint of women. She is the greatest of all the *orishas.* The great mother, giver of life. She will guard you and protect you." Margarita pushed the candle into her hands.

"Thanks, but I couldn't..."

"Take it." Margarita insisted. "You will need all the protection you can get if you insist upon living in that house."

"I don't understand."

"Oh, it is simple." She took the candle from Frankie's hands and demonstrated. "Just light the candle and place it next to your bed. Say the prayer on the back of the candle before you go to sleep. Yemaya will protect you from the evil."

Frankie shook her head. "No, I meant to say, why would I need protection from the house?"

Margarita looked at her like she was stupid. "Vibes. Bad vibes."

Frankie rolled her eyes. Obviously Margarita believed the explanation satisfactory enough. Frankie decided to leave it alone. The tiny tinkle of a bell sounded.

"A customer." Before Margarita walked through the beaded curtain she glanced back at Frankie. "That dress was made for you."

Frankie ran her hands down the length of her torso. The dress fit her to perfection. She really did want to buy it. She bit her lip and mentally counted the money in her head. It was too much.

Careful not to snag the gauzy material, she shimmied out of the dress and hung it up. Painfully aware of the dozens of eyes watching her from the shelves, she quickly got back into her clothes. The spandex top and tight jeans she had changed into made her feel like a wrapped-up sausage compared to the soft, loose material of the dress. She longed to put it back on and could imagine herself dancing in it, the material moving with her. But she had priorities. The house came first. With a sigh, she picked up the dress. Later she would contact Salvador and decline his invitation. She carried the dress up front to where Margarita sold a touristy-looking couple a copy of the *chupacabra* book.

"*Gracias.*" She waved goodbye as they walked out. Then she turned attention back to Frankie. "So, you will take the dress?"

"No. Thank you, but I can't afford it."

Margarita took the dress from her. "Nonsense. You are *familia.*"

She pulled out some tissue paper and wrapped the dress up. "Consider it a long-overdue birthday present." She delicately placed the dress into a brown bag.

"No, really. You are too kind. I couldn't—"

"I won't hear another word." Margarita waved her hand. "My mother, your grandmother, was remiss in not bringing you home when she had the chance." The woman's eyes misted up. "To think of you, all those years, growing up in the cruel, harsh world alone. No." Margarita swiped a tear from her eye.

Frankie's jaw dropped. "You knew I was alive? In foster care?"

Margarita nodded her head. "*Sí.* Mother knew everything." The words came out harsh and bitter. A haunted look came into her eyes. A million ghosts passed through her irises. Frankie felt a chill in her bones.

"If she knew I was alive, why didn't she come get me?" She couldn't help the whine in her voice. Something inside her broke. All those years in foster care, being shuttled from place to place, she had believed she had no family, no one who cared.

"No. I take it back. It is better that you were where you were." Margarita said the words with conviction.

How could she say that? Didn't the woman have a clue how hard it had been for her, how tough the system could be on a child? No. She wouldn't. No one could. But Frankie knew and that was all that mattered. Frankie straightened up. She had survived. The past was in the past. The future stood before her and she wasn't going to wonder about the whys and what ifs.

Margarita cheerfully wrapped the candle in tissue paper.

"Now, make sure to keep the candle lit day and night." She placed the glass candle inside the bag with care.

"I will. Thank you so much." Frankie hugged her aunt across the counter, warmth and affection pouring from her embrace. Margarita placed a kiss on each side of her cheeks. "Go and may the spirits be with you, *oluku mi.*"

Frankie rolled her eyes. The woman sounded like a zealot, but she couldn't fault the woman's beliefs. Frankie took the bags and headed for the door.

"Oh, Francesca. One more thing." Margarita came out from behind the counter. "When you wash the initiation gown, make sure to hand wash in cold water in order to keep the integrity of the material."

Frankie stopped short. "Initiation gown?"

"*Sí.* White is the color of purity. New initiates to Santeria wear white for a year to show their love for the *orishas.* Isn't that why you want the dress?"

"I'm sorry I hadn't realized the dress was special." She turned around and held the bag out to Margarita. "I couldn't possibly take it. I just need a dress for dancing."

"Yes, exactly. For dancing." She pushed the bag back into Frankie's hand. "The dress is made for dancing. Celebrating the spirit of the *orishas.*" Margarita looked at Frankie quizzically. "Why else would you want the dress?"

"I needed something nice to wear to a party tomorrow night. Salvador Torres invited—"

Margarita grabbed hold of Frankie's wrist. The woman's grip cut into her veins. She tried to pull her arm back. "You mustn't go." Margarita keened.

"Hey! Let go of me."

Margarita became agitated. Her nails bit into Frankie's flesh. "Stay away from that family." Frankie pulled her arm back harder. The woman stumbled into her. Face to face, she could see Margarita's fear. Full-out panic gripped the woman.

"You will pay for your sins if you go there."

Frankie twisted her wrist free. "You're crazy."

She turned and fled the shop. Margarita shouted from the door as she ran down the sidewalk. "You will regret ignoring my words."

"*Déme eso!*"

Rico held the necklace out of the shorter man's reach. The purple stone winked as it twirled on the long gold strand swinging from Rico's hand.

"Nice jewelry, Hector. Where'd you get it?"

"None of your business. It's mine. Now give it back." Sweat beaded on Hector's upper lip. His eyes darted about the small interior.

"Is there a problem here, *Señores*?" The shopkeeper smiled, but his uneasiness communicated itself in the way his hands lingered under the counter. Rico eye's narrowed on the man, guessing the guy either had a gun or an alarm button within reach.

"No problem, *Señor*. I take it my friend here came to transact business with you."

"*Sí*. Señor de la Varga is a valued customer."

"I'll just bet he is," Rico murmured. He'd taken stock of the inside as soon as he walked in. The place advertised itself as an antiques store, but the decade-old television propped next to a backgammon set on one shelf, together with a tennis racquet leaning against an electric guitar in the corner told their own tale. This place had pawnshop stamped all over it.

"You have no right to bother me. If you don't give that back to me, I'll call the police." Hector stretched his short stocky figure for an extra inch, managing only to look more ridiculous than commanding.

"Tell you what, Hector. You show me proof of ownership and I'll return it with my sincere apologies."

"Why that's... You can't..." Hector sputtered, his face turning red.

The bell over the shop door rang and an elderly couple stepped inside.

"*Señores*, there seems to be some disagreement. Perhaps, if you would discuss it outside?" the shopkeeper suggested.

"This is outrageous," Hector continued, having finally found his voice.

Rico grabbed Hector's arm in a firm grip and propelled him out the door and onto the sidewalk. "What's outrageous," Rico gritted out, "is you taking advantage of Frankie."

"I have no idea what you're talking about." Hector countered, though the sweat pouring down the sides of his face only seemed to underscore his lying.

"Then, why don't we ask Frankie? Here she comes now." With a shopping bag in her hand, Frankie hurried toward them. Rico frowned noticing how strained her features appeared even from this distance. Sensing Rico's distraction, Hector broke Rico's grip and started scurrying away.

"Hey!" Rico chased after him, surprised at Hector's ability to break his hold and by the older man's speed down the street. The booze hadn't dulled the guy's reflexes apparently, but Rico was in better shape, more than a decade younger and used to taking down criminals. He reached out grabbing the collar of Hector's shirt and yanked, pulling Frankie's uncle to a stop.

Irritation ran through him over the effort. No way was he giving the little weasel an inch. Hauling Hector against his side, Rico turned to face Frankie once again.

Hector squirmed in his shoes, obviously seeking an opportunity to escape. Rico noted the wiry muscle in Hector's arm and was determined not to underestimate the guy a second time. "I wonder how Frankie will react when she sees the necklace you were trying to pawn." Hector looked sick at the thought. "Yeah, that's what I thought."

With his grip even firmer on Hector this time, the two waited for Frankie to reach them.

Frankie switched the shopping bag from her throbbing hand. Rubbed red, faint fingernail marks still marred her wrist. She gave one last look back. Margarita was no longer on the street.

Up ahead, Frankie spied Rico gripping an indignant Hector and nearly turned around and headed in the opposite direction.

A wave of exhaustion hit her at the thought of dealing with another relative. She tripped over a crack in the sidewalk and went down on her knee. She put out her hands in front of her but her throbbing wrist didn't hold.

She heard footsteps running toward her.

"Frankie? *Querida?* *Que pasó?*"

What happened? What happened? Everything! She wanted to shout. The question should have been what hadn't happened? Ever since stepping foot on Vieques her whole world had turned upside down. Her life was supposed to get better not weirder.

Bringing her head up, she nearly choked on a laugh as she watched a concerned Rico come down the broken sidewalk at a clip, dragging a protesting Hector along with him. Not wanting to look helpless, she pushed up with her good hand and sat back on her bruised knees.

"What's wrong? Where are you hurt?" His eyes assessed every inch of her it seemed. It should've felt strange, but it felt good to have someone genuinely care about her well-being.

"I'm fine. I tripped." She waved his concern away. He put Hector aside to help her up. He asked again if she was fine. Frankie ignored his comment instead throwing a glance at Hector.

The antagonism flowing between the two men was hard to ignore. She had a faint idea that letting Hector do the shopping might not have been the wisest idea. She looked around for grocery bags. "You did go shopping, didn't you Hector?" She pinned her uncle with a look and noted resignedly the way he shifted from foot to foot.

"Oh, he went shopping all right," Rico interjected. "Only he was more interested in selling than buying." Rico shot her relative an icy glare. "Isn't that right?" Rico dug into his pocket and drew out a long chain. A purple stone winked as it caught the afternoon sun.

"My grandmother's necklace." She reached out her hand and he dropped the chain and pendant into her palm. She clasped her hand shut around the warm chain.

"You do recognize it." He made it a statement and not a question. Frankie got a sinking sensation in the pit of her stomach.

"It's one of the pieces bequeathed to me along with my grandmother's estate." She should have known better. All her life she had never had much, but what she did own she had guarded fiercely. She clutched the necklace tighter in her hand.

"You might want to rethink where you keep your valuables."

Frankie nodded her head, unable to talk. Afraid of what she might say. Her emotions rotated around inside her. Anger, grief, disappointment, confusion, all rolled together forming a ball of bitterness deep within her.

Finding her voice, she choked back the bile, "It's not all that valuable. I mean it might be worth a little something, but we're not talking diamonds or anything."

Hector, who'd been uncharacteristically quiet, broke into incoherent speech, punctuated by wild hand gestures. "It is all this peasant's fault. He assaulted me. Accused me of all kinds of base lies in front of others. It is inexcusable. You must get rid of him at once. He is not fit to wipe a de la Varga's feet."

The last was said with Hector's feet dangling in the air as Rico lifted him up in a two-fisted hold. "Listen you miserable excuse of a human being. I'll wipe the street with you. You're a liar and a thief and—"

"Rico, put him down," Frankie battled her anger, aware of the curious looks being thrown their way. Hector might have been a liar and a thief but it was her fault that they were in this mess—her desire to have a family so badly, to belong, to be part of something larger than just herself. Her foolish dreams had deluded her into believing that she could make it all work. Frankie bit back the tears. "Let's go home." She managed to squeeze out the request from her swollen throat.

Rico lowered Hector to the ground, but didn't let go of the fistful of shirt he had. He shook Hector, rattling the poor man. Hector's shirt reeked of sweat. Frankie wrinkled her nose.

"He was going to pawn off your stuff." Rico looked at her incredulously. "Probably use the money to buy some Puerto Rican rum."

Frankie felt the blow like a fist to her gut. She faced her so-called uncle, having seen enough from life to know how far addicts could go for their next fix. She didn't bother to ask for her money back. There probably wasn't any left.

Hector sputtered out a few excuses, none of which she bought. Apparently recognizing she wasn't buying his crap, his lips flattened and his eyes narrowed into slits. "That necklace is mine. I have every right to do whatever I want with it. The house. Everything. It all should belong to me." He screamed, spittle flying out of his mouth. "Who are you? A nobody. A pretender." He backed up away from Rico's reach.

Rico growled through clenched teeth. "Knock it off, Hector. I'm warning you."

"You think your boyfriend here will protect you? He won't always be around..."

"That's it, Hector," Rico hauled back his fist to punch the guy.

"Don't!" Frankie's voice cracked like a whip in the air. "He's not worth it. Please don't." The last two words came out in a whisper.

Frankie put her hand on his bicep. She could feel how tight his body was coiled. Rico's eyes glowed with icy rage. "At least let's haul his ass to jail. Press charges."

"No." She wanted nothing more to do with her so-called family.

Frankie squeezed her eyes closed and forced herself to block the pain. She didn't know what she'd expected from her newly discovered family. She closed down inside. She'd always be a foster kid. Alone. And she was better off that way.

"Let's just go."

"You're going to let him walk?"

"Yes," she said with a straight face, meeting his eyes squarely. "Could we go now, please?"

Frustration showed clearly on Rico's face. She could tell he didn't agree with her decision.

This was her problem, not his. She would deal with it. She couldn't rely on Rico to solve her problems. Like everyone in her life, he would eventually leave. She had to deal with whatever life threw at her on her own. Just like she always had.

"Hector," she stood her ground, "you're no longer welcome

at Casa Verde. I'll pack your things and have them brought to the bar." At least that was one place in town she knew he'd be. Not wanting to hear any more excuses from her washed-up relative, she started down the sidewalk.

She heard a thump and a cry of pain, but she didn't bother turning around. A second later, Rico caught up with her. He shook out his right hand.

"You didn't have to hit him."

"*Sí, querida*, I did."

She kept her focus straight ahead, her feet moving automatically down the sun-baked sidewalk. "Why?" she finally asked.

Rico lightly grasped her arm, swinging her around in her tracks to face him. "Because he deserved it and more."

His answer should have been enough, but it left her feeling empty. She searched his expression. "Is that the only reason?"

"No, *querida*. It's not the only reason." The sharp angles of his face appeared harsh. He'd never seemed more handsome to her. "Anyone messes with you, they mess with me. Like it or not, you're under my protection. Get used to it."

Her chin shot up, her natural pride asserting itself. "I can take care of myself. No man owns me."

"Too bad," he quietly shot right back. "Maybe it's about time some man did."

Chapter 8

Weariness clung to her like a barnacle on a boat. From her slumped shoulders and downcast eyes to her dragging steps, Frankie looked ready to collapse. A tidal wave of protectiveness washed over Rico and he found himself pulling her into his embrace.

What the hell was he doing?

Except he knew. He wanted to take her home—not to Casa Verde but to Isabela Segunda. Comfort her, promise to make it all better, and show her what a true caring family could be like. But he knew better. This wasn't why he was here in Punta Negra. He had to keep his head on straight. Something almost impossible to do the closer he got to Frankie.

But letting her in could lead to the death of her. His hand went to his back pocket, patting his wallet. *Remember Carla. Think of Lourdes.* Coldness settled over him chasing away the heat of the day. Five years of hounding down leads, filing reports, and conducting sting operations. So close to busting up the Cardenas ring, he could taste the success in his mouth. And then a big break.

Carla had been working as a mule, but she'd wanted out. She wanted a better life for Lourdes. She'd started by feeding Rico bits and pieces of information, testing him, seeing if he'd keep his promises. And he had—except the one to keep her safe. He'd failed her and he would have to live with that.

Two days after she'd agreed to testify and just before she and Lourdes could be whisked into witness protection, Carla was killed in an ambush.

The whole setup smelled, though the internal investigation was ongoing and no conclusions had been released. Rico'd been pulled from the case and told to take time off, as if that would make him forget. Once again, Cardenas had slipped through their fingers and another young woman was dead.

Reality cleared his senses, made it easier to shove the strange feelings he had for Frankie into a box in the back of his mind and to release her like nothing had changed between them.

Because it hadn't.

Frankie offered him a small smile as he bent to relieve her of her bag. "What'd you get?" he asked.

Her smile disappeared. She seemed disturbed. "A dress."

"You know, *querida*," Rico said, as he opened the rusty door for her, "I really don't think the party is a good idea. Why don't you stay home, and I'll go and play the good neighbor."

She paused in the act of climbing into the vehicle. "Not you, too. What is it with everyone?" She hauled herself into the vehicle and sat back in the cracked seat closing her eyes.

Rico closed the door and rounded the vehicle. Who else had been giving her a hard time? He started the engine, holding his breath that it would catch the first time. When it caught with only a small protest, he grinned. A swift glance at his passenger told him she hadn't even been aware of the small victory. Her eyes were closed.

Rico pulled the rumbling vehicle out onto the main thoroughfare and turned in the direction of Casa Verde. They'd only gone a few blocks when he changed his mind. Swinging down the next street, he made a few more turns and kept going for a few miles until he arrived where he wanted to be.

He parked and twisted in his seat to face Frankie. She'd fallen asleep. His fingers came up and gently removed a curl that stuck to the side of her mouth, feeling the silky softness against his rough skin. She shifted, her brow furrowing. Even in sleep, she appeared troubled.

He wished he could slay all her dragons.

He snatched his hand back. He killed the thought. The last time he'd gone up against a dragon, the dragon had won.

"Frankie, wake up." He shook her shoulder lightly once and

then removed his hand, knowing how much he wanted to linger and touch this woman further.

Frankie blinked and opened her eyes, her forehead creasing in confusion. She reminded him of the stray kitten his sister Pilar had brought home when she was a little girl. The little scrap of fur had spit and clawed at anything within range those first few days, just like Frankie had when he'd first met her. But a softness—a vulnerability—existed underneath all that toughness. Every once in a while, he'd glimpse it or it would ambush him with the force of a punch to the solar plexus and he'd find himself thinking thoughts that should have died with Carla.

Frankie sat up, rubbing sleep from her eyes. She glanced out the windshield and then back at him. "Where are we?"

"The next town over." He motioned to a small roadside restaurant. *La Cocinita*. The Little Kitchen, a local favorite. "It's cheap, good, and Jorge, who runs the place, can be counted on for the latest gossip. I want to know more about Hector and anyone else tied to Casa Verde. So, we eat, relax, and maybe learn something useful."

"I like the eating and relaxing part, but do we really have to ask about my family? You make it sound like we're investigating them. Right now, I want to forget the whole ugly incident."

He wished he could do as she asked. Part of him wanted to take away the wounded look he glimpsed in her eyes or ease the way she hunched in on herself as she spoke, but he needed information badly and couldn't afford to wait. "Leave the talking to me. All I want to find out is what Hector meant about deserving the estate."

"You think it's true?" She hugged herself.

"Doesn't matter if it is. Legally, the estate is yours. I simply want to know what kind of enemy Hector will make."

Frankie tucked another stray tendril behind her ear and then reached out to cover his hand with hers. "I appreciate what you're doing, but this isn't your fight. I can handle it myself." She offered him a shaky smile, but before she could let go of his hand, he clasped it between both of his.

"You're wrong, *querida*. This is very much my fight and you are in way over your head. For once in your life, let someone else stand up for you."

"I can't." Despite the sun lowering in the sky, heat and humidity filled the old truck. The combination made him perspire.

Her skin was dewy and flushed red and she swiped at her hair, trying to tame her locks. "I don't know how." The words seemed dragged out of her. "I've depended on other people before and every time they let me down. Today just proved again that I shouldn't put any stock into anyone." Her head dipped as if embarrassed by what she'd revealed.

Rico's hands tightened on hers. "We're going to go in there, get a drink and something to eat and you are going to tell me who did such a number on you. But before we leave this truck, I want your promise that you'll let me handle Hector and the trouble you're having at Casa Verde."

Her eyes searched his. He didn't know what she was searching for and didn't care. He'd wait as long as it took. He wasn't moving from this truck until he heard the words.

"I promise," she said softly.

He leaned over and kissed her lightly on the lips.

"What was that for?" She touched her fingers to her lips.

"Just sealing the deal."

Delicious *asopao* filled her nostrils. She savored the smell of the hearty gumbo chunked with chicken and yucca.

"Eat up." Rico bit into his *pastelón de carne*. He offered her a piece of his meat patty. "Come on, you could use some more meat on your bones."

She shook her head. The tasty dish before her beckoned to be eaten but she didn't feel very hungry. The day's events had left her wrung out.

Rico sunk his teeth into his meat patty. "You sure you don't want a bite?" He tempted her with a wave of his hand. The smell of the spice-filled patty made her mouth water. She caved and leaned over the small table and bit into the flaky crust.

"That's my girl. Soon you'll be looking like JLo."

Frankie laughed despite her lingering feelings. She covered her mouth to keep the food from falling out. It would take more than *criolla* cooking to get her to look like the singer/actress. "Gonna have to eat a big pot full of pigeon peas and gumbo before I can come close to curves like hers."

Rico flashed his smile. "No worries there." A pure look of carnal want crossed over his face.

Frankie swallowed the morsel in her mouth and went into a choking fit. Rico was up in a flash hitting her back and offering her water.

Tears swam in her eyes.

"You okay?"

She nodded her head, unsure if her throat would work properly.

The truth was she was far from all right. She was tired. Bone tired.

And they had yet to make one dent in the house today. Without the extra supplies they needed, it was unlikely they would get much done today at all. Each day the house went untouched meant another day the opening date for her B&B got pushed back, which translated to lost revenue. The little bit of money she had inherited would be all gone soon. She would either have to find a job on the island, which was very doubtful or she would be forced to sell the plantation and go back to New York and beg for her old job back, something her pride wouldn't let her do.

They sat in silence for a while. Rico studied the crowd while she picked at her bowl of stew. While his focus was elsewhere, she studied his profile. His eyes scanned the room, stopping on a villager here and there. His brow would scrunch up as if he were intently studying each and every detail about the person. She pretended to be interested in her soup but she found him ten times more fascinating. Frankie knew next to nothing about the man, yet somehow, somewhere deep down, she did believe him when he said he would protect her.

Reason told her she was a fool. Eventually he, like all the rest, would disappoint her too. But watching him watch everyone in the room, she felt he was protecting her right now. From what, she had no idea. The man was a total enigma. He looked like a drifter, dressing in worn jeans and faded T-shirts, and he lived on a beat-up sailboat in the bay. Everything about him screamed wanderer. Yet, her gut told her different.

She knew what it meant to be a wanderer. No place. No home. No ties. She had spent most of her life moving from one place to another. Shifted, tumbled, and forced out onto the street. Frankie bit into a particularly tough piece of meat. The juice and spices danced over her tongue but the flavor barely registered. In the years before she found her place in the world, she had known hunger, thirst, wallowed among the desperate and disillusioned.

Rico looked like he had never known one day like that. Maybe being a drifter on the sunny, sandy beaches of paradise didn't translate the same as it did in the cold, grimy city, but still all the pieces didn't add up. He talked well, he carried himself with no fear, he was chivalrous and he had cash flow and his body...his body looked, well...amazing.

He turned back in his seat and caught her staring. She spooned another bit of stew into her mouth. Some of the soup missed and dribbled onto her chin. She stuck out her tongue to lick up the juice. He picked up a napkin and wiped away the mess.

"Thanks." She leaned back in her chair to let the soup settle in her stomach.

"Save some room. We still have dessert coming."

Frankie smacked her lips together at the thought of the sweet custard dessert. "I can't remember the last time I tasted flan."

Rico flashed her a smile. "Then you're in for a real treat. Jorge makes the best on the island."

As if on queue a short lean man with thinning hair wearing an apron walked out from the back of the restaurant with two plates. He approached the table.

"Jorge!" Rico clapped the man on the back nearly sending the cook flying.

"It is good to see you." He cracked a smile. A gold tooth winked in his mouth. "When was the last time you roamed in my house?"

Rico tried to snatch a piece of dessert off the plate. The older man laughed and moved the food out of reach. "Always impatient."

Rico's eyes crinkled with affection. "Only here. The best food on the island."

The man grinned broadly and placed the plates down on the table.

"Rico, who is your pretty friend?" The older man winked at Frankie and smoothed the few wisps of hair he had over to the side.

She bit back a giggle.

"Señor Vaz meet Frankie Montalvo. She's the new owner of Casa Verde in Punta Negra."

The old man blanched. Frankie's heart sunk. Not another person who thought her place was haunted. She steeled herself for another round of ghost tales.

Instead she was greatly surprised when he held out his hand and said, "Congratulations."

"Ummm...thank you." She smiled back at him.

"Please," Rico pulled a chair from another table over, "join us."

The man turned and shouted something in Spanish back to the cooks in the kitchen. "Why not? I need a few minutes break."

He sat down. Rico plucked a sugary confection of coconut off his plate and into his mouth. He licked the sweet stickiness off his fingers like a greedy little child.

Jorge laughed loudly. "I see you still have a sweet tooth."

Rico gave a sly grin. "How is business?"

"Good. I can't complain. Tourist season is always good." Jorge gave a proprietary glance around his establishment. A waitress bustled from table to table. At the counter, patrons sipped cold beverages and cheered for the baseball team on the television. He returned his attention back to their table. "How is your family?"

"Good." Rico replied and left it at that. Frankie found it odd, but the older man didn't press further.

Rico popped another coconut ball into his mouth. He talked around his food. "Hector de la Varga? Does the name ring a bell?"

"Yes. Why?"

"He claims to be Frankie's uncle."

Jorge scrutinized Frankie. He looked at her face. Frankie squirmed in her chair. She looked at Rico. "I don't think this is such a good idea." Rico patted her hand under the table.

"Frankie... Frankie Montalvo." A light went off in his head. "You are the daughter of Tito and Ana. Francesca, right?"

Did everyone know her parents? Damn, island life was small. Frankie gave a slight nod.

"Yes, I don't know how I could have missed the family resemblance. You look just like your mother. Big eyes, curly hair, and *flaca*." He gave a belly laugh. "Even as a child she was a skinny little thing. They moved to New York, I remember. How are your parents?"

"They're deceased." She looked away, not wanting to see the pity in his eyes.

"I am sorry to hear that. Ana was a good girl. A bright girl. Tito, too. They had big dreams."

Frankie's heart raced. It had been a long time since she'd allowed herself to talk about her parents. It had been even longer since she had heard anyone talk about them so fondly.

She brought her eyes up and met Jorge's big grin. "I can see they succeeded in making one dream come true. Raising a lovely daughter."

She smiled and choked back the tears in her throat. Rico squeezed her hand and she squeezed back. "*Gracias, Señor,*" she managed to say without bawling like a baby.

She would have loved to hear more about her parents but Rico interrupted. "What about the rest of the de la Varga clan?"

Jorge scowled and shook his head in disgust. "*Tostao.*"

"What do you mean?" The word was foreign to her.

"Crazy. The daughter and the son. Both of them are crazy. Señora de la Varga was a strict woman. She believed in raising children with a heavy hand. Señor de la Varga had been a prominent man. Ran a good crop. A lot of villagers worked on the plantation, but after his death," he shook his head, "everything fell apart. Some say your grandmother grieved heavily for her husband. She went crazy. Came down hard on her children. Ana, being the oldest, got married right away and left as soon as she could. She never looked back. Hector had to drop out of law school to come and run the operations."

Rico snorted. "A lawyer?"

"*Sí*. Hector de la Varga had promise. He was a very intelligent young man. Left for the mainland to go to the university."

Frankie had a hard time perceiving Hector as a mental giant. "What happened to him? He can barely string a sentence together."

Jorge cupped his hand and tilted his head back pantomiming a man drinking. "*El Diablo* in a bottle."

"Margarita?" She almost was afraid to ask what drove her aunt.

"She is a good woman. She tries very hard to please everyone. Too bad Señora de la Varga never saw her as much. Ana had been the golden child. Margarita sort of went unnoticed. Now she is considered a high priestess or something. Very active in the community, but before her mother died barely anyone saw her come out of the plantation."

Rico looked at Frankie and then at Jorge. "Aside from one turning to the bottle and the other turning to religion, those two aren't much of a threat. So, why is everyone so afraid of Casa Verde?"

Jorge sighed. "Townspeople talk. They whisper. Some of it true and some..." he shrugged his thin shoulders.

Rico leaned in closer. Frankie followed suit.

Jorge looked left and right. He leaned into the circle and lowered his voice. "Demons."

"Oh, come on. You don't believe that nonsense." Frankie kept her voice low but didn't try to keep the revulsion out of her tone.

"Not nonsense. Ever since *Señor* died, a lot of strange things have gone on in that house. The villagers stay far away."

"Giving *el chupa* free reign." Rico looked disgusted.

"*Sí, el chupacabra*. He has been spotted all over the island. Mostly a myth, something to scare the children and keep them in line."

"Well, if enough people begin to believe then the myth

becomes real." Rico leaned back in his chair and popped the last piece of dessert in his mouth.

"But it's not a myth anymore. A young girl was found not long ago sucked dry right down to the marrow."

Frankie's flan sat cold and untouched in the middle of the table. The caramelized custard no longer held any appeal.

"All I know is that the kids want nothing to do with the house." He looked at Frankie. "I'm surprised she left anything to Ana at all."

"Honestly, I don't know why either. Far as I knew, I didn't have any family."

Jorge nodded his head in understanding. "Ana and Tito left pretty abruptly. We heard they had run off together shortly after getting married. They came back once to make peace with the old woman. I understand it went badly. Last time I saw your folks..." He counted on his fingers. "Some twenty-three years ago."

She'd have only been a few years old. It didn't make any sense. Why would they leave? What had made them head for New York, one of the toughest cities to raise a family in? A million questions filtered in and out of her mind. She wanted to ask but didn't know where to begin.

Rico leaned back in his chair. "Jorge, you are a regular town gossip."

The older gentleman laughed loudly. It amazed her such a tiny man could make such a raucous sound.

"One more thing." Rico looked serious. "Had a run in with Hector in town today. He was trying to pawn some of Frankie's inheritance. Said he had every right to the estate. That it all should have been his."

Jorge looked sad and shook his head. "Señora de la Varga didn't do right by her children. I don't know why. She came from a long line of well-to-do Spaniards. The family was not only wealthy, but also rich in history. Honestly, I can't tell you if he is entitled to the inheritance or not. That is between God and the spirit of his mother."

A shout came from the back of the restaurant. "I must go. It was good to see you again, Rico. Give my love to the family." He turned to Frankie, "And I do hope to see your face light up my restaurant another day."

Frankie smiled at the man. She would definitely be back to sample some more of the scrumptious food. The home cooking would do her well. She might even ask for some of the recipes. Goodness knew she needed a lesson or two.

He didn't get far before something he said hit her. She got up and walked quickly between the tables to catch up. "I'm sorry, Jorge. You mentioned that the family was once rich. How long ago was that?"

He rubbed his chin and thought for a while. "For as long as I can remember." Another shout came from the back. The smell of smoke wafted out from the swinging door to the kitchen. "I must go, but come back soon and we will talk some more."

Frankie would be back. She wanted to know more about her heritage, she needed to know more. Somehow she felt her life depended on it.

Chapter 9

Rico silently coaxed the old truck over the rutted driveway. Beside him, Frankie slept, having given in to her exhaustion soon after they'd left Jorge's place.

Coming around the next bend, Casa Verde loomed before them, dark and forbidding. From what Jorge had said, the warmth had long been sucked out of the place. He couldn't help shaking his head. The monstrosity needed more than money and muscle to turn it into a B&B. Didn't Frankie realize she'd be better off selling the place and using the cash to start fresh? No, of course not.

The woman was stubborn and proud.

She'd fit right in with his mother and sisters.

Scary thought, but true. The Lopez women were strong. And so was Frankie. Time and again she'd proven she was no quitter. She wasn't afraid of hard work or taking a few knocks. He'd seen the hurt in her eyes over Hector's betrayal. But she refused to be defeated.

He admired those qualities even as he recognized his job would be much easier were she to pack up and leave.

Rico pulled the truck to a halt and killed the engine. Silence, broken only by Frankie's soft rhythmic breathing, filled the cab. Rico turned his head to gaze upon her. Her wild curls had once again escaped from the clip she used, shielding much of her face. But he didn't need to see what was already imprinted on his mind. Expressive eyes, wide lips and a firm chin. All packaged in that curvy body.

She thought she was too skinny.

She was damn near perfect.

And if they didn't get out of this truck, he was liable to do something stupid. Like kiss her awake.

Rico grabbed the steering wheel like a lifeline and stared straight ahead. "Frankie, wake up. We're here." He glanced over and watched her eyes blink slowly open. She sat up and stretched. The tight material of her top clung to her breasts.

Rico snapped his eyes forward and shifted in his seat. Air. He needed air.

Shoving a shoulder against the rusty door, he pushed it open and let the air into the cab. He jumped down lightly, and reached back inside for Frankie's dress and a few other purchases he'd managed to make at the tiny store attached to the gas station. The eggs, bacon and milk would supplement what was left in the pantry.

Frankie joined him and together they headed to the back door.

"If you don't mind, I'm going to hit the sack. I want to wake up early and get to work on the house." She paused in her steps and looked up at the mansion's facade. "There's so much left to do."

Her dispirited tone twisted his heart. He wanted to tell her that all would be well. Except his gut and his head knew differently.

And he didn't want to lie to her anymore than he already had.

They'd nearly reached the back door when Rico held up his arm, blocking Frankie from moving forward. He shoved the bags he'd been carrying into her arms.

"Get back to the truck."

"What is it?" He could feel her trying to peer around him.

"The door is open. Someone could be inside. Now, get in the truck and lock all the doors."

"And what are you going to do? Play Superman? I don't think so. This is my house."

Rico snorted. "Do you ever listen to anyone?"

"In case you've forgotten, I'm the boss and this is my property. Besides, for all we know it could be Armando. He doesn't know I threw his father out. He's probably inside and simply forgot to close and lock the door."

Rico gritted his teeth. There was no arguing with this woman. She sounded too much like his sisters for comfort. "Fine," he hissed. "We go in together, but you stay behind me and you do exactly what I tell you. Got it?"

"Yeah. Sure." She tugged on his arm, preventing him from moving. "Um, just in case I'm wrong, remember even Superman wasn't invincible." She put the bags on the ground, and then hooked her finger around one of the belt loops of his jeans. The slight tug made him peel his eyes away from the darkened windows and look down upon her. In the twilight, he clearly saw her concern and fear.

"Don't be a hero," she whispered.

His gut clenched. Not too long ago he had tried to play hero and what good had come of it? He shook his head. "Don't worry, *querida*. I'm no hero."

Frankie stayed as close to Rico as she could, trying not to crowd him. This definitely wasn't her brightest idea. Kind of like when she'd told her boss off for reneging on his promise to promote her at the hotel and capped it off by quitting. Oh yeah, good move that one. With no job and rent due, inheriting Casa Verde amounted to winning the lottery.

More like the loser's jackpot.

Mentally she ticked off exactly what she'd gained by coming down to the island of Vieques to collect her inheritance. A loony aunt, a resentful uncle, and a village full of people who thought she was crazy. Then there was *el chupacabra*, the uninvited guest who'd long overstayed his welcome.

Maybe she was cursed.

Rico paused at the door and Frankie paused with him. He reached out and pushed the door inward. Frankie held her breath, not sure what she was expecting. She wanted to believe it was Armando, but lately, too many weird things had taken place at Casa Verde.

When nothing happened to them, her breath came out in a whoosh.

Rico motioned for her to wait, then jerked his thumb, indicating he would go in first. He crouched low and went in fast. Even in the darkness she could see how the muscles in his back rippled with each movement. He might be lean, but she wasn't fooled. The man had a rock-hard body and an attitude that said, "Go ahead, try messin' with me."

And she was obsessing way too much about him.

But then, he was the only one who hadn't let her down—so far.

Rico came back to the door. "All clear," he said in a low voice, "but you're not going to like it."

Any relief she'd felt was instantly replaced with a gut-wrenching twist to her stomach muscles. She entered quickly only to have her way blocked by Rico. "I'm not made of glass. No matter how bad it is I can take it," she whispered furiously.

He moved aside and she gasped.

The wanton destruction made her sick to her stomach. Food covered the counters and walls, smeared and scattered for maximum effect. Pots and pans littered the floor amid the cracked porcelain. The table she'd picked up cheap lay on its side one of its legs broken. Everywhere she looked she saw damage. Nothing appeared to have been spared.

She was barely aware of Rico moving forward. Her eyes shimmering with tears, she crossed to the windowsill where she'd placed her flowerpots.

Nada.

"Careful," Rico reminded her as glass crunched under her feet. "I want to check the rest of the house. You going to be okay here?"

"Yeah. Go ahead." She kept her voice even, unwilling to let him know how close to tears she truly was. He appraised her once before disappearing through the door into the dining room.

She should go with him. See what other damage had been inflicted on her home, but she couldn't seem to move. She hadn't had much, but it had been hers.

Who had done this?

Why?

Anger churned in her stomach at the latest violation. The will to move and to face the perpetrator flooded through her. Not bothering to be quiet, she pushed open the dining room door and walked through, bracing herself for more of the same.

The room appeared as she'd left it.

Her eyes searched carefully for signs of damage. Nothing, except...her head swiveled back to the old fashioned sideboard. Hadn't there been a small silver tray there, next to the ugly tureen that nobody could miss? She rubbed her forehead trying to remember.

But the sound of the door opening on the opposite side of the room brought her head sharply up. She snatched the dusty tarnished tureen off the sideboard and raised it for protection.

Rico slipped into the room and flipped on the light switch. His eyebrows rose at her choice of weapons, but he didn't question it. She focused on the grim set of his lips and felt her own pulse speed up in response.

"What is it?"

"It's probably better if I show you." He waited for her to put the tureen down and reach his side. "Stick close. I did a sweep of the rooms. Whoever did this is probably gone, but this place is massive. He could easily be hiding, waiting for us to get out of his way and give him a clear shot at escaping."

His words sent a shiver down her spine. Her thoughts jumped to *el chupacabra*. Could the horrible creature be behind this destruction? The thought of facing the monster, even with Rico beside her, had her longing for the safety of the truck.

Digging her fingernails into the palms of her hands to keep from giving in to her fears, she followed Rico into the front hallway and up the stairs, grateful that he'd turned on the lights. Her eyes darted back and forth the entire time, searching every shadowy corner for signs of their intruder. Would she ever feel safe in Casa Verde again?

Don't go there, Frankie, girl or you can kiss your plans for a B&B good bye.

Upstairs, under the feeble light of the single hallway bulb, Rico led the way directly to her room, where he stopped. The door stood open, giving Frankie a clear view of her clothes strewn all over. The overpowering scent of her perfume permeated the air. Slowly, she made herself cross the threshold to better view the chaos and destruction.

Her stomach knotted and her throat burned. With one

glance, she took in the slashed bed hangings, the dresser drawers that had been pulled out and their contents dumped on the floor, and her smashed jewelry box. The few inexpensive pieces she'd cherished lay in a twisted pile. Her eyes flew to the closet door, noting with relief that it stood shut, which hopefully meant the vandal hadn't had time to work his destruction there or steal her grandmother's wedding set.

She threw Rico a helpless look, uncertain what to do. Immediately, he came to her side, taking her in his arms.

She didn't have the heart to resist. Within his embrace, she felt safe, protected. She held on to him tight, feeling like driftwood on storm-tossed seas.

"You're not alone, *querida*." He whispered other words of assurance, but it was those three that cracked through the wall she'd spent so many years building and enforcing.

You're not alone.

She'd never known any other way, but at this moment, in Rico's arms, she wanted to believe. Wanted desperately to believe that she'd found a man she could depend on, someone who wouldn't abandon her when the going got rough. Someone she could trust.

She simply held on to him, letting him comfort her, wishing she had the courage to tell him what she felt inside.

And that's when they heard it. A small sound, little more than a creak. But in the silent house it might as well have been a gunshot.

Rico pushed Frankie away. "Stay here. Lock the door and don't come out until you hear me give you the okay." And with those words he was gone.

This time Frankie did as he asked. After snapping the lock in place, she sank down to the floor and prayed for the nightmare to end.

Rico didn't bother trying to be silent. He raced down the hall and stairs, aware that the front door now stood wide open.

Damn!

He tore out the door and onto the front porch, his eyes scanning the area in front of the house all the way to the trees.

Nothing. He didn't see how a perp could've made it to the forest in the amount of time it'd taken Rico to get to the front door.

El chupacabra slithered through his mind.

Yeah, right. He knew better than to fall for that garbage. *El chupa* was nothing more than legend being used by a real-life human monster.

Rico left the porch and walked to the edge of the house, constantly sweeping the area. He wished he had his gun, but he'd left it along with his badge locked up back on his boat. The faint sound of running footsteps reached his ears. He rounded the house to the back in time to see a lanky figure take off down the driveway.

The intruder had probably left the front door open to distract Rico, while taking off out the back.

Rico vented his frustration into the humid air before turning back to the house. Inside, he took the stairs two at a time, wanting to reach Frankie as soon as possible.

He rapped sharply on the door. "Frankie, *querida,* it's me. Open up. The guy got away." He heard the lock disengaging, then the door opened and Frankie flew into his arms.

"You idiot!" She wailed into his ear at the same time walloping him with her fist on his shoulder. She seemed to shudder against him and the urge to pick her up and run away from this entire mess tempted him more than he would've believed possible. Instead, he simply held her, letting her work out her emotions in her own way.

It didn't surprise him, though, when Frankie pushed away from him shortly after and thrust her chin out. She wasn't the type to give in to defeat or let others fight her battles.

"Don't ever do that again. You could've been killed. How would I explain that to your *mami*? How would I even be able to live with myself?" Her lip trembled and her big brown eyes swam with tears. She punched him once again for emphasis, eliciting a grunt. The woman might be skinny but she was no lightweight. "Stop playing Superman, *comprende?*"

Rico couldn't speak. His fingers reached up to capture one of her silky curls. It wrapped around his finger just like this woman seemed to wrap around his heart.

His heart skipped a beat.

The implications of what he'd thought hit him like a sledgehammer, cracking the shield he'd been living behind. He was beginning to care about this woman—more than was safe for her or him.

For an instant, he didn't see Frankie's face before him. He saw Carla's. The same bold approach to life. The same independent streak. The same tough-girl attitude.

With Carla, he'd told himself she was a means to an end. An informant. Nothing more. But her love for Lourdes had blindsided him. Made him see her as something more than another criminal trying to work the system. And then Cardenas had found her.

She'd been a rag doll shot full of holes by the time Rico had gotten to her.

Rico dropped the loose strand and put space between them, ignoring Frankie's questioning look. He couldn't do it again.

Couldn't lose someone because he let his guard down. Lost his focus. He'd protect Frankie even if it meant protecting her from himself.

"Do you want to report this to the cops? I'm not sure how much good it'll do, but for insurance purposes..." He let his words trail off and waited for her response.

She seemed puzzled by his sudden change of mood, but answered him easily enough. "It's not worth bothering the police or insurance company. Whoever did this sure knew enough not to damage the good stuff."

"You might say it even looks personal," Rico added. It hadn't escaped him that the only items touched had belonged to Frankie. The perpetrator had known exactly which room was hers. The whole thing stunk and it wouldn't surprise him a bit to find Hector's fingerprints all over.

"Let's just go downstairs and get the kitchen in order. That food will be real ripe in the morning if we don't get it out of the heat. Not to mention all the bugs that will see it as an invitation to a fiesta."

There it was again. That humor she managed to dredge up even when she hurt the most. He couldn't resist reaching up to lightly caress her cheek. He'd have liked to do more than that.

But kissing her, tasting those lips once more, would destroy any chance he had of keeping her at a distance. His hand dropped to his side instead. "You're the boss."

Frankie dumped another dustpan full of broken pottery into the trash bag. What a waste. Across the room, Rico continued to sweep.

"Where've you been?" Rico barked.

Frankie's head jerked in response. Armando stood in the kitchen doorway, warily eyeing both her and Rico, and looking ready to bolt at the slightest sign. He appeared dusty and weary and carried a worn backpack slung over his shoulder. His black eye and disheveled appearance reminded her of the homeless kids on the streets of New York City.

Rico propped the broom up against the wall and marched over to her cousin, clearly expecting an answer and only seeming to scare her young relative to death.

Exasperated, Frankie stomped over to Rico's side. "Simmer down, would you?" She faced her cousin and offered a smile. "Come on in, Armando. I'd offer you a drink or something to eat but as you can see, we're all out." With her arm she gestured at the destroyed kitchen.

Armando's eyes widened. He glanced quickly at Rico then edged around him. "What happened?"

"Don't you know?" Rico crossed his arms and pinned the boy with such a glare, Frankie wouldn't have been surprised if Armando had confessed just to get out from underneath Rico's scrutiny.

Armando shook his head, his eyes pleaded with her. "I don't know anything."

"You didn't know your father stole Frankie's jewelry and tried to pawn it in town?" Rico pressed.

Armando blanched and Frankie took pity on him. "Knock it off, Rico. Can't you see he doesn't know anything?"

"Maybe, but it's my guess that your Uncle Hector is behind this mess and the one in your room. He didn't like that you got Casa Verde and he didn't. Who's to say Armando here didn't help his father take the place apart?" Rico never moved, but he skewered Armando in place with his look.

"I don't know what you're talking about. Honestly. I didn't do anything." Armando turned to her, his face pinched. "You believe me, cousin Francesca, don't you?"

She really didn't want to believe that yet another relative was out to get her. Something inside her looked at the dusty lost boy and clicked. "Sure," Frankie couldn't help responding.

"You don't, do you?" Armando seemed hurt, close to tears and Frankie felt less than mold. She could recall being in foster care and wanting someone in authority to believe her, to choose her for once, but always knowing deep inside that nobody cared.

"I do believe you, Armando." This time she spoke with conviction. "I have to tell you that I told your father that he isn't welcome here. But that doesn't go for you. If you'd like to continue to stay here, that's fine by me. I could use some additional help in getting this place fixed up."

Rico stared at her, his disbelief obvious. "You're not serious, are you? His father ripped you off and probably caused all this damage and you're going to give the kid free rein to stay here? How do you know he isn't after the same thing his father is?"

"It's always like father, like son," Armando burst out. "They take one look at my father and then say that I'll never amount to anything. My grandmother said it all the time. Said she was disappointed to have me for a grandson. That's why she left the house to you even though she knew I loved this place." He hiccupped tears and turned his back.

"Armando..." Frankie reached a hand out, shocked by what her young cousin had revealed. She wanted to reach out to the boy on the threshold of manhood. But he simply pivoted and ran back out the door.

"Damn it, Rico. How could you?" Frankie whirled furiously on him.

"If you want me to apologize, forget it." Rico stated flatly, his eyes hard. "What he said only makes me suspect him more."

"Would you listen to yourself? You sound like a cop or something. He's just a kid."

"And you don't think he's capable of trashing this place? Come on Frankie. Even you can't be that naïve."

"I'm not." Anger burned in her gut, but she wouldn't let Rico think it ruled her thinking. "I spent most of my youth with the kind of kids who wouldn't think twice about trashing this place. I've seen kids steal, lie and beat the crap out of their best friend because they were told to. I knew girls who were pregnant at fourteen and others who were hooked on drugs. Add in a system that doesn't care. Fending for yourself is a bitch. And I'm one of the lucky few to get out and make it this far. So don't you dare call me naïve and don't you dare tell me I don't know what I'm talking about." She fisted her hands at her sides. Her voice snapped with fury and sadness. "When I look in that kid's eyes I see myself. I see the path ahead of him. He just needs someone to believe in him." Weariness settled into her bones. She ached inside. "You may not believe. But I do. Armando had nothing to do with this."

She grabbed the broom off the wall and shoved it back into his hands. "I'm going upstairs to clean. You can finish up down here. I'll see you in the morning." Maybe by then she wouldn't feel like breaking the broomstick handle over his head.

Rico silently cursed himself out in Spanish and English as he watched Frankie's march across the room and out the kitchen. Just what the hell kind of childhood had Frankie had? As an ICE agent, he was intimately acquainted with the seamier side of life. But he'd been an adult when he'd received his initiation into the underbelly of the world.

His childhood on Vieques had been filled with love and security. He'd never wanted or felt alone. And with six siblings and relatives all over the place, Rico had gotten away with nothing.

He'd hated it then. Now, though, he wouldn't trade that sense of family for anything.

Frankie's grandmother obviously had a warped sense of family. He didn't know why she'd left Frankie to fend for herself in the foster care system. Then again, from what he'd heard of the woman, he was beginning to think Frankie had been better off somewhere else.

Rico rubbed a hand over his face. Like it or not, Armando was about the only decent relative Frankie had left. He could understand her wanting to believe in the kid, even if he had his own reservations.

So what was he going to do?

"Rico."

He hoped she wasn't calling him to chew him out some more for suspecting the kid. He put aside the broom and walked out of the kitchen into the hallway. Frankie stood next to the stairs.

"Another step broke?"

Frankie shook her head, causing her wild mane to bounce around. "Look," she grabbed his arm and dragged him towards the darkened corridor under the main staircase. "You've got to see this."

One section of wall stood slightly ajar. It blended perfectly with the rest of the paneling. He fingered the hidden section of wall. The sectioning cracked open to reveal a small space under the stairwell.

"The broom got caught and the wall opened up. Come on," Frankie urged. "Let's look inside."

Rico pulled the door open. The space neatly tucked under the stairwell was little bigger than a closet. He would have thought it a storage closet, if not for the dusty comforter and the shackle on the floor.

Frankie squeezed in and examined the space. "What is this place?"

"Got any colorful pirates or smugglers in your past?" He joked while inside his inner alarm sounded.

Frankie wrinkled her nose. "I wouldn't know. You think that's what it was for? Contraband or something?"

Rico shrugged. "Who knows?"

Frankie bent down and picked up a scrap of linen, dirty and yellowed, that had been jammed in the corner.

"What've you got?"

"A handkerchief with flowers embroidered in the corner. It's filthy. Looks like it's been here a while."

"Come on out. I want to see how this door works." Frankie wiggled out backwards, her rear end temptingly up in the air. But his focus was elsewhere. Rico closed the door. As he'd thought, it was almost impossible to detect the seam that

133

indicated a door existed. He ran his hand along the paneling, searching for a depression or spring, some kind of mechanism that would open it. He pressed a knot in the wood. The door sprang open. He ran his hand along the inside. As far as he could tell, there was no inner device to unlock the door from inside.

Frankie pressed the knot a few times. "A perfect hiding spot. Perfect for a child to play hide and seek."

Or a perfect place to smuggle someone, Rico thought to himself. "Would be if there was a way to unlock it from the inside." He scowled. He closed the door shut.

"Well, that was fun." She stood up and dusted off her knees. "I'm going to go upstairs and tackle my room. What about you?"

At least she was talking to him. Given how they'd ended the conversation in the kitchen, he'd expected her to still be ticked off. "The kitchen is as good as it's going to get. I thought I'd go outside and check the grounds. Maybe see if I can locate Armando."

Her eyes darkened. "You're not going to accuse him of anything again, are you?"

"Relax, *querida*. If I see him, I'll simply tell him he still has a home here." 'Course he'd also let Armando know that messing with Frankie meant messing with him. He figured the kid would get the message.

Frankie's mouth widened into a smile that knocked his breath away. She threw her arms around his neck and hugged. "I knew you weren't a complete jerk." She kissed his cheek, let go of him, and headed for the stairs. He watched her, feeling bemused. This woman had him tied up in knots and he didn't have a clue what to do about it.

Frankie stretched her back, working out the kinks in her muscles. Rico had been gone quite a while. She wondered if he had found Armando.

Her eyes swept the room one last time, noting that it appeared virtually spotless. The scent of perfume, which had nearly knocked her out earlier, no longer blanketed the room since she'd opened the windows to air it out. She doubted, though, that she'd buy that particular brand again. Too many bad memories attached.

Leaving the light on, she left and headed back down to the first floor. She went out the front door and stood on the porch, letting her eyes adjust to the night.

She stared across the barren front lawn to the edge of the forest. Night insects chirped, leaves rustled and she'd never felt further from her New York City roots.

The wind ruffled her curls and caressed her skin. Casa Verde was now her home. She should have felt pride and happiness in the thought.

Instead, she felt troubled.

Did she truly deserve ownership? Didn't Armando have as strong a claim as she had?

Her head hurt thinking about it. Wearily she moved off the porch and walked around the silent house. "Rico," she called out. No answer. She rounded the corner to the back and paused to examine the area. No sign of Rico or Armando.

Where was everyone?

She hugged herself, rubbing her arms. Not that she was afraid or anything.

Bushes plastered against the side of the house rustled with movement. Frankie's mouth went dry. It was probably some night creature scavenging for food.

Even as she thought it, she edged towards the back door. Had Rico locked it? She didn't know.

The air burst with an explosion as something huge hurtled from the bushes.

El chupacabra!

Not wanting to chance the door being locked, she ran for the front of the house. She could hear the harsh breathing of the creature behind her. She'd only needed one glimpse of those gleaming eyes to know what chased after her.

With a burst of speed, she went for the porch, more afraid of what was behind her than the treacherous planks under her feet. Her hand closed around the doorknob. She pushed the door open and slammed it closed behind her. She threw the locks.

Where to hide?

She could hear the creature outside, its heavy footfalls clawed at the wood. Her body trembled. She went for the stairs and stopped. She would be trapped upstairs. Her eyes searched frantically for a hiding place.

The secret room! She ran for the enclosure below the stairs, glad she'd taken time to learn the secret to opening the door. Her fingers worked frantically to push the indentation in. The door sprang open and she ran inside, pulling the door closed and shutting herself in the dark.

For long seconds, she stood frozen, barely able to hear beyond her own breathing and the pounding of her heart.

A loud crash reached her ears. The creature had smashed through the front window. She stuffed a fist in her mouth to keep from crying out. She scooted back and pulled the blanket over her head. She sat, pulled up her knees and hugged them to her chest, burying her head to keep the fear at bay.

She heard the creature thump his way up the stairs and curled herself up even tighter. Would he know she sat in the dark underneath him? Smell her sweat and fear through the wood?

Time seemed to slow. Each second dragged out to an unbearable hour. Banging and crashing shattered the air. She could sense his rage pouring down upon her as he searched but couldn't find her.

She fought the hysteria that threatened to overwhelm her. She didn't know how to get out of this room and wasn't sure she'd even be able to get her feet to move for fear the creature would pounce on her.

She didn't want to die in this cubbyhole.

Her heart thumped against her ribcage. Her worst fear worked its way to the surface. For the first time she couldn't handle the situation alone. She'd take back all her digs, all her stupid pride. She'd even give him a piece of her heart. She needed him. She needed a hero. She needed Rico.

Chapter 10

The sounds of Puerto Rico echoed in the night as *coquí* frogs sang to their mates and crickets chirped. Rico shone the flashlight he had grabbed from the house down onto the sandy path. Two deep grooves ran parallel on the soft earth. He followed the cut trail, just as he imagined Armando had. The boy's sneaker prints lay fresh in the dirt. Rico could trace the course the boy took back and forth into the abandoned mangroves, but it seemed he wasn't the only one. More than a few other prints ran along the sandy road. But most curious of all was the tire marks he had noticed from the night before. By the depth of the tread marks and the amount of mud that had been churned up, mostly likely the vehicle had come during the most recent summer shower. The sun had since baked the earth dry, preserving the tracks.

An owl hooted above him and took off in search of prey. The moon, round and bright, hung in the starry sky like a lantern. The moonlight made little difference in the mangroves, but the old road had been cleared of trees many years ago and made for an easy trek through the groves, a far cry from those on the opposite side of the property. Rico could see how Casa Verde had once been a profitable plantation. Aside from the thick foliage growing wild on the orange trees and the rotted fruit that lay on the ground, the groves on this side were sectionalized. Straight rows of trees spaced evenly apart, separated down the middle three feet along the side and in the front and back by sandy ditches, the channels of irrigation neglected, choked with weeds and bone dry.

Signs of a better, more prosperous time long past still popped up occasionally on the path—a shovel propped up on a tree waiting to be retrieved, a basket woven from palm husks discarded in the road, a moth-eaten straw hat casually hung on a tree limb. The legacy of the de la Vargas, like the fruit, lay rotten and abandoned on the ground.

The trail began to thin and ended abruptly. A wall of trees and brush signaled the end of the plantation. Rico whisked the flashlight around. He searched for a way forward but found none. The tire tracks ended too. A blanket of darkness enveloped the mangroves beyond the plantation. His flashlight barely penetrated through the thick foliage.

If the boy had gone into the wild tropical forest he might be in trouble. Instinct told him Armando was savvier than that. He maneuvered silently around the trees and over roots, his senses attuned to the night.

The dense vegetation soon cleared, revealing another route. Unnoticeable from the main road, the path coursed around a large, ancient ceibo tree. Gnarled, twisted limbs hung low next to the earth, long elegant fingers reached for him. The majestic tree stood alone in a circle of sand. Silvery moonlight touched down onto red blossoms.

Bent at the hip, yet somehow brilliant and beautiful as the bold native Anahí, the tree stood proud in defiance of the black grove trees surrounding her. An oddity among the others, the tree's fat limbs dug deep into the soil, rooted and stubborn like the legendary tribeswoman who had been burned to death rather than capitulate to the invading Spaniards. All but the stars, which winked in the clearing above, remained still within her presence.

The faint hum of a truck engine broke the spell. He turned around, but not without a last glance at the tree before he headed back into the mangroves. The land became marshier and the trees closer together the further he went. Using his sense of hearing, he followed the noise. Shouts and whistles soon joined the din drowning out the sounds of the night creatures.

He cut the light and moved silently, careful to stick close to the trees to avoid being noticed. From over to his left, a cigarette flared to life. Rico froze. He scanned the area for the presence of others.

Taking a chance, Rico moved cautiously closer. His feet sank into the soft mud, the ground beneath him shifted. He went down into a crouch and moved like a jungle cat on all fours. He kept low and out of sight stealthily moving from tree to tree until he couldn't get any closer without alerting the guard. The man could be nothing else by the way he carried a semi-automatic weapon with ease that bespoke familiarity.

The scent of cigarette smoke wafted to Rico's nostrils. Another guard walked over and lit up.

Not the brightest pair of guards he'd ever met, but that didn't make them less dangerous. Somebody should have told them that smoking not only affects night vision, but that they might as well be wearing a large target on their forehead saying "aim here". Still, the darkness of the mangroves kept their identities well hidden.

Rico couldn't hear what they were saying. Getting any closer risked detection. But he wanted to know why they were traipsing around Frankie's property.

He crouched down beside the tree and strained to hear their conversation. Bit and pieces filtered through the night air.

"*La chica*... I don't know why he cares so much."

The other man sucked hard on his cigarette. He plucked the cancer stick from his mouth and threw it into the dead leaves on the ground. "Probably dead." The two men laughed.

"...get paid tomorrow." The other man threw his cigarette. "Better get back...don't lose more of the shipment otherwise..." he ran his finger across his neck. "Señor Cardenas won't be happy."

"*Idiota*! Don't say his name. We know nothing. *Comprende*?" The other guard nodded and held his gun closer, his hand dangerously close to the trigger. He turned and looked in Rico's direction. Rico plastered himself against the tree.

"*Vámanos!*" The taller guard shouted. Rico waited a beat before checking to see if the other man had followed. An engine revved in the distance. Rico crept from his spot and edged closer. He saw the red of the taillights fade away.

The raucous sounds of the mangroves resumed.

Rico stood still, his body frozen. His mind in turmoil.

Cardenas. A common name.

Could it be?

He rubbed his hands over his face. Weary from the direction his mind was going. "Damn," he cursed under his breath. He wondered when his thoughts, his life, his world, everything morphed to revolve around his job. Had the world gone insane or had he?

Somehow the world he dealt with at ICE had invaded his fabric of being to the point that nothing in the universe didn't go untouched by perverts, predators, drug lords, criminals and the sleaziest of society.

They'd mentioned *la chica,* the girl. Did that refer to Chita, another girl, or even Frankie? He hadn't missed the reference to "dead" either. His blood ran cold at the thought.

A shipment. Tomorrow. Time was running out. Rico mentally ran through a list of goods that would require heavy manpower. None of the goods he could think of were *good.*

Was there nothing in his life that remained pure, unharmed?

He made a mental note of the location the guards had been. He'd have to come back during daylight to see if they'd left any evidence behind. Any clues as to what they were transporting.

Then he'd have to decide whether to tell Frankie.

Oh, hell. Frankie!

How long had he been gone? Time in the mangroves didn't seem to exist. Rico turned around, got his bearings and headed straight for the path. After a few wrong turns, he found his way back down through the orchard.

Knowing the guards were loose in the forest, Rico took his care on the return trip, but didn't slow his pace.

Once he broke through the trees bordering the edge of the backyard, Rico jogged to the house, anxious to see Frankie. He entered through the kitchen, not having bothered to lock the door earlier. Why hadn't Frankie? The house was quiet. He glanced at the clock on the wall. Midnight.

She must have fallen asleep. It bothered him that she hadn't checked the locks, but the day had been a long one. Too long. He'd talk safety with her tomorrow. He washed his face and hands in the kitchen sink, removing the stink of the mangroves. Tired, he headed for the stairs. A quick shower and eight hours of shuteye would do him good. Hopefully by then the kid would come to his senses and return to the house if he hadn't already. For Frankie's sake, he hoped Armando did come back safe. As much as he suspected the kid of being bad news, he still felt sorry for him. Maybe Frankie was right and he should give the kid a break. Hell, with a father like Hector, any attention the kid got probably didn't amount to much.

Rico passed the front door, noting the locked door. Glass crunched beneath his shoes. His eyes shot to the window. He reached for his knife in his back pocket. He flicked it out.

His world narrowed down. The man in him wanted to call out for Frankie. The agent in him knew better.

Swiftly, silently he traversed the hall, switching on lights, peering into one room and then the next on the first floor. Frowning, his stomach muscles tightening, he began the climb to the second floor. Following the same routine, he checked all the rooms. Everything looked normal. All the chaos from earlier had been cleared up, nothing out of order.

He went down the back stairs trying to hold back the panic. Where the hell was Frankie? Had she been taken, snatched from under his nose?

Would he find her with her life's blood seeping away, unable to stop the flow, unable to save her? Would he be forced to relive those last few minutes with Carla all over again?

Dios, please no.

Rico closed his eyes to shut out the memories. He tightened his grip on the knife. If he got her back alive he was going to keep Frankie Montalvo glued to his side, if that's what it took to keep her safe. If she resisted, he'd fight back harder. This time he wouldn't fail.

"Ow!" Frankie shook her hand, then stuck her throbbing finger into her mouth. That was the third nail she'd broken in this hellhole.

She didn't know how long she'd sat frozen in fear, unable to do more than breathe and pray for deliverance.

But, as usual, the only person she could count on was herself.

Rico had gone off who knew where. She didn't want to think about *el chupacabra* getting him.

Finally, she'd built up enough nerve to come out from under the covers. Sealed completely in darkness, the tiny room seemed to press in all around her. She'd never been claustrophobic, but right now all she wanted to do was claw her way out.

She pressed her face against the door. At least she wouldn't suffocate. While exploring the space with her hands, she'd found a small vent. Not that suffocating was her biggest worry either. Hot and thirsty, she knew there were other ways to die, but at the moment it sure seemed like a pretty crappy way to go.

Again her fingers traced the seam and all around, searching for a release mechanism. Surely, whoever had designed this room had installed a means to exit.

Frustrated, she banged with both hands against the paneling, a sob escaping from her throat.

"Frankie?"

Though muffled through the wall, she still heard her name clearly and she knew that beloved voice.

"Rico! I'm in here." She pounded the door with her fists. "Get me out!"

The door abruptly opened and she fell out, nearly colliding with the floor. A muscular arm caught her instead, dragging her against a hard chest.

"Damn, *querida*, you really scared me this time."

Frankie savored the sense of warmth and security—like a pet lost in the city who finally makes it home. Laying her head against his shoulder, she let her body relax and absorb his strength.

His hand smoothed down her hair and traveled the length of her back, sure strokes that eased the tension from her body.

"Hector came back." His voice a low growl, "Did he touch you?"

Her body jerked at the question, "No."

"Good because I would have to kill the bastard." Rico pulled her further into his embrace as Frankie continued, her words rushing out of her in one breath. "Not Hector. *El chupacabra.*"

"*El chupa* is a legend." Rico gently her unruly curls. He kept her close. She didn't mind. The thud of his heart, solid and reassuring, soothed her anxieties.

"A week ago, I would have said the same thing, but I saw him." Her voice sounded small like a child afraid to admit that she was scared.

Rico stopped stroking her hair.

"Get your stuff."

"What?" Frankie pulled back enough to see the cold rage in his eyes.

A shiver ran up her spine.

"Get your stuff. We're leaving."

Frankie unfolded herself from his embrace and stood up. "I am not leaving my house." Rational or not, she wouldn't run. Casa Verde was her home. If she ran now, she would continue to run just as she had run from one foster home to another. She put down her foot. "No."

"No?" Rico unfurled from the floor, each muscle moving and rolling as he pulled his full six-foot frame up. He stood looking down on her.

She backed up a step. "You're right. *El chupa* isn't real."

Rico grabbed her by the shoulders and turned her around. "No, *el chupa* isn't real, but someone real enough smashed your window in."

Frankie gulped hard. Glass glittered, strewn all over the hardwood floor like droplets of water. The beautiful urn she had worked so hard to polish also lay on the floor, cracked in half.

Rico jerked her back around. His head inches from hers, he met her eye to eye. "You may think you are tough enough to handle this on your own but you're not." He bit out the words. "I want to protect you, Frankie. But how can I when you insist on facing the monsters head on?"

"You can't let the monsters win." Frankie raised her voice. "All my life I've been running away from one problem just to come up against another one. Damn it, Rico, I am tired of running."

Rico pulled her into his embrace and rested his cheek on top of her head. "I know, *querida*. I'm tired, too."

She heard the sorrow in his voice, the weariness and the strain.

For a moment they stayed that way—him leaning on her and her leaning on him. He didn't seem like Rico the laidback contractor anymore.

No, this man in front of her was tough. Dangerous. A stranger.

Her heart flipped over, recognizing the truth of her feelings.

It didn't matter who he was, because she was falling in love with him.

She didn't want to and it wasn't in her plans, and what if he left her like everyone else did? She didn't think she could handle that. She stared up at him, drinking in his features—memorizing them—because deep down she knew there was no future for them. She wanted, needed roots, while he wandered the seas on a boat.

She tucked her feelings away, to be examined later. For now, she would enjoy his protection, his care, and his touch.

Rico's thumbs caressed her cheeks, then his head dipped down to brush a light kiss upon her lips. It sent tingles down to her toes.

He held her gaze with his own.

"Pack a bag. I want to be gone in five."

"What about Armando? What if he comes back and we're not here? He might get worried."

"Armando's resourceful. Somehow I don't picture him sticking around."

Frankie dug in, resisting Rico's efforts. "Wait. Where are we going? Maybe we should leave a note."

He shook his head. "Not a good idea. Whoever is trying to hurt you might get hold of it."

Frankie bit her lip. Conflicted, she wanted to stay, but realized Rico was right. Whoever was out in her yard tonight hadn't just wanted to scare her. The fight in her drained out with the last of her adrenaline. Her body felt weak. She slumped down on the stair landing.

"So, where are we going?"

"My boat."

His boat. She gulped. "Um, that thing didn't look so big. How many rooms does it have?"

"Cabin," he corrected, his mouth quirking in a smile. "One cabin. One bed."

∞

"Are you sure it'll hold the both of us?" Frankie eyed the boat warily.

"Sure." Rico put his foot up on the side of the small yacht, grabbed hold of the rope railing and pulled himself aboard the sailing vessel. The boat rocked back and forth in the water. He held out his hand and Frankie passed the small bag with her to him. "She's a little old but in great condition."

"What's her name?" Frankie asked, trying to shake the butterflies fluttering in her stomach. The idea of sleeping cradled in the sea with nothing but pieces of wood nailed together freaked her out.

"Sea Hag."

"Great." Frankie didn't know whether to laugh or run back to the truck and sleep there for the night. Casa Verde looked a whole lot safer and in better condition than Rico's floating shack.

"Never been on a boat before, huh?"

"Um, let's see. I have this issue with water." Frankie shook her head. "What do you think?"

He straddled the rope and held out his hand. She stretched out her arm and put her hand in his. She looked down at the darkened waters between the boat and the dock. The floating dock bobbed up and down. If she slipped, she would fall into the crack and be crushed, or worse, drown.

He tugged gently on her hand. "No need to be afraid," he softly reassured her.

Frankie mustered up the courage to put her foot up onto

the fiberglass siding and hoisted herself over the side of the yacht.

Waves rolled under the boat from a small watercraft vessel motoring into the marina. The side of the boat rubbed against the rubber on the wharf's pilings. Rico grabbed her around the waist and pulled her squarely onto the yacht.

"Don't worry, I've got you." He held her close. Her fingers clung to the thick cotton of his T-shirt. Back and forth the boat listed until the last of the waves subsided.

Rico released her, taking her hand in his. He picked up her bag and they moved along the side to the back of the boat. *"Cuidado,"* he cautioned, warning her to step over ropes, rigs and other things associated with sailing.

Light from the marina flooded the docks, making it easy for them to walk around in the night, but Rico didn't stop to show her his home. He simply went straight down a hole in the boat like the rabbit in *Alice in Wonderland.* She bent down to look in.

"Come on down. Watch your head."

Frankie went down the narrow steps, mindful not to knock her head on the opening. When she touched down, she was greatly surprised to see she could stand underneath with no problem. From the outside, the boat looked small, but really was moderately spacious below.

"So, you going to show me around the place?"

He clicked on the electricity. Bare bulbs flared to life.

Rico flashed her a smile with a little pride thrown in. *"Mi casa es su casa."*

And it was like a miniature house, or more like a studio apartment. Plain, simple, narrow and long. The layout of the design made the boat functional.

"Down here is the cabin." He walked over to one side outfitted with a tiny sink and electric double burner cooking range. "Note the clever use of ergonomics for the galley." He winked at her. "Fancy word for kitchen." Rico put a cup under the tap and turned the faucet on. "Fresh water." He turned around and handed her the cup. "Take a seat." He swept some maps off a square table bolted to the wall, large enough to accommodate two. "Eating and navigation area." Radio, sonar and other electronic equipment she couldn't identify littered the shelf above the table. He opened up one of the bench seats and put the maps inside. "There is limited space for large stores of water and food. So, I use whatever space I have available."

Frankie sipped the water before putting it down on the table. "Any chance you have something stronger in one of those cupboards?" she asked wryly. Her nerves were still jumping from the narrow escape she'd had.

Rico assessed her for a moment, then reached overhead to open a compartment and pulled out a bottle of Scotch. "Will this do?"

"Yeah, thanks." She held out her now empty cup and allowed him to splash in a small amount. He grabbed another cup and poured some for himself. She took a sip, feeling the burn work its way down her throat.

"You want anything to eat?"

Frankie shook her head. It was well past midnight and her stomach heaved at the thought. She'd lost her appetite about the same time *el chupa* had put her on his menu.

Rico shrugged apologetically. "I'm starved. Must be all that adrenaline. I'm going to make a quick sandwich. Sure I can't interest you in one?"

"No, thanks. I still haven't digested our dinner from earlier."

"Why don't you go stow your bag in the saloon," he pointed to the narrow point at the front of the boat, "while I make some chow."

She pulled aside a thin tarp curtain. A wooden sign dangled above the triangular alcove with engraved gold letters that clearly stated Captain's Quarters.

"Guess this is the one bed." Frankie plunked the bag down on the twin-size mattress neatly squeezed into the hull of the ship. Two portholes and a little cabin light decorated the wall, along with snapshots of exotic animals.

She fingered one. "You take these?" she called back over her shoulder.

"A hobby of mine."

"They're beautiful." Each picture appeared perfectly focused. The details were so sharp and clear that she was in awe of his skill. Frankie wondered how long he would've had to wait around to capture the perfect close-up shot of a parrot's face. How steady his hand would have had to be to pick up the fine details of the snake's skin. The precision and timing to snap a *coquí* frog leaping mid-air.

"Come on. Grab your drink and we'll head topside." Through the open curtain, she saw him hold up a plate with a fat ham and cheese sandwich. "Sure you don't want a bite?"

"No," Frankie said with a small smile. She appreciated his trying to put her at ease. And she wished she were simply here on a date. Two people getting to know each other. It sounded so normal, so far from the nightmare she'd been plunged into. She retrieved her cup and headed for the stairs. Maybe the night would bring answers and peace. Maybe.

They sat together in silence. He'd greedily wolfed down the sandwich, proud that he'd managed to coax Frankie into at least one bite. Frankie sat with her knees up to her chest admiring the night sky. Stars twinkled in the cloudless heavens. A sea breeze blew softly, ruffling her hair. He watched as she reached up to tuck several strands behind her ear. Rico leaned back on his elbows and stretched out his legs and let the serenity of the night soak in, erasing the tension of the day.

"It's absolutely beautiful," Frankie murmured beside him. "I can't believe how bright the stars are, how fresh the air smells."

"It's even better on the sea. Out there, no crowds, no noise, no polluted air. Just you and the sea."

"Doesn't it get lonely?"

Rico turned his head. Frankie gazed at him, her eyes tinged with sadness. Why? For him? Or was it simply a remnant of all that had happened today? He didn't like thinking she felt sorry for him. He faced back to the dark ocean. "I suppose some people might find it lonely. I don't. It keeps me grounded. Reminds me that there's still beauty in the world, unspoiled by man's greed and evil."

Frankie stirred beside him, making him wonder if he'd said too much. "It sounds simple, doesn't it?" she spoke softly. "Hide yourself away from everyone and everything. Then you don't have to deal with all the messy stuff. Emotions. Relationships. Demands from others. But then, you're left with nothing. An empty space in your heart." She turned her head towards him, laying it on her knees. "And the hole keeps getting bigger until all you're doing is going through the motions of living." She gave a short laugh. "Sorry, I don't know what made me get philosophical all of a sudden. Forget about it."

He didn't think he'd be able to. Her words had an uncomfortable ring of truth in them. Not wanting to think about it further, Rico straightened. "It's really late. How about we turn in?"

Her eyes widened in the moonlight. Nerves stared back at him, though she rose promptly enough and made her way back to the entrance that led to the deck below.

"Watch your step," he warned as she carefully made the descent.

"Umm..." Frankie held back. He could see her trepidation.

"Chill, *querida*." He moved to the side of the boat and unclipped a latch on the wall. A bed big enough for one opened up. "I'll take the spare bunk."

He wanted to reach out and touch her. Hold her. But he knew it'd be a mistake. Already she was getting under his skin. If he touched one spot of her silky smooth skin, he'd be a goner. Because Frankie Montalvo could make him forget.

And he couldn't afford to forget.

Didn't deserve to. He'd failed Carla and Lourdes. He'd have to live with that mistake for the rest of his life. His fingers curled at his sides and he forced himself to ignore the heat in his loins and the fire in his blood.

"Good night." Rico lay down on the spare bed, his arms folded under his head, and listened to the waves lap against the boat. The night settled down but his mind refused to rest, continuing to play back the scene in the mangroves and his fear when he'd found Frankie missing.

Like it or not, the woman had crawled into his heart, filling up one of those holes Frankie had talked about. He hadn't looked for it, and sure as hell didn't want it. So what was he going to do about it?

He'd punched his pillow for the umpteenth time, when the curtain drew back. Frankie stood at the foot of the bed, her nightshirt barely covering enough of her legs. He swallowed hard.

Rico slid upwards, the sheet he'd used for a covering slid down to his waist. Her eyes focused on his naked chest.

"What do you need, *querida?*"

"I can't sleep. Every time I close my eyes, I see that...that thing. That monster chasing after me."

Rico threw the sheet off and stood only in his boxers. "You want a drink?"

She shook her head, her eyes mutely pleading with him.

He took a step closer, pitching his voice low. "What do you want, *querida?*

"Hold me," she whispered. "Just until I fall asleep." She held her hand out.

Rico shook his head. "I don't think I can," he admitted hoarsely. "If I get in that bed with you, I'm going to spend the night making love to you so you won't have room to think about anything other than my mouth on yours, my hands touching all your secret places and me inside you, taking us both to heaven." His hands fisted at his sides. "I want you too much, damn it."

Frankie licked her lips. Rico followed the movement hungrily. Her eyes closed briefly and he saw her drag in a breath. The moment in time seemed to hang between them.

"Promise?"

"What?" Expecting her to turn him down, he was confused.

She took a step forward, her light shirt clinging to her curves. God, how he wanted to strip it off her.

"Promise me you'll take us to heaven."

His head snapped up, understanding her surrender. He reached out and tugged her into his arms, locking her in his embrace. Bending his head, his lips only a few inches from hers, he looked into her eyes and saw his own desire reflected back.

He closed the distance. When his lips touched hers, white hot lightning exploded through him, rocketing him skyward.

Who knew heaven resided here on earth?

Chapter 11

Rico's mouth devoured hers, making coherent thought impossible. Vaguely, she sensed his hands skimming up the back of her thighs, snagging her oversized T-shirt and dragging it up. The cooler air hit her sensitized skin, eliciting a delicious shiver that traveled down the length of her spine.

His hands continued to lift the shirt while his tongue plundered her mouth, and all she could do was hold on. His mouth left hers briefly to pull the shirt up and off, leaving her standing there in bikini panties and nothing else.

Frankie didn't consider herself shy, but her lovers had been few and far between. Sex had been fulfilling and fun, a giving and taking of pleasure. It hadn't mattered.

She'd never allowed it to.

But this time was different. She'd fallen for this sexy-as-sin beach bum. For the first time in her life, she felt unsure. The armor she normally wore had been stripped away like the cotton T-shirt on the floor.

"You are so beautiful. I've dreamed of you this way."

Heat rose, flooding her cheeks at his words. "I'm *flaca*," she denied. "Too skinny."

His hands splayed against her back, pulling her in close. His head dipped until she could feel his breath on the rim of her ear. "You're absolutely perfect, *querida*."

His tongue rimmed her lobe. He sucked gently, while his fingers caressed her skin in light strokes up and down her back.

She could feel herself melting and he'd barely touched her. Frankie let her eyes drift shut. Her head fell back to give him better access as his mouth left her ear to place a trail of hot wet kisses along her jaw and down her throat.

His hands traced the curve of her waist. His fingers danced up over her ribcage until his thumbs rested below her breasts.

"So sweet," he murmured just before taking her nipple into his mouth, suckling and tugging, creating a pull that arrowed down to her core.

Her knees buckled. "Rico," she whimpered. His heat and male scent surrounded her. She wanted this. She wanted him. Her hands pulled at him.

He chuckled even as his other hand tweaked her other nipple, driving her crazy with need. "Impatient, aren't we?" But he didn't tease her any further. His lifted her bottom, telling her to wrap her legs around him, and moved them the few steps that took them back to her bed.

She could feel his erection pressed against her. She arched up, pushing against him, felt him harden further and smiled when he shuddered.

"Wait, *querida*." She heard him fumbling with a drawer at the side of the bed, but she was too busy biting, licking and kissing his throat. At the same time her hands feverishly explored his back and every inch of skin she could reach.

"You're overdressed, Lopez," she whispered in his ear.

"Not anymore." His boxers flew off and then he was peeling her panties down her legs. He rolled on a condom. She stared at him looming over her. Wide shoulders, a trim waist, and those wicked brown eyes. The man was one lethal package.

Frankie lifted her arms.

He moved over her, nudging her legs apart. Bracing himself on his elbows, he looked down at her. "Tonight, *querida,* is for us. No memories, no regrets, no demands."

She barely heard his words, so caught up in the fire consuming her.

"Now, Rico. Please." She'd never needed like this before, barely recognized the stranger begging for release. Her body craved his touch and when he entered her she rocketed skywards—all the way to heaven, just like he'd promised.

Wet. Hot. She surrounded him. Squeezed him. In and out he buried himself in her heat.

Her breasts pressed up against his chest muscles. He didn't know how she could think she was less than perfect. He had only to look at her to get hard.

Those wild curls, amber eyes, and tough-as-nails attitude, all contained in an irresistible body. He'd been toast from the get-go.

And he was going up in flames.

Since stepping back on Vieques, his heart had been enclosed in a block of ice. Now, he could feel it start to thaw. He hadn't wanted to care, but she wasn't a woman you could easily ignore or dismiss.

Frankie had worked her way under his skin to the point she had him going crazy.

And now he had her in his bed. He sure as hell didn't deserve her, but he wasn't strong enough to let her go.

He wanted this night to last. His body had other ideas.

"Look at me, *querida*." His muscles rigid, the blood pounding through his body, he forced himself to stay in control. Her gaze, flooded with passion, finally held his. "I promised you a trip to the heavens. I want you with me the whole way." Slowly he withdrew. His mouth came down hard on hers as he plunged back inside her.

Her hands clawed at his back, her body shaking. She milked him over and over until his muscles quivered in exhaustion. Rolling to the side, still connected, he slid a hand along the curve of her torso, waiting, watching.

A cat-like smile crossed Frankie's mouth. Her eyes opened. "Rico?"

"*Sí, querida?*"

Laughter lurked in her eyes. Her fingers trailed a blaze of need along his shoulder that had him sucking in a breath. "Heaven is a big place. I really don't think one visit is enough." She leaned over him to kiss the path her fingers had created.

"You don't, huh?"

"Definitely not." Her hand gently stroked down his chest,

flicking his nipple. "I think it's going to take more than one trip. Several, in fact."

He could feel himself hardening inside her all over. Rolling onto his back, he took her with him. He reached up, wrapping one of her long tendrils around his finger and tugged, bringing her head down until her lips hovered above his own. "You're the boss, *querida*. Lead the way."

Frankie rubbed her eyes and stretched, even as her body cried out for more rest. The gentle rolling of the waves beneath the boat nearly lulled her back into sleep, but she resisted the temptation to languish longer in bed. She reached out to stroke the lazy jungle cat who had rocked the boat with her last night, but Rico was gone. The smell of fresh-brewed coffee filled the cabin. Figured the man would be an early riser.

She stood up on shaky legs and adjusted to the sway of the boat. Sunlight spilled down through the open hatch door. The deep rumble of Rico's laugh floated into the cabin from the deck above. It washed over her, seeping into her pores, reminding her of the pleasure she'd received in his arms. Her lips turned up in a smile.

She dressed quickly, the smell of coffee luring her out of the room. The bed he'd pulled out blocked the path to the tiny galley. She could climb over it, but it would be easier to put it away. Besides, as much as she wanted to go up on deck and greet Rico, she dreaded it. What if last night had been nothing special for him, a one-night stand?

She pulled up the bottom section of the bed and folded it inward, still thinking about the man upstairs. She'd fallen for him hard—harder than she'd fallen for anyone ever in her life.

She shoved the rest of the bed back into place when she heard the sound of keys dropping. She searched the floor and easily spied the keys for her dilapidated truck. Next to them lay Rico's wallet. A few items had fallen out of his billfold. She picked up her keys, automatically pocketing them. She grabbed the remaining items and began stuffing them back into the well-worn black leather. A couple of business cards slipped easily inside.

The last, though, was a picture. She should put it back, but she couldn't help staring at it. Just like the pictures tacked to the wall of the cabin, the crinkled around the edges photograph was a perfect close-up, taken with the same steady hand and focus. Colorful and bright, a young woman and child hugged together tight, their smiles wide for the camera, their eyes filled with joy. Simple, yet tender.

A loving picture.

Frankie felt her heart squeeze.

Who were they?

Her teeth worried her bottom lip as she returned the wallet to the table, the picture laying face up beside it. She snagged the cup on the counter Rico had thoughtfully left out for her and poured herself a coffee, her eyes straying back to the photo. Could it be a sister and his niece? But why only the one picture when he claimed he had a huge family? Another thought slid in, one she shied away from.

Frankie finished up the last of the bitter-tasting coffee, knowing she couldn't hide below any longer. On impulse, she snatched up the photo, tucking it away in her pocket. The only way to know for sure was to ask. She might not like the answer, but better to face the truth than to hide in the sand. She climbed up the ladder determined to put a good face on, even as tiny cracks formed in her heart.

Another beautiful day in paradise greeted her topside. The sun shone brilliantly, seagulls circled and called out to one another in the blue sky. It was Saturday morning and the marina bustled with energy. A family packed up gear and food on the boat next to them. A little girl smiled and waved. Frankie waved back. It seemed the day couldn't be any sunnier, except for the black cloud of insecurity that hung over her head. At the front of the boat, Rico sat in a canvas sling chair. He had his back to her and she could hear him talking to someone on the phone.

Her interest piqued. She didn't know boats were equipped with telephones. She walked up silently behind him.

He had a cup of coffee in one hand, his other occupied with the keys on his laptop. He put down the mug to switch the Blackberry from one ear to another. "No. I'm telling you there is a road that leads in and out of the mangroves." Rico grunted. "How am I supposed to know if you can zoom in or not? You're the techie."

She squinted against the glare on the screen, trying to make it out. The picture looked like an aerial shot of someone's property. Her property!

Frankie felt hot under the collar and it wasn't from the sun bouncing off the bay. She wanted answers and she wanted them now.

"*Buenos días.*"

Rico hit a key and the screen went blank. "Jared, I've got to go." He cut the connection.

Rico leaned back and flashed her a smile. "Morning, *querida.*"

His charm had no effect on her. Kind of hard to feel anything when you felt numb.

"I have to say, I never knew the life of a freelance contractor was so lucrative." She walked around him and ran her finger over the shiny chrome laptop.

"Helps with navigation," he stated matter-of-factly.

Frankie crossed her arms over her breasts. "Oh, really. You sail over sea and land?" She eyed the cell phone in his hand. "I see executives in the city walking around hooked up on these things. Can't get enough, so addicted to their crackberry. Want to tell me why you need one?"

Her stomach in knots, she kept her gaze on his, refusing to back down. His face hardened. A shutter came down. He would lie to her. She didn't know how she knew it, but she did and the cracks in her heart widened further.

"Who are you?" Before he could stop her, Frankie snatched the Blackberry out of his hand. With her thumb she scrolled through the names on his address book. Row after row, names flew by. "You have a lot of friends for a drifter.

Rico stood up and took the cell phone back without a word.

"So tell me. Are you a drug dealer?" She thumped him on his bare chest. His skin was hot compared to the icy, coldness in his eyes.

"Huh? Well are you?" Her voice, tight and high, attracted a few stares from the family next door.

Rico's nostrils flared. "No." He spoke so low it sounded like a growl.

"Then tell me why you have such nice stuff?"

He avoided her questions, instead opting to pack away his laptop and phone in a protective bag.

"Actually I couldn't care less about your toys."

She pulled out the picture and dangled it under his nose. "Care to tell me who they are? I didn't snoop if that's what you're thinking. It was on the floor next to your wallet." She held herself stiffly, bracing herself for who knew what. A bunch of lies probably. "So who are they?"

He took the picture from her hand and stuffed it into his back pocket. "No one." A cloud passed overhead, blotting out the sun for a second and casting his face in shadows.

"No one?" She laughed harshly. "Right." She backed away from him. Emotions tumbled inside her like clothes caught in the spin cycle. "Just tell me this isn't the family Jorge was talking about. Please, tell me you're not married." Coffee burned inside her gut at the thought.

"No! I'm not married." He shook his head. "Frankie you have to believe me, I would never..." He reached for her.

Frankie stepped back. "I don't know what to believe." She left him alone and went down to the cabin to get her luggage. A few minutes later she returned topside. Rico stood at the helm of the boat. He gripped the steering wheel. He stared out at the open sea at the mouth of the bay unaware of her presence.

Frankie's heart clenched inside her chest. No doubt Rico wanted to be rid of her. Free to go and sail off into the ocean blue. What else could she expect from a man without any roots?

Her anger propelled her forward. She threw her bag over the side. It fell down on the floating dock with a thump. Rico's head snapped up, he called out to her to wait, but she didn't stop. Unlike last night, she didn't hesitate. She grabbed hold of the rope and went over the other side and jumped onto the floating dock. The water surrounding her only made her want to leave Rico and his stupid boat behind.

Rico stared at her from on top the yacht. "Frankie, it's not what you think."

"No? Then what?" She wanted him to explain himself. Reassure her that she was wrong. Instead, he stood mute.

She grabbed her stuff, waved her hand in the air without

looking back and headed for her truck parked in the lot. Each step took her closer to home and one step farther away from him.

How could she have been so stupid? How many times had she seen girls fall for a pretty face and a few lines, only to find out later the guy was walking trouble? She'd always believed she was smarter than that. Had always taken time to get to know a guy real well before she let him anywhere near her bed. At the very least she'd had the brains to keep her heart locked up tight. No chance of getting hurt that way.

Until now. Until Rico.

Until she'd fallen for a smooth-talking guy with more charm than should be legal.

Estúpida! Imbécil! Idiota!

The floating dock beneath her feet trembled. She knew Rico was coming, but she didn't slow down.

"Hey, not so fast." He grabbed hold of her shoulder.

She shrugged off his hand. "Leave me alone."

Rico edged around her and blocked her path.

"Move it or lose it." Standing tall, she jutted out her chin and drew back her bony shoulders.

"Okay. If that's what you want." He moved to the side. Frankie stormed up the gangway. Rico walked behind her, following her to the truck.

"Get lost," she hissed, aware of the stares from another couple in the parking lot.

Rico's face went hard. "We need to talk."

"So you can lie to me some more? No thanks." She balled her hands into fists at her side, her carryall banging against her leg. "I don't need your help anymore. I can take care of myself."

"*Querida,*" he ran a finger over her collarbone, "I thought I took care of you pretty good last night."

She smacked his hand away. "I'm not your *querida.*" She opened the truck door and threw her bag in before hoisting herself up into the seat.

"Hey! Where do you think you're going?"

"Home." She yanked the door shut, locking it, and pulled

the keys out of her pocket.

Rico knocked on the cab window. The air was stifling and she should roll it down, but she didn't want to give him access. She ignored him and his muffled pleas to open up.

Frankie threw the truck in gear and backed out of the space. Rico planted his hands on his hips and glared at her. Fine. Who cared? The man deserved to eat her dust.

She didn't need him. She didn't need anyone.

Rico swore, pivoted on his heel and ran back to the boat. He needed to lock up and find wheels. He couldn't believe how badly he'd blown it with Frankie.

He'd taken a chance calling Jared earlier. He'd known better, but it hadn't stopped him from dialing the number. Time was running out and he needed info fast.

He'd meant to keep one ear out for Frankie. He'd gotten so caught up in those damn aerial shots that he'd missed hearing her come up the ladder. She'd taken one look at his laptop and cell phone and two and two made five.

She'd thought he was a drug dealer! The idea of being compared to something as low as the scum he took down sickened him. The image of Cardenas popped into his mind. The man was ruthless, heartless, a liar and a murderer. He paused for a moment.

Frankie wasn't far off from the truth.

It wasn't like he'd been honest with her from the start. She thought him a freelance contractor. What else was the woman supposed to think? Rico nearly groaned at his own arrogance and stupidity.

He found his wallet on the table. Pulling the photo Frankie had questioned him about out of his pocket, he started to put it back in his wallet only to pause and stare at the two faces. Lourdes was only three, a sweet little girl who'd been a ray of sunshine in the ugly world he'd lived in.

He'd promised to protect Carla and failed. Her death lay at his feet. His conscience could never be absolved.

And Lourdes? God, Lourdes. He couldn't bear to think of her.

He had to make things right with Frankie. Some way. Some how.

He'd do anything to keep her safe. Except tell the truth.

Frankie drove the vehicle up the driveway, barely aware of the mansion rising before her. Physically and mentally drained, she couldn't seem to focus on what she needed to do. She parked the truck and simply sat in the cab until the sweat trickling down her face induced her to leave.

Her muscles protested as she climbed out of the truck. She ached all over, an unwelcome reminder of the night before.

Slamming the door closed, she trudged up to the house, her bag in hand. Curious to see if Armando might have come by, she peered into the shadows of the sagging porch. She sighed. No Armando. She had hoped to see him sleeping on the rocking chair, instead there was a large bundle of red roses with an envelope attached.

"Who would...?" Aside from Rico she had no idea who would send the flowers. She turned the letter over. No name. *Nada.*

Maybe it was from Hector apologizing for his bad behavior. Though she highly doubted it. She didn't see the man spending money on anything except his precious booze.

Frankie dropped her night bag onto the porch. Using her fingernail, she slit open the envelope to pull out a square card. Turning it over, she saw it was a formal invitation from Salvador Torres for tonight's party. She'd completely forgotten about the event.

Chewing on her lower lip, she considered it. She really wasn't in the mood for company. But did she really want to be by herself tonight? A party would take her mind off Rico and maybe give her a chance to meet some of her neighbors.

The sound of footsteps on gravel caused her to whirl around, her heart leaping into her throat. Relief coursed through her at the sight of Armando, with his faded backpack slung over his shoulder, shuffling towards her.

"Armando, are you okay? I was worried."

The young man stopped in his tracks and nodded, his black and blue eyes lowered to his feet. He toed the ground before finally looking her in the face. "I'm sorry about running out. I'm sorry about what my father did to you."

Frankie saw the shame cross Armando's face and cursed Hector under her breath. "You aren't responsible for your father's actions. And I don't judge you based on them either."

"I don't want to go back with him," he burst out. "I don't know much about fixing a house, but I can learn." The look in his eyes pleaded with her, nearly breaking her heart. "I thought, in exchange for room and board, I could maybe help or something..." His gaze dropped away, his shoulders hunching as if preparing himself for rejection.

Frankie went down the steps, closing the distance between them. "You are welcome to stay as long as you want, Armando. We're family." For the first time since meeting her various relatives, she felt comfortable with the relationship. "I'd be happy to have your help and later we can talk some more about what you might like to do with yourself in the future." His head came up and she was relieved to see the worry ease from his face. "Let's go inside and get you something to eat. You must be starved."

Together they climbed the steps to the porch, Frankie's emotions no longer weighing as heavily.

"Nice flowers. Who sent them?"

"Salvador Torres."

Armando frowned as he glanced from her to the flowers.

"What? *Qué?*" she asked in irritation.

"Well, he's got something of a reputation. What's Rico going to think?"

"What Rico thinks doesn't matter to me," she said in a very sweet voice. "He won't be back." She ignored the twinge in her heart. She'd made her feelings to Rico clear. And if he had the nerve to show up, she'd send him packing. "Come on, Armando. It's just you and me, kid."

Frankie wielded the hammer with ease. She imagined Rico's head on the top of each nail and pounded. She'd let him play her for a sucker and she deserved what she got. *Wham!* If she hadn't been overwhelmed by this place and all the crazy stuff that'd been happening, she'd never have looked at him

161

twice. *Wham! Wham!*

Okay, she definitely would've looked. The man was total drool material. Only a dead woman wouldn't have looked. *Wham! Wham! Wham!*

The sound of a throat clearing reached her. "Um, Frankie, you mind if I take a break? I thought I'd grab a bite of lunch and head outside, if that's okay with you."

Frankie wiped the sweat away with her wrist. Armando had worked hard, hauling the lumber inside and measuring what she needed. "Sure. Just be back by two. I figure we can get in another couple of hours of work before I have to get ready for tonight."

"You still planning on going?"

Frankie sat back on her heels. "Yeah, of course I'm going. Why wouldn't I?"

Armando held up his hands in a sign of peace, grinning as he did so. "No reason. But he might have something to say about it."

Frankie shot to her feet. "He who?" From the front window, she spied Rico getting out of a midsize white sedan and felt her blood pressure rise.

"Catch you later," Armando threw at her as he scurried out of the room.

"Coward," she yelled after him as she marched to the front door and threw it open. "Go back where you came from. No trespassers."

Rico looked at her. She knew she looked sweaty, with her curls out of control, and a hammer gripped in her hand. His gaze paused on the hammer and then he had the nerve to grin.

"You planning on using that?"

"I'm real tempted."

Rico stopped at the bottom of the porch steps. She couldn't make out his eyes behind the dark glasses. Why had he come?

"Frankie, we need to talk."

"No, we don't. Now go away."

He stepped onto the porch, tugging off his glasses as he did so and tucking them in his shirt pocket. "You got anything to drink? I've got a mean thirst." He walked past her and into the house.

Emotions churned within her. She wanted to throw the bum out. But the moment he'd taken off his shades, she'd seen something in his eyes, worry, concern, and all she wanted to do was wrap her arms around him and make it all go away.

God, she was pathetic.

She followed him into the entryway where he'd stopped. He stood in front of the bouquet she'd set on a small table, the invitation in his hands.

"Hey, that's mine. You've got some nerve opening another person's mail." Frankie snatched the invitation from his hands.

"You're not going."

"What?" She stared at him in disbelief. His mouth thinned and his eyes hardened as he glared back. "Look, let me spell it out for you. Last night was a mistake and, even if it wasn't, it sure as hell doesn't give you the right to dictate my actions. I'm going." Frankie deliberately moved close to the roses and inhaled. The blossoms' fragrance, strong and sweet, filled her nostrils.

"Fine," Rico gritted out. "Then I'm going with you."

She stopped smelling the roses. "Excuse me? No. I don't think so."

"Too bad, Señorita Montalvo. You need an escort to the party and since you have no relatives to take you, then I am obligated to see you there myself."

"That's ridiculous! Nobody does that anymore!" She felt like pulling out her hair.

"Island custom dictates that a single female going to a party needs a chaperone. Of course, if you don't want me, I can put in a call to your aunt Margarita or your uncle." Rico crossed his arms over his chest and smirked at her.

He knew darn well she'd never ask Hector for help. As for Margarita, Frankie recalled the scene in the boutique when her aunt had flown into a fit after hearing about the party. Was Rico telling the truth? Did she really need a chaperone or risk offending people? But if he wasn't, then what reason would he have for wanting to attend the party? Her gaze narrowed thoughtfully over him.

Maybe letting him come wasn't such a bad idea. She could keep an eye on her pseudo-contractor and see exactly who he talked to and what he was up to.

"All right," she agreed. "You can take me. Be ready to leave by seven-thirty. The party starts at eight."

She walked away, not bothering to wait for his response, pleased by the puzzlement on his face at her easy capitulation. He'd expected more of an argument from her. Well, he wasn't getting one. He'd kept her off-center since the day they'd met. It was about time he got some of what he'd been dishing out. She'd lost trust in Rico Lopez. Maybe tonight, she'd finally learn the truth about the man she'd fallen in love with.

She prayed it was a truth she could live with.

Chapter 12

Chinese lanterns strung along towering ceibo trees lit up the night. A warm tropical breeze from off the coast carried the sweet scent of gardenias and jasmine and the distinct smell of saffron rice. The gentle wind ruffled the hem of the finely embroidered linen tablecloth heavily laden with dishes. Waiters dressed up like penguins hustled between the guests. Handsome men of distinction and beautiful women of elegance milled around the lush Caribbean estate of Salvador Torres, their conversations mixed and mingled with the chirping songs of *coquí* tree frogs.

Rico took it all in while his eyes made a second sweep of the guests to ensure he knew no one. Since his home base lay in New Jersey and his family didn't normally run with the movers and shakers in Vieques, he hadn't expected to see any familiar faces. But you couldn't be too careful. He'd learned that lesson the hard way.

Beside him, he felt Frankie stiffen as he escorted her through the numerous people crowding the terrace. "What is it, *querida*?"

"I'm not your *querida*. That would imply we have a relationship. What we have is a one-night stand that I regret."

His hide should've been tougher but her words pierced the shell protecting his heart. He'd hurt her. Badly. And he didn't have a clue how to make up for it.

He watched Frankie lift her chin and walk regally down the terrace steps to the brightly lit lawn. It occurred to him that she seemed nervous. His Frankie, who was never at a loss for words, looked like she wanted to bolt at the first opportunity.

Rico placed a hand on her back, soaking in the feel of her warmth and her smooth, silky skin. Leaning close, he whispered into her ear. "You are the most beautiful woman in this place."

A hint of a smile tinged her mouth and he felt the tension in her muscles ease beneath his palm.

She stepped away from him, saying under her breath, "You're a liar, Lopez," but the laughter coloring her voice took away the sting of her words.

He didn't know why she didn't believe him. Didn't she see how the men followed her every movement? In the simple white dress that clung to every curve, she appeared an angel with a body made for sin. Already, Rico's blood pressure was heating. A pendant lay between the swell of her breasts, her only concession to jewelry. Her hips swayed to an internal rhythm as she walked, while a small pearl bag dangled from her wrist. She'd done something fancy to her hair. His fingers itched to undo it and he recalled, in detail, their lovemaking when her curls had caressed his skin.

Rico could feel himself hardening at the memories. *Focus, Lopez.*

He meant to follow her but movement up on the terrace caught his eye. The host of the evening stepped out, accompanied by three men. A short older man with a cigar shook Salvador Torres' hand and then clapped him on the shoulder. Rico sucked in a breath.

Cardenas!

His blood ran cold. The murdering bastard was within his reach.

Rico's fingers fisted at his side, a red haze filling his mind. He'd always walked the side of justice, believed in the system despite its flaws. Only, men like Cardenas knew how to work the system and get away with murder.

The Venezuelan businessman thought himself invincible and above the law. So far he'd been able to slip through every organization's fingers, no one able to pin him on smuggling charges. Not the DEA, FBI, ICE or any other homeland security department.

Years of collecting data, seeking out leads, hunting out

warehouses and mountain retreats had turned up little yield. And then Carla offered to turn evidence. She wanted out of a desolate world filled with drug traffickers, pimps and prostitutes. She'd wanted something better for her daughter and had trusted him to keep them safe. Only she'd paid with her life. Despite Rico's promise to protect her and her child, Cardenas had been faster than him.

Staring at the man he considered his enemy, Rico vowed to see justice done one way or another.

Seemed Cardenas, even under scrutiny by every major federal agency in the United States, couldn't kick old habits. Gustav Cardenas loved the lavish life—heaps of money, dirty cash earned from other people's misery—he relished the limelight and friends in high places. No matter his reputation, Cardenas still garnered invitations to the best parties and continued to rub elbows with the rich and famous. Apparently Cardenas counted Salvador among his friends. Made Rico wonder what kind of raw goods Salvador exported.

Rico maneuvered closer, all thoughts of Frankie forgotten. When a space opened up, he slipped in, maintaining a sharp vantage. He snagged a glass from a passing tray and, with his free hand, extracted his Blackberry. Quickly he sent a text message to Jared informing him of Cardenas' presence. The other agent would get the ball rolling.

But Rico had no intention of waiting.

The group broke up with Cardenas and the other man rejoining the party while Salvador conferred with yet another man who stood at attention. Security detail, Rico thought. He'd noticed several well-dressed goons in strategic parts of the house and grounds.

Salvador finished issuing his orders, opened the terrace doors and stepped back inside the room where he'd been meeting with his notorious guest. Rico blended into the shadows. He had every intention of finding out what lay behind those doors.

Frankie had never felt more out of place.

What was she doing here? Had she really thought she could fit in? The closest she'd been to people with this much money was when she'd manned the front desk of the hotel she'd worked for.

She fingered her dress, aware of the glances of dismissal other women had shown her. Pride fortified her backbone. She pretended not to notice, determined to enjoy what she could of the evening and leave as soon as possible. Besides, whatever these women might think, Rico thought her beautiful.

And this matters why? Didn't you call him a liar? Didn't he abuse your trust? You're not even sure he's not a criminal. Hello?

"Oh, shut up," she mumbled under her breath. A girl needed something to boost her courage. A waiter passed with glasses of white wine. Frankie took one, and half turned, expecting Rico to reach for one as well.

She stood alone. Gripping the glass, she searched for him amongst the guests nearby. Surely he'd simply stopped to pass small talk with an acquaintance or something, except he was nowhere to be seen.

He'd ditched her.

Her fingers tightened on the stem of the wine glass. If Rico Lopez was standing in front of her right now, she'd pitch the entire contents in his face.

She didn't know what he was up to, but he obviously didn't want her to see it. Well, too bad for him.

She navigated through the crowd with purpose, determined to find Rico. She couldn't believe he'd given her the slip so easily. What was he involved in and why did she care? Getting involved with the guy hadn't been one of her sanest moves. Sure, he talked sweet about a mother and several brothers and sisters, but that didn't mean he couldn't be up to his neck in something ugly. Something she wanted no part of.

She made it to the top of the terrace steps and made a beeline for the doors. She'd start inside and work her way out again. One way or another, she'd find that bum.

A hand wrapped around her upper arm, halting her progress. Frankie's head whipped around, ready to do battle, only to find herself staring into the enigmatic eyes of her host.

Her free hand crept up to her throat. "Señor Torres, you startled me."

His eyebrows rose in question. "My dear Francesca, when

did we become so formal? I insist you call me Salvador." His arm slid down hers in a caress that made her nervous. His hand captured hers and he lifted it to press a kiss in an old-fashioned gesture. "Come," he said. "I have some gentlemen who wish to make your acquaintance."

"That is very kind, I'm sure, but I really wouldn't—"

He waved away her protest even as he pulled her forward, tucking her hand into the crook of his elbow. "These gentlemen have heard me speak of you and Casa Verde. They wish to meet you. That is all. I would not want to disappoint them."

Frankie gave in to the inevitable. She'd meet these men and then resume her search for her wayward contractor. As they moved along the terrace, Frankie couldn't help notice the way men and women deferred to Salvador. Those women who had dismissed her of little consequence before now regarded her with envy. Go figure.

Really, what was wrong with her? Here she was hanging on the arm of an extremely eligible bachelor, not to mention a wealthy one, yet her stupid heart was tangled up with a good-for-nothing beach bum. She needed counseling is what she needed.

They approached a group of older gentleman. Salvador introduced her to each in turn. She gave a wan smile. Her hotel training proved useful as she easily memorized each man's name, automatically noting identifying traits, such as Señor Cardenas' love of cigars, judging from the lit one in his hand and the two others in his breast pocket.

"We were about to sit and eat. Please join us."

"Oh, I couldn't—" Frankie began only to be drowned out by Salvador's agreement.

Salvador gazed down at her, a glitter in his eyes. "I would be heartbroken were you to refuse."

Frankie didn't know what to do. Rico, the rat, had abandoned her. If she offended the host, would she have to walk home in three-inch heels?

Pasting a smile on her face, she graciously accepted.

Rico stayed hidden in the shadows, watching the flow of people along the terrace. Earlier, Salvador had finally exited the room, locking the terrace doors behind him. Immediately, he'd been joined by a man with a suspicious bulge under his suit jacket. Rico observed several guards scattered around the house and property dressed in dark suits to blend in with the guests. This particular guard must have been assigned specifically to Salvador, because he maintained a protective stance towards his employer, all the while sweeping the surroundings for threats.

Rico held his patience, wanting to be certain that Salvador didn't return. From his vantage point, he could see the guests dancing and mingling, and even caught sight of Frankie for a moment, craning her neck as if searching for someone. Him.

His conscience rode him hard. He didn't like leaving her without an explanation when she was so uneasy with the company. She already had reasons for not trusting him. His behavior tonight likely sealed the deal.

Discipline from years on the job kept him in check. He couldn't afford to let thoughts of Frankie distract him.

Easily he adopted the pose of a guest, moving in and out of groups, working his way back up to the top of the terrace stairs until he was once more inside Salvador's elegant home. Several guests wandered in and out of archways. Above, ironwork graced a gallery that overlooked the huge salon. People traded comments over the priceless antiques and works of art together with the latest gossip.

Rico pretended the same, all the while checking out the cameras placed so discreetly that most guests were probably oblivious of them, only the tiny red dot on top indicating they were working.

It made his job harder but didn't deter him.

Though he'd e-mailed Jared before he left his boat about his plans to attend the party, along with a complete account of all that'd happened and his conclusions so far, Jared was in New Jersey. Not exactly what you'd call close back up. Rico imagined that his latest mail about Cardenas would have his fellow agent lighting a fire under several butts. But Rico couldn't afford to worry about what might be happening someplace else. Chita's life could very well hang in the balance and whatever info might be in the room Salvador came out of could be gone by the time a warrant was served.

Rico's mind sped to connect the various bits of information he'd collected so far. Last night's activities in the mangroves took on even greater meaning with Cardenas' presence in the area.

And it wouldn't bother him a bit to take Torres down as a side note. He hadn't liked the guy from the start. Particularly Torres sniffing around Frankie, and if that made his attitude unprofessional, so be it. His Latino blood didn't easily forget or forgive another man going after his woman.

Rico let out a breath. Focus. He needed to focus or he'd be useless. He spotted another security goon doing a sweep and kept his attention firmly on the sculpture of a bird in flight before him. Once the guy passed, Rico entered the hall and continued in the direction he wanted. He'd counted the windows on the terrace and had a fair sense of the room's location.

Salvador's home contained a main section flanked by two wings. Rico needed to get into the east wing.

He moved confidently down the hall as if he belonged. A door suddenly opened and a woman stepped out. She flashed him a smile even as she straightened her tight sequined dress. From behind her, another man exited, tucking his shirt back in his pants. He glared at Rico, grabbed the woman's arm and pulled her back along the hall. Rico flashed her a smile and a wink as she looked back at him.

Around the next bend, he calculated. Up ahead the hall ended. Stairs led up and probably connected to the gallery above. A sharp right, though, took you into the wing.

Only one camera covered the hallway, alternating left and right. Not very efficient. Salvador might spend bucks on his art, but it looked like he pinched the occasional penny when it came to security. Probably figured no one had the *cojones* to steal from him. Rico'd run across that type before.

At the end of the hall, Rico made as if he were heading up the stairs. He climbed two treads and stopped. He'd timed the camera's movement. Certain it was pointing in the other direction, he made his move. He jogged down the steps and, with his head averted from the camera, slipped around the corner into the next wing.

In contrast to the bright lights that bathed the main house,

171

only one sconce lit this hallway, creating deep pockets of shadows. Rico melted into a doorway and waited. Listening. Sensing.

A lone camera stood sentinel. It didn't move. The red light indicating power didn't glow. Maybe he'd gotten lucky tonight. Maybe Salvador's penny pinching had led to a faulty system.

He was about to move when a breath of sound caught his attention. His eyes, now adjusted to the dim light, picked out a man's bulk exiting a room several doors down. Julio!

What was the attendant to Señor Torres doing here? Rico watched as Julio glanced furtively left and right then moved farther away.

Rico waited a few more minutes to make sure there were no more surprise visitors and went directly to the room Julio had exited. This had to be it.

He pulled out his lock-picking tools, but on a hunch tried the door. It opened. He entered the darkened room questioning once again what the senior Torres' attendant could have wanted in here. Little light filtered in through the drawn drapes and Rico didn't dare chance turning on a lamp. He fished in his pocket for his penlight.

If there were cameras in here, he didn't have much time. The guards would see his light on the screen. Still, he didn't see any red glow.

He flashed the light in front of him and saw the shiny dark top of a desk. Not a scrap of paper marred the surface. The only object visible was a laptop. Rico didn't consider trying to boot it up.

He took a moment to guide the light around the room, noting the spartan decor. A large potted plant sat adjacent to the desk. Against the wall, he made out a low sofa facing a glass-top coffee table accented with a jade dragon. A large portrait with strong Asian influence in its style dominated the opposite wall. Aside from two leather chairs facing the desk, the room provided no hiding places.

That left the drawers or a hidden safe.

He turned his attention to the desk. The time he'd been inside the room ticked off in his mind. He couldn't afford to stay much longer. With a handkerchief, he carefully pulled the drawer handle, expecting it to be locked. The drawer slid free, jolting him. Uneasy with his fortune, he perused the contents, finding stationary embossed with Torres Traders, Ltd., some business cards and loose change.

Nothing. Damn.

He closed the drawer, leaving it as he found it. One more drawer. After that, he'd get out.

The drawer opened, yielding manila folders stacked one after another. Rico pulled one out. A neat computer label with the initials LGH topped the folder. Inside, he found business receipts for various shipments of textiles. On the surface it all looked legit.

It was too much to hope evidence would be lying out in plain sight. He replaced the folder and slowly pushed the drawer half way in when he noticed the discrepancy in proportions. He pushed his hand down on the bottom of the drawer and heard a soft click. Looking down, he observed another well-concealed drawer pop out. He reached inside the hidden compartment and pulled out a folder. Inside contained sheets of paper with names and dates.

His eyes narrowed as he scanned the top one. Rico recognized a few of the names. They matched the names Jared had sent him on the report of missing girls.

One name in particular stood out. Chita Santos.

The date indicated tonight. Rico had an idea what was going down. Whatever the girl had gotten herself mixed up with, she was up to her neck in trouble. Cardenas' cartel was notorious for using young girls as mules. And that was only one side of the business. His stomach knotted when he thought of Cardenas' other operations.

Carefully he replaced the file, cursing himself for not having brought a camera, and closed the drawer. Any evidence he removed would be inadmissible without a warrant. No way was he letting slime like Salvador Torres get off on a technicality.

Time was up. He needed to get out. He'd only taken two steps across the plush carpeting when the door burst open, and Rico suddenly faced two men armed with very deadly semi-automatic weapons who didn't look like they wanted to make friends.

"Put your hands up, *Señor,* and do not move. There is someone who will wish to speak with you."

"I think there's been a mistake," Rico said, raising his hands in obedience. "I was simply looking for the bathroom. Perhaps one of you gentlemen would point me in the right direction?"

"Where you are going *Señor*, the bathroom will be the least of your worries. Now get moving."

Frankie and Salvador sat at a table that clearly had been reserved for his group. While everyone else went to the buffet tables to get food, Salvador simply whispered to a man he called to his side and soon plates filled with various delicacies covered the white tablecloth. Frankie sat quietly, listening to the men speak. Salvador blended in well with the surroundings. He appeared to be a king in his castle, from the manicured rolling lawn, the sculpted bushes, even to the finest detail of the monogrammed bone white china and silverware. Frankie had thought Casa Verde impressive. She hadn't understood the meaning of the word. Her entire mansion probably wouldn't even take up one wing in Salvador's house.

Salvador placed samples of everything on her plate, encouraging her to eat. She tried, but her appetite wasn't strong, partly due to Rico's disappearance and partly to recognizing that she was way out of her league at this gala. Smiling once again at Salvador, Frankie took a bite of the *lechón asado.* The roast pork was perfect, yet it lacked the richness she had tasted with Rico at Jorge's *Cocinita.* In silence, she continued to eat, tuning out the conversation in order to listen to the old-time melodies from the hired band.

The night dragged on. Frankie had no idea how much time had passed. She wondered if it would be rude to make her excuses and leave. She would kill Rico for putting her in this position. He had the car keys, which meant she needed to rely on Salvador to see her home.

"Please accept my apologies for not being a better host," Salvador spoke suddenly. "I'm afraid I get caught up talking business."

"Really, it's okay. I understand you're busy."

"Never too busy for you, *mi paloma*." His arm slid around the back of her chair so that his hand could caress her shoulder. "You look like a dove in white."

Frankie reached for her champagne and took a nervous sip. The music changed and the bandleader took the microphone in his hand and called for people to come dance.

In the middle of the yard, beneath the muted glow of the red and yellow plastic lanterns, couples embraced and swayed to the music. Frankie listened to the crackle of the man's voice as he celebrated his country. "How beautiful it is to live in this dreamland! And how beautiful it is to be the master of the *coquí*'s song!"

"*Mi Tierra Borincana.*" She smiled at the sentiment of the words.

"Beautiful, isn't it?" Salvador said and then hummed a few bars.

"Yes. When I was little girl my father used to sing me to sleep with this song." Frankie's eyes misted, but she quickly blinked her eyes to rid them of the ridiculous moisture. "He sang whenever I had a bad day."

"Your father sounds like a good man."

"Yes, he was. He loved it here. He had hoped to come back to Puerto Rico, retire and build a house. Guess that dream now extends to me." Frankie frowned. Having taken in the sights and sounds of Vieques, she could not fathom how her father could have left such a place behind for the cold, polluted hustle and bustle of New York City.

"You speak of him in the past tense."

"My father passed away some time ago."

Salvador raised an eyebrow. "Your mother?"

Frankie nodded her head. "As well."

Salvador studied her for a second. She squirmed under his gaze. "Come. Let us take a walk."

She pretended to look at the antique watch she picked from her grandmother's belongings, the hands permanently stuck in position. "It's been a lovely party, but I must go. The house needs so much work..."

His eyes went dark. "I insist." He got up and held out his hand for her to join him.

Frankie didn't want to offend Salvador. So far he had been the only one on the island to show her any hospitality. And somehow she had a gut feeling that Salvador got what he wanted.

Frankie gave him a half smile and hoped that would satisfy the man. It did. He placed his hand on the small of her back and led her away from the table.

They hadn't walked far when they came upon Salvador's father. Distinguished and gray, Señor Torres sat in his wheelchair dressed up in a stuffy tuxedo, staring out blankly into the night. Julio stood attentively by his side, his keen eyes moving over the crowd before settling on his boss. Salvador exchanged a few words with him, chatting over the older man's head as if he was there, but Frankie could tell no one was home. Señor Torres' situation hadn't improved since she last saw him. But at least he was well taken care of. It spoke volumes of Salvador that he saw to his father's comfort in these difficult twilight years. Family obviously meant something in the Torres world.

Unfortunately for Frankie, all she had learned from her family on Vieques was that she couldn't rely on anyone. She could only trust in herself. Something she had been doing for a very long time.

A man strode up to them. "Señor Torres, I must speak with you." He moved forward and in a low voice spoke to Salvador.

Frankie let her eyes drift over the crowd. She hadn't seen a sign of Rico since he'd dumped her earlier. Where had he gone? Not that she intended to listen to any explanations. He wasn't worth her time.

"Forgive me, Francesca. A matter of business has suddenly come up. I'm afraid it must be dealt with immediately." He smiled down at her at the same time he lifted her hand to his lips for a kiss.

"I'm sorry too, but there is no need for you to apologize. It really has been a wonderful evening, but—"

"Julio, here, will see you back to the table. I insist."

There he went with that insisting again. The men down

here really needed an attitude adjustment when it came to women. "Actually, Salvador, I'd really like to go home. Perhaps Julio or someone else in your employ could..." She didn't like the idea of going home with a stranger, but the man worked for Salvador and instinctively she knew no one would touch what Salvador had claimed for himself.

Of course, Salvador's claims would have to be dealt with another day. For tonight, she'd put up with it.

"As soon as my business is complete, I will see you safely home." He squeezed her hand briefly and walked swiftly away.

Frustration gnawed at her insides. Julio waited expectantly, while the senior Torres' expression remained blank. She had no choice but to allow the duet to accompany her back to the table.

Rico was dead meat, she vowed.

She found the table deserted, except for Señor Cardenas and a man who stood a couple feet behind him, stiff as a board. Señor Cardenas beckoned her to sit in the empty seat next to his. Reluctantly, she did. Up close she could see that the man was younger than Señor Torres and older than Salvador. He wore his black hair slicked back, sported a diamond stud on his tie and a Rolex on his wrist. When he smiled, a gold tooth winked at her. At least he hadn't lit up his cigar. Thank God for small favors.

"Señorita Montalvo. Salvador has told me all about you. He did not do you justice." The man reached over and covered Frankie's hand with his own, his thumb rubbed along her wrist.

She pulled her hand back and placed it in her lap, scrambling for words. Back in New York, she'd have told him exactly what would happen if he touched her again without her permission, but this wasn't the city. This was a world with rules she didn't understand.

Señor Cardenas chuckled. "You misunderstand, my dear. I merely wish for us to dance. Shall we?"

Frankie wanted to refuse, but she felt like such a fool that she nodded instead. She hoped Salvador finished his business soon, otherwise she'd walk home. She couldn't take much more.

Cardenas reached out and cupped her elbow as he led her to the dance floor. The strong odor of cigars, too much aftershave and sweat bombarded her. Her stomach lurched. Behind them, she sensed rather than saw the other man following in their wake. Cardenas stepped onto the dance floor and took her into his arms.

"It is a beautiful night. You are young and sweet. I am old and rich." He laughed. Frankie smiled weakly, though she didn't think it funny at all.

The music changed into a salsa. He put his arm around her back and pulled her near. She put her right hand in his left hand and tried to keep distance between them. Her effort paid off, but not by much.

"Señor Cardenas, please." She hated how breathless she sounded. Frankie was not as adept at the dance and tried to keep up, but she feared for her toes. Her father had shown her how to dance. He had been the best salsa dancer. The older gentleman wasn't bad, just a little more free in style.

"Call me Gustav. Don't be shy. You can get a little closer." Frankie cringed at the suggestive note. The thought of holding his hands during the dance was grossing her out enough. She looked around for Rico, Salvador, anybody who might save her. The rhythmic music of the maracas and drums beat a wild tempo. Gustav moved his hips from side to side, his legs and feet moving in time with the music and more than once he ground his pelvis into hers.

The music stopped. Everyone clapped. Frankie extricated her hand from Gustav's death grip and moved off to the side.

Frankie eyed Gustav warily and turned back to the crowd. Something about the way he leered at her made her shiver. She wanted to leave and she wanted to leave now.

Relief pounded through her when she spied Salvador coming towards her. As soon as he reached her she made her request, not caring that she sounded almost desperate. "Would you please take me home?"

"Yes, of course. Is everything all right?"

No, it's not all right, she wanted to scream. Rico had deserted her and she'd had to play nice with Gustav the Gross. And speak of the devil.

Gustav joined them, slapping Salvador on the shoulder. "I accept your offer, including the bonus."

Salvador smiled. "I knew you would see it my way. We can discuss details later."

Gustav smiled at Frankie. His eyes moved down her body as if he were cataloging her assets. He made her skin crawl. "Until we meet again, *Señorita.*"

"Not likely," she muttered to his back.

"Did you say something?" Salvador asked.

"Nothing important. What kind of business do you do with Señor Cardenas?"

"We trade in priceless dolls," Salvador said smoothly. "Shall we go?"

Priceless dolls? The idea of that slimy man dealing with dolls was too ludicrous for words. Oh well. None of her business. Happily, she could finally make tracks from this place.

"Um, Salvador. I came here with my contractor, Rico. Somehow we got separated during the party. Anyway," she rushed on, "if he should ask for me, please let him know that I've gone home."

"Of course. Do not worry. I will see to your escort myself."

The interior of the Mercedes was quiet except for the hum of the air conditioner. Butter soft leather seat cradled her weary muscles and her sore toes. She slipped off her sandal and rubbed her toes. Salvador turned onto the narrow back road, halogen lights cut through the darkness.

Frankie looked at the house looming in the dark, a few lights dotting the windows, but the sense of homecoming wasn't there. It stood alone, neglected and forgotten. A feeling she knew all too well. The only ghosts here were the ones that hung in the cobwebs of her memories.

Salvador pulled the car into the driveway and parked. He unbuckled his seatbelt and turned his body toward her. He skimmed his hand down her arm. She shifted closer to the door, disturbed by his touch. Most likely because of the yucky encounter with Gustav, she reasoned. Besides, having had her head messed with by Rico, she wasn't about to jump into another relationship any time soon. Only stupid women did that.

And falling into Rico's bed after knowing him only a few days doesn't qualify you for membership in that club?

"You are very lovely, Francesca."

Startled out of her thoughts, Frankie turned her head to regard her companion. Salvador's eyes gleamed with interest even in the darkness.

"Thank you." She didn't want to offend her neighbor, but she really needed to get out of this car and put some distance between them.

"Yes," he continued, "much too lovely to be spending your days working like an *hombre*." He fairly spat the word. "I would be happy to make an offer for this property, to take the load off your beautiful shoulders. It would be an honor and a pleasure." He practically purred the last.

Frankie's mouth dropped open. Were all the men around here throwbacks to the caveman? Somebody needed to drag them kicking and screaming into the modern world where women stood up for themselves, had more than the occasional thought, and could wield a hammer with the best of them. "I really don't know what to say, Salvador. No wait, yes I do. No, thank you. This is my home and I intend to stay. I'm also quite aware of the work that needs to be done and have no problem with doing it. This," she said, waving her hand down her dress, "is not me. I don't do parties. I'm tough, strong, and not afraid of breaking a sweat. And I sure don't intend to be run off my property by scary legends of *el chupacabra* or offers of salvation."

"My apologies if I have offended you." He smiled innocently. He skimmed his hand over her fingertips. "It is just that such a beauty like yourself shouldn't have to slave." Salvador picked up her hand and kissed up her arm. She cringed back before he could reach her lips.

"No, look, I'm sorry too. I probably said more than I should've." She faked a yawn. "I can't believe how late it is. My cousin is probably up waiting for me." She grabbed a hold of the door handle and opened the door. Before he could protest, she scooted out and shut it.

The click of Salvador's door being opened sounded behind her. Frankie nearly groaned. What would it take to get rid of the guy? She turned to politely send him on his way, when a shadow detached itself from the darkness of the front veranda, causing Frankie's heart to slam in her chest.

Had *el chupacabra* come back for her again?

Chapter 13

"Tía Margarita, what are you doing here?" The air whooshed out of Frankie upon recognizing her aunt.

"Where is your young man? Why are you with *him*?" Her voice came out strident, thin. Frankie winced at the tone.

With her sandals dangling from her hands, Frankie walked barefoot towards the porch. "He's not my man and I suppose he's still at the party." There was more she could say but Salvador stood nearby listening.

"*Buenas noches*, Señorita de la Varga." Salvador's smooth baritone broke into the night air.

"You must go. It is not proper for my niece to be with you alone. Please go."

"Margarita—" Frankie protested half-heartedly. Admittedly, she wanted Salvador gone, but the idea that she needed to be protected from all men irritated her.

"Do not worry, Francesca. Your aunt is perfectly correct. I must return to my guests." He smiled over the car door at her, his expression polite but amused. "I will see you again soon. Good night to you both."

The car rumbled back down the drive as Frankie wearily climbed up the stairs to the porch. "Why are you here, *Tía*?"

Her aunt clasped a necklace with one hand while her other fluttered helplessly in the air. "I was worried. You do not understand so much." She lapsed into silence.

Frankie prayed she wouldn't have to endure another emotional scene. Digging in her bag for her key, she used it for an excuse to not have to continue the conversation. A

182

conversation going nowhere, anyway, she thought sarcastically to herself.

Key in hand, she opened the door, glad that she'd left the hall light on so that she wouldn't return to a darkened house. "Would you like to come in?"

Her aunt hovered nervously behind her, her eyes darting at every shadow. Finally she took a step over the threshold, rubbing the necklace in her hand. "I hate this place," she burst out. "Can't you feel the evil?"

Frankie squeezed her eyes shut and strove for patience. "I know you're not comfortable here, but this is my home now. Give me a chance. I can turn this place around. I can do it."

"You have a good heart, Francesca. Your mother would be proud of you." Margarita reached out and laid her hand on Frankie's arm, a gesture of tenderness that caused a knot to form in Frankie's throat.

"Thank you."

"I must go now. Why don't you come back with me to town? It is safer there."

"I have Armando here. I'll be fine," Frankie refused gently.

"Armando's a boy, what can he do? You don't understand the kind of evil that exists in this world." Her aunt's voice became desperate, her fingers digging into Frankie's arm.

"We'll be fine," Frankie repeated, pulling her arm away at the same time. They'd have to be.

"I must go, Francesca. But you are welcome in my home any time, day or night. You will find refuge there." Her aunt finished by murmuring some kind of prayer, kissed Frankie on both cheeks, and left.

Frankie blew out a breath. If one more person got in her face, she just might scream.

She padded up the stairs. At the top she flipped on the light. Instead of going to her room, she turned in the opposite direction. Armando's door stood shut. Frankie tapped lightly. When no one answered, she opened it and peered inside. A crack in the curtains allowed a slim slash of moonlight in, letting her make out a lump under the covers. It was late and after all the work they'd done, it didn't surprise her that he'd passed out for the night. She was exhausted too.

She closed the door softly and moved back down the hall. Though it gave her comfort knowing Armando slept not far away, she missed Rico.

There she'd said it.

She missed the bum. He'd made her laugh. Made her feel alive. And amidst all the craziness and attacks, he'd made her feel safe.

But like most people in her life, he'd turned out temporary. She'd been foolish to let her guard down and invite him into her heart. She'd be doubly foolish to forgive and forget.

Feet dragging, she entered her room. The curtains on the bed blew in the soft breeze coming from the open window. Frankie pulled the pins from her hair, letting her curls cascade down her shoulders. A serenade of cricket chirps filtered in from the night. Peaceful and serene, she didn't bother to turn on the lights, afraid the night lullaby would stop. Too tired to wash up, she changed quickly into a tank top and matching shorts pajama set and collapsed on the bed.

Had it only been last night that she'd found heaven in Rico's arms? She'd never given herself completely as she had with him. Never trusted anyone with her heart.

And the first time she had, it'd been handed back to her with a big crack.

Stupid. Stupid. Stupid.

Frankie hugged the pillow close and let her emotions spill out. Tears leaked from her eyes no matter how hard she tried to stop them. She prided herself on being tough and now look at her. Pathetic.

Eventually, she cried herself to sleep.

A shift in the bed jolted her awake. "Rico?"

Her eyes groggy with sleep, she rolled over. A shadow loomed dark and large at the edge of her bed. *El chupacabra!* Before she could react, the creature leaped and landed on her, knocking the breath out of her lungs. Clawed hands grabbed her arms and pinned them to the bed. Her legs free, she kicked and made contact with the beast's crotch. With a yowl, it rolled off her. She scrambled up from the bed but didn't get far. The beast tackled her from behind and she landed hard on the hardwood floor. Hot and rank, the creature breathed down the back of her head. From behind, sharp fangs plunged into her neck. Stinging pain shot up her nerves. Frankie bit down against the clanging in her brain. She had to get away. Under its weight, she bucked and squirmed enough to roll free. *El chupa* hissed and lunged again. Nails out to defend herself, she went for the eyes. Frankie grabbed onto the head and scratched. *El chupa's* skin pulled off. It took a split second for her mind to register. It wasn't skin at all, but a mask that dangled from her fingertips.

Her vision swam. Her limbs grew sluggish and heavy. The last thing she saw before she blacked out was her attacker's face.

El chupacabra was Hector!

℘

Frankie woke slowly. Cold. She felt so cold. She tried opening her eyes, but the world spun around too much.

Something was wrong. Very wrong.

She tried to think, but her brain felt fuzzy, like she'd had too much to drink. Only she was always careful not to drink too much. The drumming noise around her rattled in her brain. Her head pounded. Her tongue felt thick, her mouth dry. What had happened to her? A groan escaped her lips as she tried to move, but her hands were firmly shackled in chains attached to a metal pipe.

"Shhh. Do not make any noise to bring them back. Please." The whisper sent Frankie's heartbeat skyrocketing. Who was in this place with her? Where was she? And why did the plea to not "bring them back" make her limbs shake?

"I'm going to be sick," Frankie mumbled, her stomach beginning to heave. She managed to get on her knees, her eyes blinking to bring the room into focus. Hands gently clasped her shoulders and aided her as far forward as the chains would allow so she could vomit away from her body. A strange rattling sound penetrated her consciousness, but she couldn't think about it while her stomach rebelled.

Where was she? Frankie thought desperately, as she expelled the contents of her stomach into a watery hole in the floor. She still couldn't see straight and it took her a moment to realize that they were rocking.

Her stomach empty, she collapsed weakly on the floor, her arms dangling awkwardly above her head.

"Are you okay?" a soft voice asked. Frankie forced herself to really examine her surroundings and the person with her.

She gasped when her gaze fell onto a young girl of sixteen or seventeen huddled on a hard metal bench against a wall. She was beautiful despite the dark, ugly bruise marring her cheek and her swollen lip. The girl's brown-eyed gaze met Frankie's for one brief, all too penetrating moment, in which Frankie saw hell reflected back at her before the girl's eyes dropped to the floor.

Sick with apprehension, Frankie's eyes moved around the small area, horrified to discover four more girls. One lay in a fetal position on the floor between motor engines. Two others clung to one another on a makeshift bed of oily rags, their eyes meeting hers and then sliding away, while the fourth rocked back and forth, her arms hugging her knees as tears poured down her face.

She'd stumbled into a nightmare. The rattling sound occurred again and Frankie realized with growing horror that every one of the girls had chains binding one foot to the other. The ugly reality set in along with the smell of fumes and heat from the boats engines.

Harsh fluorescent lights blinked on and off with the sway of the boat. The engine room felt cramped with six of them taking up every bit of space.

Panic set in at the thought of being in the middle of the sea. Even if she got loose and escaped, there was no place to go. She couldn't swim. And even if she could, the idea of shark-infested waters terrified her even more.

"What is this place? Who are you all? What is going on?" The questions poured from her lips.

The girl who helped her simply shook her head. "It is better you don't ask questions," she said before her gaze darted away.

Frankie had no illusions about the situation she'd been thrust into. All the girls bore signs of violence and she was certain not all of it was on the outside. Emotionally, they appeared to be barely hanging on by a thread. The smell of fear mixed with the stale air. Frankie felt suffocated in the tiny prison.

The sound of a key turning in the lock acted like a gunshot. The girls seemed to shrink into themselves. Frankie, who'd never considered herself a coward, found herself wanting to hide.

Except there was no place to go and these girls had endured more than enough.

Though her legs trembled, Frankie forced herself to her bare feet and faced the door as it swung open.

ℬ

The blow snapped his head back, rattling his brain. Darkness flickered at the edges then retreated. Rico ran his tongue along his teeth checking they were all there. Blood trickled down his chin.

Grim and Glum, as he'd dubbed his captors, paced in front of him in the luxury-appointed cabin of a mid-sized motor yacht. Grim rubbed his knuckles in a caress, waiting for the signal from his partner that he could belt Rico again. Glum poked through the contents of Rico's pocket laid on top of the built-in cabinet.

He'd been stripped of his jacket and bound with his hands behind him to the chair. Good thing he'd left his badge locked up in his boat. The only ID they'd find would be his New Jersey driver's license.

"What were you doing in Señor Torres' study?" Glum asked.

"Looking for the bathroom. I told you."

"I don't believe you and neither does he." Glum nodded, a sharp silent command.

This time the blow was to the stomach. Rico would've doubled over from the pain, but the ropes tying him to the chair held him in place. His head dropped forward. Sweat beaded his brow.

Glum flicked open Rico's knife. He put it down in exchange for the lock-picking tools. "Interesting collection you got. Not what party guests usually carry."

Rico brought his head up. "I'm a handyman. I like to be prepared." He shot off a cocky grin. It nearly killed him, but damn if he was going to give these goons any satisfaction.

"You're a fool, *Señor*. You'll never see the woman again. Already she has chosen to be with Señor Torres."

His captor's words ripped fresh wounds inside, but Rico kept his expression blank. The only chance he had of saving Frankie was to pretend she meant nothing to him.

Rico quirked his eyebrow, the equivalent of a shrug. "The woman means nothing. A job, free room and board."

Glum laughed, a harsh sound that filled the room. He grabbed his crotch in a suggestive manner. "Then you won't mind what I plan to do with her very soon. I can show her what it's like to be with a real man."

Panic flashed through him momentarily. The image of Frankie's body, bloody and lifeless, swam in his mind. The bitter taste of failure flooded his insides.

The door opened suddenly and unseen hands shoved Hector into the room. He stumbled then straightened himself, a white oversized handkerchief clutched in his hand that he used to wipe the sweat beading his forehead. His gaze darted around the room, widened upon catching sight of Rico, then slid away like the rat he was. Behind him, Salvador entered the cabin.

Rico stared at Frankie's uncle with growing rage. "You're her family," he growled out.

Hector blanched but kept his eyes averted. "Salvador, you must see that I've done as you asked. Now it is your turn to honor your promise." He blotted his face, crushing the cloth in his hand when he finished. "The money. Where is my money?"

"But what is the hurry, my friend. Don't you wish introductions?" Salvador's smile resembled a shark's.

Hector backed up a step and shook his head. "No. I don't want to know anything. I did what you asked. You owe me."

"I owe you nothing. You brought a traitor into my midst."

Hector backed away further, shaking his head. Sweat dotted his forehead. "No. I don't know what you're talking about. I only did what you asked—try to scare Francesca into leaving the property so she would sell."

"You son of a—" Rico spat, only to get a punch in the stomach for his effort.

"This man was caught in my private study. What do you know about it, Hector?"

"Nothing. I don't know anything. I swear." Hector's voice and hands shook. He stepped back again and came up against the solid wall of Glum.

Salvador flicked a speck off his evening jacket. "Perhaps I should question your niece. I'm sure she'll be willing to give answers. If not, my friends here will make sure she talks."

"You hurt her, Torres, and I'll see you rot in hell," Rico vowed.

Salvador laughed. "I think you will be going there a lot sooner."

ॐ

"Where are you taking me?" Frankie struggled to pull her arm from the brute who'd entered, unchained her and, without a word, had dragged her from the room.

The guard simply ignored her. He yanked her along a narrow passageway. She heard a second guard shout at the girls to shut up before locking the door.

"Let us go! Please." She knew her pleas fell on deaf ears, but she had to try. She could barely keep the terror down, the sight of the large black deadly weapon he carried a clear warning of how much danger she stood in.

He pushed her forward. She put her hand against the wall to catch her balance. He merely jerked his gun up, directing her to go upstairs. A crewmember in full dress whites appeared at the top. His gaze slid insolently over her body. The simple outfit she wore gave inadequate protection against his perusal.

The hall opened into a small salon. Lush, ornamental furniture with gilded inlays over cherry-wood cabinetry and high-tech entertainment equipment filled the space. It even had an elevator, if you could believe that. The vessel clearly outclassed Rico's craft in size and appointments, but she'd give anything to be back on that bum's boat. She'd even give him a second chance to explain. That was if she ever saw him again, for that matter, if she lived to see anyone again.

Frankie's mind boggled at who could possibly afford the tricked-out yacht. The answer to her question soon became evident.

Señor Torres sat in one of the cushioned chairs alone, his empty wheelchair rested folded against the wall. The elderly man's glazed-over eyes stared out the panoramic glass window at the black waters of the Caribbean Sea. Julio, his attendant, was nowhere to be seen.

The guard pushed her from behind. She walked forward, finally stopping at a door near the front of the boat.

"Knock."

Frankie stared at the door before her. What was going to happen to her? Her knees shook.

"Knock," he ordered again.

She did as she was told. The door was jerked open and yet another man with soulless eyes faced her. He shifted slightly and Frankie gasped.

She felt a push between the shoulder blades that nearly sent her sprawling over the threshold into a master suite cabin twice as big as Rico's and three times as posh. Salvador greeted her.

Hector cowered in the corner, sweat dripping down his face, while Salvador watched her with a predatory look. She barely noticed him. Her gaze took in Rico strapped to a chair, beaten and bruised. Blood stained his white dress shirt, while a brute of a man stood behind him with a deadly knife pointed at Rico's jugular.

"We've been waiting for you, Francesca." Salvador's gaze lazily swept over her body, lingering on her bare legs.

She'd never been more scared in her life. Her eyes met Rico's, seeking guidance, but he refused to acknowledge her, his entire being focused on Salvador.

The sound of the door closing snapped her to attention. She stepped sideways to avoid contact with the man who'd told her to enter. She watched him take up a post against the door. On top of a built-in cherry-wood cabinet, she caught sight of Rico's black-handled switchblade and Blackberry.

Help was only a push button away, she thought hysterically.

Her nails dug into her palms and she reached for every ounce of courage she'd ever possessed. After a deep breath, Frankie raised her chin and faced her neighbor.

"So beautiful. So treacherous," Salvador murmured as he slowly circled her. He reminded her of the snake Rico had killed in her room, watching her every movement, waiting to strike.

"Why am I here? What do you want?" Her New York accent sounded thicker in her false bravado.

Salvador's hand shot out, grasping her nape, his face only inches from her own. "I'll ask the questions." His hand squeezed and, out of the corner of her eye, she saw Rico strain against his bonds, only to have the guard cuff him in the head.

She forced down her fear and the need to defend herself. Street instincts and defense classes had taught her how to take down an attacker. But the odds were against her now. Better to let them think she wouldn't put up a fight. She'd find an opportunity. She had to.

"Let me go," she ground out.

Salvador tightened his grip and stepped closer, his gaze never leaving her face. "Your friend over there is an undercover cop. DEA, FBI, perhaps? Are you one too? "

Frankie's eyes flew to Rico's in disbelief. Shock held her immobile. Was it true? Somehow it all clicked. The gadgets, his looks, the Superman complex, she shook her head for not putting it all together earlier. He'd lied to her. Frankie bit back tears. She hung her head, unable to look at Rico. The stupid image of having a family and home shattered. What in her right mind had made her believe that she could have it all? Dreams, nothing but dreams. Her gut churned.

Another step and Salvador stood flush against her. She could feel his arousal and shuddered.

"I've never done it with a cop," he whispered in her ear. To punctuate his words, he ground his pelvis into her abdomen.

"Back off, Torr—" Rico barked out, only to be cut off. Hearing the sharp sound of a slap gave Frankie a fairly good reason why.

Frankie's gaze was glued to Salvador's. She could tell her

fear fed his sexual excitement. The faces of the broken girls in the other cabin ran through her mind. Her stomach knotted.

"Once you have told me what I want to know, you and I will get better acquainted," Salvador continued. "I look forward to teaching you obedience like I do to all the women before they are sold. Unfortunately, my time is short. You and your friend have upset my plans. Usually, I ship the girls to Venezuela in a fishing boat, but for you I have made an exception." He brushed a strand of hair off her forehead. "Señor Cardenas has paid extra to have you delivered personally. He has taken a shine to you." Salvador turned up his nose. "A beautiful face, though a little too skinny for my taste. Still, there will be plenty of men willing to pay for your services once Cardenas finishes with you." He laughed, a warped sound to her ears, his breath hot on her cheek.

With his free hand, he ran his thumb across her mouth. His hand traced a path downward. Salvador's smooth hand latched onto her breast through the thin material. He pinched and squeezed, his arousal evident as he pressed himself against her stomach. It took everything she had not to react, to show her repulsion.

Anger flitted across his face at her lack of response. "You'll be begging for me by the time I'm done with you," he hissed.

"Salvador, please," Hector whined in interruption. "I've done my job. I brought her here for you. Pay me. It is time a true de la Varga resided in Casa Verde."

Betrayal. Anger. Indignation rose up from her gut.

"You call yourself *familia*! Doesn't it mean anything to you? May one of Tía Margarita's *orishas* curse your soul for all time," she spat at him. "Betrayer!"

She saw neither shame nor remorse, only hate in his bloodshot eyes.

"Betrayed? I was the one betrayed. My mother disinherited me! Her only son. What right had she to pass our heritage to you? A nobody. You don't even appreciate its history. You want to foul it with strangers." Spittle flew out of his mouth as the words burst forth. "Oh, yes, I heard how you intend to turn Casa Verde into a low-budget hotel for the riffraff. You dishonor our name. I won't allow it." He shook his fist in the air and stalked towards her.

The sound of clapping sliced the air. "Bravo Hector. Your outrage has made my plans so much easier."

Confused, Hector stopped in his tracks. Frankie caught the wisp of fear that crossed his face. He licked his lips and spread his hands out in a gesture of peace. "We are neighbors, Salvador. I have done as you asked. I used the costume you lent me to take her. Everyone will believe *el chupacabra* is responsible. I think it best you pay me and I leave."

"Of course, Hector. Thank you so very much." He snapped his fingers. "Raul, pay the man."

Frankie barely registered the popping sound. Her uncle's eyes widened and a red stain spread fast across his chest. Another gunshot followed. A round hole appeared in the middle of Hector's forehead.

Screams remained frozen in her throat. Trapped by fear, she stood paralyzed.

Hector's body hit the floor with a thud, breaking the spell that hung over the room. A whimper escaped from her, the only other sound.

Salvador's cold-blooded eyes turned on her. "I suggest you tell me what I need to know, Francesca, or your friend is next."

Chapter 14

Sweat trickled between her breasts. She didn't have any information for Salvador, but if she told him that, he'd kill Rico.

Her mind raced for a solution, while her eyes bounced around the room for inspiration. She couldn't bear to look at Rico, knowing she might be the catalyst for his death. Her eyes landed on her uncle, lying in a pool of blood. Her stomach lurched.

An idea formed. It'd be a risk, but what was her choice? Let Rico die? Allow herself to be raped and sold into slavery by a madman? *No!*

"I'm going to be sick," she said, stumbling to a corner of the cabinet. Her stomach rebelled. Frankie braced her knees and doubled over.

Salvador backed away from her in distaste. "Get the body out of here, Raul. Toss it overboard. You," he pointed to the other guard, "Go get something to clean up this mess."

Frankie bent over and continued to heave. Weak and tired, she sat back on her heels. Raul dragged Hector by the heels out the door, while the other guard got busy with the stain on the floor. From the corner of her eye, she could see Salvador had turned his attention back on Rico. With everyone's attention focused elsewhere, she made a particularly bad retching sound, bent over double and scooped the knife off the top of the cabinet. Her heart pounded and her head spun. She clutched the knife close, afraid of discovery.

Salvador returned his malice to her. "I'm waiting, Francesca, and my patience is limited."

Keeping her hands wrapped around her waist, the knife tucked out of sight, Frankie considered her next move. "Look, I'm not a cop or anything like that—"

"That's too bad. Get rid of him." The remaining guard went for his gun.

"No! Wait!" Frankie shouted.

She stumbled up on shaky legs over to Rico, collapsing between his legs. Frankie wrapped her arms around him and laid her head against her chest. "We're lovers," she rushed out. "He likes to talk in bed, to brag. I know more than he thinks. I can tell you stuff." She turned her head to meet Rico's eyes. They were furious. "I'm sorry," she said in a loud voice, playing the part of desperate lover even as she pressed against him, slipping the knife into his hand.

His fingers closed over it. She felt the steady beat of his heart, breathed in his masculine scent mixed with sweat and blood, and gathered courage.

Salvador's hand thrust into her curls, grabbing a handful and yanking her to her feet. "Enough of this foolishness. Tell me—"

A knock sounded and the door opened. "*Jefe*. Señor Cardenas has arrived."

The man stood at attention waiting for his orders. Salvador thrust Frankie away. "Tie her up on the bed." He moved to the door only to pause. He gave her a predatory look. "One way or another, I will get answers out of you." Frankie dug her feet into the thick carpet, but the guard easily overpowered her and tossed her onto the bed. Salvador sneered. "And if my method doesn't work, I'll let him slice up your boyfriend and feed him to the sharks—piece by piece."

Frankie swallowed the whimper that crawled up her throat. She wouldn't let these bastards break her. She forced herself to breathe normally, to concentrate on finding any advantage, any opening that she and Rico could use. And if worst came to worst, she would survive.

She'd been a survivor her whole life. No matter what living hell these men thought up, she'd find a way to escape, she vowed. The guard finished tying her off and left the room. Immobilized by the ropes, she could only raise her head an inch off the bed. From her position she could see Rico. He sawed at the bindings. His efforts doubled. She could see the strain on his face as he hurried to cut through the rope.

"I'll get us out of here," he whispered through gritted teeth.

Frankie kept silent. Anger tumbled around in her. She'd made love to this man, yet he was a complete stranger.

"Did you hear me? I promise..."

"Don't promise me anything!" she shot back. Her anger spilled out of her with tears held too long in check. Duped and deceived, she didn't want to believe. As a child, she had believed her parents would be with her forever, they had died. As a teenager, she had believed that her family would come and claim her, they had abandoned her. As a woman out of the system, she believed she could make it on her own, she'd struggled every step of the way. In Puerto Rico, she'd hoped she'd finally be able to build her dreams, they'd turned into nightmares. With Rico she'd believed in a family, hope for a future filled with love.

Frankie cut off the thought. There was no future, not with Rico, or anyone. They were going to die. Salvador would make sure of it. She turned her head away. Hot tears ran down into her hair.

"Listen to me, Frankie." Rico spoke softly, gently. "I never meant for you to get involved. If I could turn back time, I would."

"Well, you can't." The words choked with tears. "You lied to me. About everything." She turned back to him. Chocolate-brown eyes stared back at her. "Tell me the truth, Rico. Who are you?"

He stayed silent for a moment. He blew out a breath. "I work for Immigration and Customs Enforcement for the Department of Homeland Security in the United States."

"And what about the woman and child in the picture?"

"The woman was an informant. She agreed to testify against Cardenas in exchange for witness protection. Cardenas had her killed. She died because of me. Now her daughter, Lourdes, has no one who gives a damn about her," he said bitterly. "But that's not what's important here. My reasons for being in Vieques have nothing to do with my job. It was never my intention to drag you into my world."

Frankie sucked in a breath. "Yeah, right. Do I look stupid or something?" Her heart squeezed inside of her chest, afraid to hear his answer.

"No. I am." Pain clearly showed on his face. "When *Mami* asked me to find Chita, I should have left it to the police. Instead, I agreed to play hero." He cut through the last of the bindings. Rico jumped up from the chair and sliced through her ropes.

"Who's Chita?" Frankie tugged off the rope and rubbed her aching wrists.

"She's a distant cousin. *El chupa*...correction, Salvador kidnapped her." Rico helped her off the bed. "She must be on the boat. The girls are scheduled to be smuggled out of the country tonight."

"I saw some women. They were in bad condition."

"Where?" His voice rose in urgency. With the knife out, he stood off to the side of the door, listening to the outside.

"In the engine room. There are guards everywhere. How are we going to save them?" She stepped back toward the bed when the handle turned. Her eyes flew to Rico who signaled for her to stand back.

One of the guards walked into the room. Rico grabbed him and pulled him to the side, at the same time using his leg to kick the door closed. A quick blow to the back of the head and the guard lay incapacitated on the floor.

Rico used the cut piece of rope to tie the man's hands behind his back. He tore off a strip of bedding and used it for a gag. He then frisked the guard and retrieved a pistol and a second knife.

"Come on, let's get out of here." Rico held out his hand to Frankie. She hesitated.

"You have to trust me."

She bit her lip. Her intelligence battled with her emotions. The trust had been broken along with her heart.

His dark eyes remained steady on hers. "Please."

She'd never been good at reaching out. Never been good at letting another person in, having been burned too many times.

But, God help her, she needed Rico. Not just to get out of this horrible place. It was much more elemental than that. So though her head shouted warnings, her heart insisted she take a chance.

Frankie stretched out her hand. Their fingers interlocked. Her gaze met his, silently begging, *don't hurt me again.*

He must have understood because he dragged her clasped hand up with his own to cover his heart. "I'll keep you safe, Frankie. Or die trying. That I can promise."

Cautiously he and Frankie made their way out of the room. Rico could hear shouts from the outside deck. Through the porthole he made out lights from another watercraft that bobbed outside on the dark sea. If they could get off the boat there was a chance to be rescued. Once on shore he could contact the Coast Guard and save Chita and the other girls. He ducked down low. Frankie followed suit. Slowly, they made their way up the winding staircase to the main deck. A galley befitting a first-class chef stood off to the side. They made their way past the dining room into the main salon. Keeping low, they crossed half the room, using the plush chairs as cover. The sliding glass doors at the stern of the boat waited, open and empty. Rico grabbed hold of Frankie's hand and sprinted to the end.

A dark figure blocked their escape. Foul cigar smoke puffed up.

Rico pulled Frankie behind him. His hands free, he braced himself for action.

"Cardenas," Rico snarled out his enemy's name through his teeth.

Cardenas took the cigar out of his mouth and waved it towards them. Rico had half a mind to shove it down the bastard's throat.

"What a pleasure to meet you again, Agent Lopez." Rico's body jerked at the identification.

Cardenas smiled. "Oh, yes. I know who you are. I recall you well. You gave my organization lots of trouble, particularly when you persuaded Carla to testify." He sucked on the cigar, blowing the foul air everywhere. Cardenas eyed Frankie.

"You seem to steal away my most prized possessions."

Instead of cowering, Frankie stepped up beside Rico not backing down against the man.

"I'm no one's possession!"

Pride welled in Rico's chest, along with fear. Frankie would go down fighting and so would he, but this was never how he wanted it to end for her. She deserved so much better than this.

Frankie's hand stole into his own. Shock ran through him as he felt her quick squeeze. She was letting him know that she trusted him. That whatever happened, she would stand beside him. He wanted to howl at the moon at the unfairness of putting the woman he loved in danger. Emotions burned a hole in his chest, but he forced his mind to clear.

He'd said he would protect Frankie or die trying. And he would.

Ice in his veins, he went for his gun.

"I wouldn't do that if I were you." Salvador approached from behind, accompanied by the guard who'd killed Hector. Raul pointed an automatic at Rico's head.

Salvador walked up behind Rico. "You two are getting on my nerves."

Salvador grabbed Frankie into his arms, plastering her up against his side. She struggled to free herself.

Raul slugged Rico in the side of the head with the gun. Rico heard Frankie's cry as the force of the blow drove him to the floor. The goon yanked out the gun Rico had taken earlier from the other guard. Rico rode the pain, realizing Raul had missed the two knives he carried.

Blood trickled from a wound in his temple. On his knees, he observed Cardenas step out of the shadows into full view, his features weathered with age and the stamp of cruelty. Jewels on his hands and wrist winked in the light. Cardenas stoked on his cigar. A deep crease marred his brow. "How a nobody like you can get so close to me, I'll never understand."

Rico thought of all the suffering Cardenas had caused through drug smuggling and human trafficking. "You should be behind bars with the rest of the animals. Better yet, on death row."

"Ah...but you see. No one can kill me. I'm invincible." Cardenas cocked his head to the side, a sneer on his lips. "Something Carla knew. No one betrays me and lives."

Rico's blood ran cold. He risked a glance at Frankie, willing her to follow his lead. He had to calculate his moves carefully if they were going to get out of there alive.

"You kill a federal agent, there won't be a rock big enough for you to crawl under."

"Perhaps," Cardenas agreed with a feral smile. "But then you won't be around to know. Kill him," he ordered as he turned to exit the glass doors.

Rico rose up in one fluid move and, flicking open the knife, threw it at the guard. "Now," he yelled at Frankie even as he dove for the gun that clattered to the floor, as Raul sank to his knees, the knife buried in his throat. Rico heard Frankie struggle with Salvador. His hands gripped the weapon and he came up off the floor, keeping the gun trained on Salvador.

Salvador had Frankie in a headlock, a small caliber gun pointed at her temple. "*La mato!* I'll kill her."

Blinding light swept through the cabin. Despite the glare, Rico never moved his eyes or weapon from Salvador. "Bay Constable. Cut your engines," an authoritative voice boomed over a bullhorn.

Cardenas rushed back inside the room. From inside his linen jacket, Cardenas pulled out a gun. He moved behind Salvador, making it impossible for Rico to get off a shot. He couldn't take a chance of hitting Frankie.

A crewman shouted from the entrance of the stateroom. "*Policía!*"

Salvador cursed. "Tell the *capitán* to go to full throttle." Salvador backed up, dragging Frankie with him. "No heroics, lover boy." He punched the elevator button. "It's been fun but the party is over."

The brass door pinged opened. Cardenas, Salvador and Frankie got in. Silently, the doors slid shut. Rico moved and hit the button. The elevator was heading up to the flybridge.

Rico rushed out the back. Two boats bobbed along portside. Big beams of light flooded the night, illuminating the boat. A man in a marked Coast Guard jacket blared over the megaphone. "Prepare to be boarded."

The engines revved and lurched forward in the water. Sea spray hit him in the face, the dress shoes he'd worn to Salvador's party slid on the slippery deck. He ducked down as the sound of gunfire exchanged in the night. Rico moved swiftly, holding onto the side railing. He reached the aft of the boat and climbed the ladder up to the upper deck. Wind whipped at him. The boat cut through the water. He guessed the motor yacht was pushing seventeen knots. Fast and dangerous, the engines were being worked. There was no way the captain could maintain running at this high speed. Trying to outmaneuver the better-equipped Coast Guard boats, the yacht cut a path through the waves, sending the hull of the ship skipping across the water. Rico slipped and slid backwards on the deck. Up ahead, he could see Salvador operating the hydraulic crane. The wind whistled in his ears, making it impossible to hear anything. Cardenas angrily waved his gun. Frankie clung to the railing for dear life, while her hair blew wildly around. The boom fully extended, it would be a matter of minutes before the men would have the hard-bottomed inflatable outboard dinghy in the water.

He wouldn't let Cardenas get away. This time the man was going down.

Frankie clung to the railing, terrified to let go. The boat chopped through the waters and, if she hadn't lost everything in her stomach earlier, she would now. Her stomach rolled.

Wind lashed at her face, easily penetrating her light outfit. She didn't know what Salvador was doing, though she watched uneasily as he attempted to lower a small boat over the side. At the speed they were going, she didn't see how he could manage it.

She eyed the dark water with dread. Visions of drowning filled her mind. They were going to have to pry her hands off this bar, because she was not moving, no matter how much they threatened her.

She'd rather die by a bullet than in churning black waters.

Standing only a few feet away with his gun aimed at her, Cardenas screamed for his guards. From below, gunfire sounded. And somewhere close by, Rico waited for an opportunity.

Even if she couldn't see him, she knew he was there and knew he would try to rescue her.

He'd promised.

And she believed him.

The boat suddenly swerved, doing a massive U-turn. In the distance, faint lights dotted the coastline. They were headed back to shore. The Coast Guard boat chased alongside. She waved her arm to capture the men's attention on the other boat. Salvador's yacht jerked ahead to avoid collision. Frankie lost her grip and slid across the deck. Cardenas lost his balance as well. The engines slowed.

Her fingers wet with sea spray, Frankie crawled across the floor until she grasped hold of a chair nailed to the deck. She squeezed her body between the small control console and the chair. It didn't offer a lot of protection, but it was sturdy. She held on with all her strength. Hopefully with the police breathing down their necks, Salvador and Cardenas wouldn't have time to look for her.

Cardenas signaled to Salvador to cut the control. The dinghy was in the water!

Salvador shouted over the wind. "Where's the woman?"

He turned and spotted her.

If she could hang on a few more seconds...

Rico's coming. Like a refrain, the words repeated themselves over and over.

Salvador started toward her, his gun pointed out.

Rico appeared like a demon in the night, rising up seemingly from nowhere, his stance menacing. He propelled himself forward, catching Salvador around the middle. Both men went down, sliding across the shifting deck. Weapons drawn, each tried to disarm the other. Stronger and faster, Rico rolled over onto the man's chest. He slugged him in the jaw. He grabbed the man's gun and threw it over the side of the boat. The yacht bounced over a wave, dislodging Rico. Salvador rolled away.

Frankie held tight to the metal pipe securing the chair. How much longer would it be before law enforcement boarded the vessel? Would they get off alive?

Out of the corner of her eye, she caught movement. Cardenas inched closer until he was directly in front of her hiding spot. Rico and Salvador still fought. Rico's attention on his opponent, his back faced Cardenas. Gustav raised the gun, his intention clear. She couldn't let him do it. She couldn't let Cardenas kill the man she loved.

"No!" Frankie screamed and launched herself at her kidnapper. Her momentum combined with the slippery deck forced them both against the rail and right over the side.

Frankie screamed. Her body hit the water like a brick. The impact knocked the air out of her lungs. She kicked and grabbed for purchase. Air. She needed air. Frantically, her arms flailed in the water until she broke the surface. She gulped down seawater. Waves churned up in the wake of the boat crashed over her head, carrying her farther away from the boat. Farther away from help. She was going to drown!

Chapter 15

"Frankie!" Rico shouted.

Salvador went for the stairs. Rico went to the railing. Below, the outboard inflatable bounced in the wake of the boat. Anxiously his eyes searched the water. He spotted her floundering. She couldn't swim!

Rico jumped up on the rail and leaped into the waters below. Caught in the turbulent wake, he fought against the undertow. With bold strokes, he sliced through the water. He shouted her name. No reply. Terror unlike any he ever felt before gripped him. He couldn't lose her.

The image of Carla's lifeless body flashed in his mind. The image changed and morphed. Instead, he held Frankie. He would never see her beautiful face alive with fury, passion and laughter. Cold dread filled him. He wouldn't let another innocent life die because of him.

A short blast sounded. The Coast Guard flashed the spotlight over the water. A life ring tossed into the water bobbed on the waves. There! Near the end of the inflatable, barely hanging on, Frankie struggled to keep afloat.

"I'm coming, *querida*."

With his head up, he swam swift, sure strokes towards her. He grabbed onto the life ring. A few feet away, her eyes closed and her lips pale, Frankie clung with one hand to the slick raft.

A wave smacked into the tiny vessel. Too weak to hang on she sunk beneath the surface.

"Frankie!"

Rico dove under. Kicking his feet as hard as he could, he dove down deeper. Hand extended he made contact. He tugged with all his might towards the surface.

They broke through the water. He pulled her up against his chest into a lifesaving hold. She gasped in a breath.

"That's my girl. Breathe." He held her tightly, afraid she would be swept away again. Another wave carried the floating ring within reach.

"Hold on tight," he instructed her, hooking her arms around the ring.

"Don't let me go," she rasped out.

"Never." He wrapped his arms around her, holding her up as he treaded water. Another small raft carried men their way. They would be rescued. "I'll never let you go again."

On the bow of the Coast Guard ship, as the sun broke over the horizon, warmth slowly returned to her body. Wrapped tight in a blanket, Frankie closed her eyes and savored the feeling of being in Rico's arms. He hadn't let her go once since their rescue.

Men and women dressed in jackets bearing the initials ICE on the back swarmed around the boat.

A familiar face approached, carrying cups of hot coffee. Rico stiffened against her back.

"Special Agent Rico Lopez? I'm Special Agent Julio Castillo." Julio offered them the two cups of coffee then extended his hand for Rico to shake.

"I'm sorry about not getting to you two sooner," Julio said. "I've been undercover for a year, posing as Señor Torres' attendant. Operation ICE PREDATOR has been in the works for some time as we tried to gather evidence against Cardenas and his crime organization. Lucky for you, we decided to move last night and shut him down."

Rico nodded his head. "I guess I have you to thank for those cameras not working in the east wing."

"The party seemed the best night to slip in and out. You're welcome."

"What about the girls?" Frankie suddenly asked, recalling

how terrified they'd been.

"Don't worry. They're being transported to a medical facility on the mainland. The police will interview them and take their statements. They'll be reunited with their families or provided assistance if they have none."

Relief flooded into her along with the hot coffee. "And Salvador?"

Julio smiled. "He's in custody. He's going away for a long time. Agents are already searching his mansion and I heard they found three different *el chupacabra* costumes. That explains the attacks on the girls. Too bad one girl was a diabetic. She went into insulin shock and died."

"Salvador probably had her body drained of blood thinking to hide cause of death and stoke the legend even more," Rico said. "Explains why the autopsy was sealed."

"You know about that, do you?" Julio leaned against the rail. "Pretty busy for a guy on vacation."

"What about Cardenas?" Rico continued, ignoring the spoken jab.

Julio shook his head. "Shark bait." Another officer called Julio over. He gave a one-fingered salute and excused himself.

Frankie looked out over the shimmering calm waters of the Caribbean Sea. "Do you think he's dead?"

Rico remained silent for a moment, scanning the surrounding waters. A helicopter flew in overhead. Men in a search boat dragged nets through the water. Divers dove over the side of another boat.

"I want to believe the bastard is dead, but something inside me says he's going to pop up somewhere else. Meaner, stronger and deadlier." His voice was laced with rage and the coffee shook in his hand.

Frankie turned in his arms and took the mug from him. She put it down and placed her warm hands on both sides of his face. "Look at me." She searched his brown eyes for the man buried beneath the anger.

"Cardenas is dead. There is no way he could have survived."

"You don't know Cardenas the way I do. I had a chance to

kill him and I didn't." He pulled away from her. Signs of aggravation and frustration marred his features, while his body shook with anger. He went to the railing and looked out at the shoreline, slowly getting closer as they entered the harbor. "He killed Carla. He could've killed you."

Frankie went to him. She hugged him around the waist from behind and laid her head against his back. "But he didn't." The thought of falling into Cardenas' hands again sent a shiver down her spine. "You kept your promise."

Rico exhaled. He turned within the circle of her embrace. He wrapped his arms around her and drew her closer. "I promise. Whatever happens from now on, I'm going to be there for you."

A lump formed in her throat. Tears welled up in her eyes. She blinked them back. For so long she had waited for someone to say those words but she knew they were just words. No one had ever bothered to stick around. Frankie slid out of his embrace.

The Coast Guard vessel pulled into the harbor. More officials waited on the docks. "You don't have to promise me anything."

Rico stepped toward her. His eyes filled with uncertainty. He opened his mouth to speak but was cut off. Julio approached with another man. Older, more distinguished, he wore a badge around his neck.

"Special Agent in Charge Lorenzo Phelps from the Puerto Rican Division." The other man held out his hand. They shook.

"Sir," Rico stood his ground. "I can explain."

The man put up his hand. "Not to me—other than any information you have on Torres and Cardenas. Your boss might be another story." He shot Rico a sympathetic grin. "I got a call from your SAC in Jersey. Seems another agent felt you were in way over your head. I'm sure your SAC will be interested in hearing your explanations."

Rico winced. "Looks like I'd better head back to Jersey soon."

Phelps clapped Rico on the back. "I could use a good man like you on our team. If ever you decide to return to Puerto Rico, look me up." He pulled out a card and handed it to him.

Another couple of agents came over, blocking Frankie's view.

She took the opportunity to sneak away, leaving the boys alone to discuss whatever ICE agents discussed. Her time with Rico had been nice, but the real world waited. For her, here in Vieques. For Rico, somewhere in New Jersey.

The boat pulled into the dock. An agent approached her for questioning. She took one more look back at Rico, laughing among his fellow agents. He was back in his world. Time she returned to hers.

"Goodbye, Rico," she said silently and disembarked.

Chapter 16

Frankie walked out onto the wrap-around veranda, the smell of fresh paint mingling with the tropical breeze. The early morning hours were peaceful, but she didn't know if she'd be able to watch another sunrise without being reminded of Rico.

She sat down on the old wooden porch swing, now sturdy thanks to the amount of labor she and Armando had been doing on the house.

More than a week had passed since her nightmare adventure. Days in which there'd been no word from Rico. Instead of dwelling on the past, she had put all her efforts into building her future. She had enough experience to know that promises weren't meant to be kept. Except the promise she had made to herself to turn Casa Verde into a home.

A cloud of dust announced the arrival of a visitor. Her heartbeat picked up only to immediately slow as she recognized her aunt's car.

"Good morning, Margarita." Her aunt joined her on the porch. "What brings you out early?"

"I wanted to check on you and Armando." Her aunt fingered the beads at her throat. She appeared uneasy.

"I'm fine. Armando is doing better. I've made sure he knows that he has a home with me for however long he likes. We'll be fine," she said with more confidence then she felt. Frankie knew better than anyone else how devastating it was to lose a parent, even if that parent was a criminal. Armando had taken his father's duplicity hard, but she'd assured him that she didn't hold it against him. Still, she knew it would be a while before he could come to terms with the loss.

"Would you like to go inside? I can make some coffee."

Margarita waved the suggestions away. "Thank you, Francesca. I'd prefer to stay outside."

"All right. Then why don't you have a seat beside me?"

Her aunt gracefully sank down onto the swing next to Frankie. Her hands fluttered nervously in her lap. Once again Frankie was reminded of a small bird. Fragile. Delicate.

"*Tía?* You wished to say something?"

"*Sí. Sí.*" She lapsed into silence again. Frankie waited quietly, not wanting to pressure the older woman.

"This is very difficult for me." She raised her head and, with eyes filled with pain, looked directly at Frankie.

"If you don't wish to talk about it, you don't have to." Frankie had no idea what her aunt wished to discuss with her, but she had no desire to cause the other woman pain.

Margarita sucked in a breath and touched the beads once more. "No. It is best that this be spoken. It has been hidden too long." She shifted in her chair and faced out towards the mangroves.

"I used to love this house. This plantation," she began. "When my father, your grandfather, was alive, it was a different place. Vibrant. Productive. When Papa died it all changed. Mama changed."

Frankie kept quiet, not sure where all this was leading, but willing to let Margarita say what she wanted to say in her own way.

"Mama became obsessed with the de la Varga name and position. She didn't know how to run a plantation and soon all our workers left, but that didn't stop her from lecturing us on what was due our position."

"That must have been hard," Frankie murmured.

Margarita gave a small smile. "Your mother would slip out of the house to meet your father. Oh, there were fireworks when my mother found out. They ended up eloping. They came back to stay here for a while, but my mother made their lives so difficult, they decided to leave again." Margarita looked down at her lap. "I wish they had taken me with them," she said fiercely.

"I'm sorry," Frankie reached over and lightly squeezed her

aunt's hand, wanting to comfort her in some way. She had no memories of that time. She barely remembered her mother who'd died when she was very little. And her father had rarely spoken of his Puerto Rican roots.

"It's not your fault, child." Margarita patted Frankie's hand in acknowledgment. She looked up and out at the mangroves as if searching for a measure of peace. "I used to slip out as well. No one waited for me. I simply created my own world in the mangroves. I used to dream of my very own prince who would come and take me away." Her features tightened and Frankie knew that the memories coming were not good.

"That's where he found me," Margarita whispered.

"Who?" Frankie's stomach knotted in dread.

"Señor Torres. He ruled this town. Only he had more power than my mama. His wife was always ill. We rarely saw her. It was said that Señor Torres beat her because she could not give him children." Margarita bowed her head. "All I know is that he came upon me in the mangroves. He raped me."

Oh, God. Frankie reached over and pulled her aunt into her arms. Margarita began weeping. Frankie felt tears prick her own eyelids. It seemed a while before Margarita was composed enough to continue.

"I didn't tell my mother. I didn't dare. But then I couldn't hide the changes to my body. Mama noticed. Accused me of being someone's whore. I was with child. I confessed what had happened. She beat me and locked me in a small hidden room under the staircase."

Margarita took out a handkerchief from the small bag she carried and daintily wiped at her eyes. "With Señor Torres' wife alive, there was no question of marriage. My mother kept me hidden. She told the townspeople that I was visiting a relative. Once the baby was born, Señor Torres came by. Apparently my mother made a deal with him. The baby for his word that no one would ever speak of the evil he had done."

Frankie felt sick to her stomach. The more she learned of her grandmother, the more she wanted to renounce her claim to the house.

"You're saying that Salvador was—"

"—my son." Margarita finished. "That was why I did not

211

want you to attend the party. Over the years, I've seen the blackness in Salvador's soul grow. I prayed for him." She stared down at her hands, several tears coursing down her cheeks. "I did not want the blackness to touch you. Can you forgive me?"

Once again, Frankie drew her aunt into her embrace. "There is nothing to forgive. Nothing at all."

"But if I had told you the truth from the beginning, perhaps you would have stayed safe," Margarita pursued.

"I don't think so. Salvador had his own agenda. It's over and done with. We have to let this go and move on." Holding her aunt by the shoulders, Frankie put some space between them so she could look her aunt in the face. "Thank you for telling me. If there is anything good that came out of this nightmare, it's that I gained an aunt and a cousin. I have family."

And she did. Whatever might or might not happen with Rico, she could say with sincerity that she was not alone. She had a family.

❧

Why haven't you gone after her?

You haven't called her yet? What's the matter with you? Maybe we should call her for you.

His sisters' words rang in his ears the entire drive from Isabel Segunda to Punta Negra. God save him from opinionated women, he thought in disgust.

Actually, someone up there was probably having a good belly laugh over his predicament, because here he was ready to take on a woman with a mouth and mind that equaled every single Lopez female.

Casa Verde came into view. He remembered his first impression of the place. He'd thought Frankie crazy.

But if anyone could turn this place around she could.

And if anyone would be willing to take on a slightly worn-at-the-edges federal agent, it would be Frankie.

But would she want him?

He parked the rental and sat a moment to build up

courage. After being debriefed on what had happened, he'd flown up to Jersey to square things with his boss. And when he'd returned, he'd gone home to make peace and explain what had driven him away from his family.

He should've called Frankie. Had even picked up the phone several times, only to hang up. He sucked in a big breath. Well, it was now or never.

Frankie stepped out onto the porch. Rico stared. She was so beautiful. And he'd missed her.

Rico got out of the car. She eyed him warily. He could understand. "Hi," he said.

"Hi, yourself."

She wasn't going to make it easy for him, but that was his Frankie—full of attitude and grit.

"Why are you here?" she asked when he stood at the bottom of the porch steps looking up at her. She tucked a stray tendril behind her ear and then crossed her arms in front of her chest. "I mean, you don't owe me anything." Her foot began tapping a rhythm on the wooden planks.

"Now that's where you're wrong, *querida*. I owe you my life."

Her teeth worried her bottom lip. "I don't understand. You're the one who saved me."

Rico waved her words away. "But you saved my soul. I hated Cardenas so much, I'd lost perspective. He nearly pulled me into the darkness, but you led me back into the light." Rico took the few steps up to the porch. Frankie backed up. "Come on." Rico grabbed her hand and led her to the swing seat. She scooted away when he sat down beside her.

"You asked me why I'm here," Rico continued. "I put in for a transfer to the San Juan office. I thought I could come visit you, but now that I'm here, I know that's not what I want."

"I see," Frankie said, ducking her head to hide the pain he saw flash in her eyes.

"No, you don't." He reached over to tip her chin up. "I love you, Francesca Montalvo. I would prefer it if you made your home with me in San Juan, but this is your heritage, and if turning it into a B&B is your dream, then it's my dream, too."

Her gaze flew up to search his. "When I first came here,"

she said seeming to pick her words slowly, "getting this place up and ready meant everything to me. But I've learned a few things about myself, about what really matters. I want a home. A family. I want to plant roots, whether here or in San Juan."

"Does that mean—"

"I love you Rico Lopez. When I fell into the water, I didn't think I'd ever get the chance to say that to you."

Rico leaned over, spearing his hand in her wild curls. "I'm glad you did," he said, "because I love you back. I need you." He kissed her gently, enjoying the taste of her, the feel of her beneath his fingers. He tucked her under his arm, her head resting on his shoulder.

"What do you want to do with this place?"

"Sell it. Get rid of it," she said decisively. "Whatever money I get I intend to split with Armando and Margarita. They deserve it."

Rico nodded, content to rock and stare out over the mangroves.

"What about you?" Frankie asked. "Have you really gotten over what happened to that woman, the informant who was killed?" She tilted her head to look up at him.

"I will always regret that I couldn't save Carla, but I won't let it take over my life. I've put it behind me," Rico assured her.

"You know, I was thinking." Frankie's hand dropped down to his jean-clad leg and began stroking softly. "About that little girl in the picture."

"Hmmm?" Rico felt each stroke create a slow burn in his gut.

"She's a little girl trapped in the system. I've been there. No one saved me. But maybe we could try to save her."

Jolted, Rico stared down at her. "You'd seriously consider it?"

"I don't know what kind of mother I'll make, but I want to try. I've spent too much of my life keeping my heart locked up because it hurts bad to lose people you love. But life is about risk and I'm willing to take one if you'll be there with me."

"*Dios*, Frankie, I love you so much." He crushed her in his embrace. "I will always be there for you," he said thickly.

"That's good to know, Lopez," Frankie said breathlessly, a few minutes later. "I won't let you forget it. I've got a temper, in case you didn't know." She grinned.

Rico groaned. "You're going to try to rule me like all my sisters. I'm sure they'll get in line to tell you all my bad points, too."

Frankie laughed. "I can't wait to meet them."

"They can't wait to meet you either." He saw the question in her eyes and nodded. "I told them I intended to propose. They expect us for dinner tomorrow."

"Tomorrow?"

"Yes," Rico replied as he laid small kisses along her shoulder and neck. "Where's Armando?"

"Margarita insisted on taking him out for clothes." He could feel her skin heating up under his touch. "Um, Rico what are you doing?"

"Making love to my soon-to-be wife. Don't make me wait, Frankie."

Her arms circled his neck. "I don't want to wait either. I've waited much too long already. A lifetime it seems."

Hand in hand they entered Casa Verde, laughter and joy trailing in their wake.

About the Author

To learn more about Gabriella Hewitt, please visit www.gabriellahewitt.com. Or you can send an email to Gabriella Hewitt at gabriellahewitt@hotmail.com.

*Caught in the sights of a killer, David and Miranda fight for life—
and the chance to love again.*

Love on the Run
© 2007 Marie-Nicole Ryan

Miranda Raines thinks she has found a safe haven in Oxford, England, until Scotland Yard DCI David French knocks on her door with terrifying news. Her ex-husband, a convicted murderer, has escaped from prison and he's coming for her.

Miranda, who for years has harbored a secret love for the driven Chief Inspector, has no choice but to trust him. She just hopes she can guard her own heart at least as well as he guards her.

After thwarting her ex's first attack, David spirits Miranda and her young son out of England and the three of them end up on the run across Europe. David has no intention of falling in love again, but with each passing day Miranda awakens passions he thought long dead.

Could this be their forever love? With a killer on their trail, they may not live long enough to find out.

Available now in ebook from Samhain Publishing.

Enjoy the following excerpt from Love on the Run...

After dinner on the flagstone terrace, Randi helped Mina clear away the dishes and load the dishwasher.

"I'm glad you came back," Mina said. "Jamie would've been quite all right, but I'm not sure you would have."

Randi stopped in the middle of folding a towel. She shook her head. "No, I was a wreck. I don't think we went ten kilometers on that bike, and I bawled like a baby the whole time."

Mina smiled and placed her strong arm around her shoulder. "You are losing that pinched look you had when you first came to us."

"That bad, huh?"

"Not bad, but still it was there."

"I do feel safe here," Randi admitted.

"You must relax because David will protect you and your son. It is very obvious to these old eyes how important the two of you are to him."

Mina's words gladdened Randi's heart, but surely the older woman was exaggerating. "He's been absolutely wonderful, but..."

"Time will tell, my dear. Be patient." Mina removed the towel from Randi's trembling hands. "Let's go outside and enjoy this nice fall evening. The men shouldn't have all the fun."

℘

On the terrace Randi eased down into a lounge chair and watched David and Jamie wrestle in the grass. A sensation of pure contentment stole over her and wrapped her in easy comfort.

She turned to Mina. "Dinner was wonderful, Mina. Thank you for having us. For everything."

"It is my privilege. I'm so glad that David thought of us. So rarely do we have visitors from the U.K.—at least none we are so happy to see." Mina turned to her husband. "Jean-Luc, why don't you play some music for us?"

Randi's ears pricked. "Music? Oh, yes, please."

Jean-Luc grumbled, but with good nature, "She doesn't want to talk to me, so she asks me to play. I am wise to her tricks." The older man hauled his cumbersome self out of his chair and ambled into the house, returning a moment later with an old violin.

David turned to Randi, a wide grin spread across his handsome face. "Did you know Miranda plays?"

"Bon!" Jean-Luc declared. "You will play for us, Ran-dee?"

"Yes, but you must go first. I warn you I'm very rusty."

Jean-Luc drew the bow across the strings, then frowned at the sound. "Just a little adjustment." He tightened the E string and drew the bow again. "Parfait!" he pronounced, and then launched into an old folk tune which Randi immediately recognized as Sur le Pont d'Avignon.

After the rollicking tune which had young Jamie up on his feet, dancing, Jean-Luc paused and extended the violin toward Randi. "Now you must play us something from your country, s'il vous plaît."

Randi nodded her assent and took the violin from Jean-Luc's gnarled hands. "I'll play you our state song." She drew the bow across the violin, the melodic strains of The Tennessee Waltz filling the night air.

After she completed the waltz, Jean-Luc stood and clapped. "Bien, Ran-dee! C'est bon."

"Mummy, play Rocky Top. Jean-Luc, you'll like that one. It's bouncy."

Randi looked from Mina to Jean-Luc to David whose eyes were actually closed. It was the first time she'd seen the taut lines of tension erased from his lean face.

"Rocky Top, Tennessee it is," she said with a nod, then launched into the sprightly tune. Jamie sang, charmingly off key, "Once I had a girl on Rocky Top," then fell to humming when he didn't know the words, but intoned, "Rocky Top, Tennessee," during the chorus.

Randi lost herself in the energy and rhythm of the country

tune, until it came to an end.

"Encore, encore!" Jean-Luc prompted.

"Something classical, dear?" Mina suggested. "I believe David told me that you play with chamber groups as well."

"All right." Soon the lyrical strains of the second movement of Beethoven's Violin Concerto rose through the valley, soaring into the night. Swept up in the mood and imagery of the music, Randi became the violin, the music. When the last note faded, she heard a collective sigh of appreciation.

"That was simply lovely, dear," Mina told her, pulling her sweater tighter around her shoulders. "Why don't we go in? It's getting too cool for these old bones. Besides, I think your son has fallen asleep."

Randi nodded. "He's been conditioned. Whenever he has trouble going to sleep, I play for him until he does."

℘

Randi tapped on David's door. She heard sounds of his moving about through the door, then it opened. Apparently he'd been getting ready for bed. His shirt was unbuttoned and pulled out of his jeans. Her breath caught in her throat when she caught sight of his broad, muscular chest and washboard abs. She felt his arms surround her, pulling her into his strong embrace.

"You played beautifully," he murmured in a voice so soft and seductive it sent ripples of desire to the pit of her belly.

"Thank you," she said, as he maneuvered her into his bedroom and kicked the door shut behind him.

"It's paid a few bills," she quipped before she could stop herself. Lord, why was she so nervous? David would never hurt her, not physically anyway.

"Is Jamie asleep?"

"Yes, he's all tucked in."

"Have you come to tuck me in?"

She bit her lip and tilted her head to the side. "You're a big boy. Do you need to be tucked in?"

"I might do." He closed the short distance between them, his gaze never leaving her eyes. "Depends on who's doing the tucking."

"And would it be presumptuous to assume the who would be me?" she asked, trying to keep her tone light so he wouldn't know how scared she really was. She was just no good at sex.

Stefan had told her so countless times.

"No, you'd be right on target."

His lips brushed across the top on her head. "Miranda, will you stay with me tonight?"

She pulled back and looked up into his warm gray eyes and swallowed hard before answering, "Yes."

Oh Lord! Had she really said yes?

His lips, warm and demanding, descended against hers. Every bone in her body liquefied with the heat of his kiss. He wanted her. The reason didn't matter. She wanted him, too.

Together they fell backward onto the bed, his hands skimming under her sweater and caressing her breasts though her bra. His kisses were hungry and demanding. She opened her mouth to his. His tongue swept into her mouth. He tasted of the strong French coffee he'd had at dinner.

One expert twist, then his hands, warm and gentle, were all over her again. The memories of their earlier bathroom tryst flooded back. Too late to stop, even if she'd wanted. And she didn't. Her ex had never been this kind or gentle. Forcing the bad memories and fears far, far away, she gave her trust again to David.

Suddenly they both were tugging at her sweater. Over her head it went along with her bra, tossed somewhere. He rolled her nipples between his thumbs, then applied his lips and teeth, raking them ever so tenderly, teasing them into taut buds of screaming sensation. An unfamiliar heat spread down her belly and centered between her thighs.

She gasped, "Oh." Hands shaking, she slipped his T-shirt over his head, taking care not to disturb his bandage. She gazed into his eyes and saw the passion and desire burning there. She shivered. Her fingers splayed over his chest. His flat male nipples drew into tight nubs. She kissed one, then the other.

He let out a groan and her name, soft as a sigh. He pressed against her, his rigid erection straining against the confinement of his jeans. His hands worked at the button and zipper of her jeans, easing them apart. She raised her hips, allowing him to slip her jeans and panties down over her hips.

She kicked off the jeans, giving him access. He quickly found the warmth between her legs, his caress gentle, yet urgent.

"You're lovely," he told her, kissing her inner thigh. Shivers ran through her, fanning the heat of her desire into a blaze.

He pulled away. "No, don't go," she protested as he stood.

Glancing down at his jeans, he grinned. "I'm not going anywhere." He unzipped and shucked his jeans in record time.

He stood before her, his lean-muscled body tense. More excited than ever, she reached out and touched him, marveling at the texture of his arousal—rigid steel covered in the softest of silken skin.

"Easy," he gasped, his lips claiming hers again.

Their bodies matched, warm skin to warm skin, lips to lips.

hot stuff

Discover Samhain!

THE HOTTEST NEW PUBLISHER ON THE PLANET

Romance, fantasy, mystery, thriller, mainstream and more—Samhain has more selection, hotter authors, and everything's available in both ebook and print.

Pick your favorite, sit back, and enjoy the ride! Hot stuff indeed.

WWW.SAMHAINPUBLISHING.COM

Printed in the United States
124256LV00001B/100-102/P